A Hadley Falls Novel

Ashley Kay

Copyright © 2021 by Ashley Kay

All rights reserved.

No portion of this book may be reproduced in any form without written permission from the publisher or author, except as permitted by U.S. copyright law.

To the girls of **Pencils & Lipstick CWC...**
I couldn't have done this without you!

To any of my family who is picking up this book.
This is your ONE warning.
Put it down and walk away. I love you!
-Ashley Kay

Foreword

All characters, places and settings of this book are works of fiction.

TRIGGER WARNING: This book contains references and a subplot that deals with domestic violence.

Contents

1. Katy — 1
2. Katy — 7
3. Connor — 19
4. Connor — 25
5. Katy — 37
6. Connor — 49
7. Katy — 60
8. Katy — 75
9. Connor — 82
10. Katy — 99
11. Connor — 118
12. Connor — 125
13. Katy — 131
14. Katy — 140

15. Connor	147
16. Katy	166
17. Connor	179
18. Katy	188
19. Katy	199
20. Connor	204
21. Connor	215
22. Katy	221
23. Katy	229
24. Connor	240
25. Connor	250
26. Katy	260
27. Connor	272
28. Katy	285
29. Connor	294
30. Katy	306
31. Connor	318
32. Katy	323
33. Lily	332
34. Katy	340
35. Connor	345
Epilogue	351

Coming Soon...	355
About Author	357
Let's Get Intimate!	359

Katy

Chapter One

"Take off the dress," he growls into my ear from behind me, grazing his teeth down my lobe. A strong hand grips my hip in a bruising hold while the other slowly pulls at my zipper.

My blood heats with anticipation. Warm breath at my neck sends a tingling sensation over my chest. My nipples tighten and scrape against the fabric. His hands release the clasp behind my head and the ends tumble down my back, caressing my skin and exposing my heavy breasts to the night air.

A sigh escapes my lips. His rough palm brushes the underside of my breasts kneading them together. My mystery man drags his fingers across my aching pink flesh. My back bows and a moan rips from my throat.

The rubbing turns to pinching and pulling. My hips writher and rock to his movements. The man's right hand inches down brushing my belly before landing on my sex.

"Oh god," I cry out.

His warmth melts into me sending a shiver right to my clit. Fuuuck. If he enters me...

RING! RING!

What the fuck? The cool, dark room is gone, replaced by my plushy, warm bed. Bright light from outside peeks underneath my black out blinds.

Ugh.

Whoever is calling is a dead man.

Before I can finish the mental ass chewing I'm giving my mystery caller, the ringing starts again. Fuck. I reach for my phone. The screen says Noah.

Huh? Shouldn't he be at work?

"Hey babe, I missed you last night," I say, trying to keep the annoyance out of my voice.

"Had a meeting. A VIP I couldn't pass up. You know how it is." Not really, unless his clients cover themselves in flour and call it work.

"Sounds like fun." I attempt to sound supportive. Noah works for an investment firm. Stocks, bonds, IRAs. The terms make my head hurt and turn into white noise after a while.

"Dinner went fantastic, that's why I'm calling."

My heart drops and I freeze, pulling my covers up like a shield. He's calling about work? Not for me?

"Pack a bag and be ready by six o'clock tonight. The client invited me to join them and a few high-ranking executives from the firm. They extended the invitation to significant others at some swanky country club in San Diego."

"Noah, hold on, what are you talking about? Today is my birthday! My first three days in a row off in forever. We had dinner plans tonight and I planned dinner with my friends tomorrow, remember. Little Greyson's party, then a night out with Elise and Ryan." My voice cracks and I slam a pillow over my face to keep the sound inside. What's wrong with him? How can he expect me to blow off my birthday?

"Sorry babe, this client comes first, if I land him on my own can you imagine the perks? I'll be a shoo-in for the partner promotion. Be ready to go at six. Tomorrow night can be all about you. After dinner with my colleagues we can hit the town." Noah reassures me, completely disregarding my feelings.

"I won't be ready at six. You can go, but I made plans. Before you get angry. I'm not mad, I understand better than anyone, work is work, but I'm not canceling. I'm gonna celebrate my birthday with my girls." *Don't show your pain. Keep it in.* Noah scoffs through the phone. No way can he be angry.

"What did you say? You bet your ass you are coming. Katy this isn't some dumb kid game this is my career. You will be ready to go at six. Cancel the damn birthday plans, now. This deal is an opportunity of a lifetime for me, and I need my girlfriend by my side. They want a family man."

"Hold on there, I'm not a child you don't get to order me around. And a family man wouldn't demand his significant other miss out on their birthday so which is it?" I snip throwing the small square pillow on my bed across the room. "Are you a family man or not?" I taunt.

"Don't." He spits like a warning.

"Don't what Noah? I don't want to go and you can't make me. I'm a grown woman. No amount of yelling, or berating is changing my mind." Feet tapping along a hard surface float through the phone. Each pass sounds more irritated than the last.

"I'm really surprised in you." Huh? "You are acting like a selfish little girl, I thought you were ready to be an adult." He jabs. "Do you care nothing about our future? This weekend is make or break for me so, don't you think of embarrassing me." He hisses into my ear.

Who the hell is this man and what did he do with my sweet boyfriend?

"No. I'm not coming. End of story." I keep my voice calm, but I'm firm and refuse to give in.

The last few months play back in my head. How can he act so hurtful? Was everything he said all a lie?

A loud crash of glass rings through the phone. "Screw this shit Katy! You made it perfectly clear to me you aren't ready for a real relationship. I'm so done with your innocent ass. I need a woman who understands my needs come first. Not some inexperienced little brat who can't please a man. We're done, I don't need you or the shitty sex." He slams the phone and I stare at my screen in utter shock.

What the hell just happened?

I unlock my phone and shoot a quick 911 text off to Elise. Complete with a cake and coffee emoji, my secret code for melt down. Meet me now. She takes less than two seconds to respond.

ELISE: *Common Place in 20*

I jump out of bed. Turn the shower in my adjoined bath on high. The best thing about this condo, not having to leave my room for a shower.

"Fuck," I shout to no one as boiling hot water hits my back. That's what I get for not checking.

Oops, I hate when I over heat the water. I reach behind me to adjust the temperature. As soon as its cools I turn under the spray and let warmth wash over my face and into my hair.

When the stream grazes my nipples, my stomach jumps, sending a bolt of pleasure straight to my still sensitive nub. Remnants of my dream fill my mind. The mystery hunk commanding me to take off my dress. My thighs are slippery, slick with the desire leftover from my dream.

Do I have time? *Do you care?* Nope.

I grab at my aching nipples and give them a gentle tug, heat pulls in my core, making my walls tighten with need. My left hand explores my sticky folds. My fingers slip over my clit and dip into the opening of my sex.

One brush across the tight bundle of nerves and my knees go weak. I brace myself against the shower wall in preparation of my impending orgasm. I pull hard and long on my nipple, swiping my thumb over my nub until I explode.

Blinding euphoria sweeps over my body, I have to use force to keep myself upright as I ride the waves of my orgasm back to reality.

"Whoa." I shutter, letting the water beat my back while I catch my breath.

Relief finally achieved,I grab my loofah, favorite body wash and clean myself up. How did a faceless, imaginary man make me burn so hot? I've never felt that before.

What about with Noah?

The second I think his name, my mood sours, all my thoughts turn to the breakup. Damn, how was he so cruel?

I'm a damn fool. He sleeps with me and less than a month later he turns into a complete asshole. What the hell?

When Noah found out about my virginity he put me at ease. He took the pressure off being a virgin. Our first time together, my first time period was awful. Nothing like I expected. There was no passion. I didn't come, not even close. Afterwards, Noah expected me to praise him or something. I still don't understand the whole deal about sex. I have more fun alone.

Am I broken? I've only been able to make myself come before. Only me.

Stop! Today is a celebration day. Yes, screw Noah. Time to go meet my bestie and stop sulking.

Katy

Chapter Two

The second I step into Common Place, my go-to morning spot in town, the fresh ground coffee aroma surrounds me in a delicious hug as if to say welcome back The line is to the door with people on their phones or fidgeting in place while they wait for their morning fix. I have to carefully dodge around people attempting to exit back onto Main Street.

College students and teachers sit at long wooden banquet tables with their books splayed out in front of them, clicking away on their computers and tablets.

Tables with couples make my chest tighten like a stab straight to my heart. Why today? My fucking Birthday. Okay, I take that stab back, I'm more angry than sad.

I walk right past the metal kitchen wares and happy wall signs. Happiness can suck a dick; I snicker to myself.

Elise sits at our favorite sofa in the corner away from any other patrons. Perfect, less chance of being overheard. I flop down on the couch next to her. My eyes go wide at the giant piece of cake waiting for me.

One of my favorite sweet treats! Three layers of super moist chocolate cake, filled with chocolate fudge icing. The cake is finished with a chocolate ganache coating that is poured over top leaving a clear finish. My mouth waters, I wet my lips, grab the plastic fork and dive into the cake. Pure heaven explodes in my mouth.

"Oh, my god!" I groan.

Elise clears her throat with a small cough.

I glance up. She is staring at me, one eyebrow crooked. I give her a chocolate-covered cake smile. She isn't impressed so I cover my mouth to finish the delicious bite.

"Should I save your Happy Birthday hugs for later?" Elise squints one eye and shrugs.

"Noah broke up with me." I say in a rush, expecting pity in her eyes. Instead, her nostrils flare. Oh crap, Elise is mad. I go into detail about the phone call, Noah's demand, him dumping me and of course his goodbye telling me I'm horrible in bed. When I finish, I take a deep drink of my coffee and a larger bite of cake.

"What the hell. Screw Noah he's a total dick." Elise pointing at me. "No one should be dumped on their birthday. And no man should ever tell the girl who let him pop her cherry, that she's a crappy lay. I mean, that shows more poorly on him than you!" She raises her voice as she slams her hands down on the table, knocking me out of my funk.

"Fucking hell, Elise! Want to say that a little louder. I don't think the lady on the other side of the cafe can hear you." I peer over my shoulder. "Nope, with the evil eye she is shooting us, she totally heard."

"Don't care who hears, he's a dick, now we can find you a real man."

"Seriously, please no. I don't want another man and don't smirk at me like you're planning something. This morning blindsided me. Noah said all the right things. Okay, I didn't think he was all that talented in bed, but I don't have anything to compare him too. I hoped the passion would come. Now I'm rambling, ugh." I lay my head in my hands, hating how whiny I sound.

Sometimes I can be a little self-conscious in the sex and love department. Comes with the territory when you're the last of your friends to lose your virginity.

"Excuse me, how am I making this worse?" she huffs. "Are we not sitting in your favorite coffee shop, stuffing our faces with cake and lattes? I'm planning an extra jog for eating this."

"Oh shut up. You are hot and I'm sure Ryan won't mind a little extra to hold on to while he's banging you. He looks like a strong guy," I wink at her, then flinch expecting something to fly at me.

"Dirty bitch." She screeches as a bright pink blush blooms over her chest and up her neck. Elise hurls her wadded up napkin at me, all while sticking her tongue out.

Knew it. She's way more modest than I am and talking about certain things always earns a sassy response. Keep it clean and she throws light stuff. Being a dirty mouth chick, I've learned to duck.

Some days I don't know how I function without this woman. Elise Grey has been my best friend since high school. We are total opposites but we click. She's model tall, with beautiful brown eyes, silky espresso colored hair, which she styles in a cute little bob. She is the most loyal, soft-spoken rule follower a girl could ask for.

Then there's me, I stand five feet high, have dark chestnut hair and green eyes. My body has more of a coke bottle shape with extra padding compared to Elise's slender frame. I curse a lot and sometimes bend the rules. She is the prude to my inner dirty old lady, forever shushing me and turning red at the things I say.

"Oh I know." Elise wails, once again bringing me out of my own thoughts. "Why don't you go out with Ryan and me tonight? I want you to hang with him more, plus, you will love the bar we are going to. Ryan's friend owns the pub. He loves Whiskey and Single Malt, so the selection is huge."

"I love a good Single Malt."

"Say you'll go. You need a night out and Ryan's friend is pretty hot, maybe you'll like him." I roll my eyes at her, after Noah I'm not going out looking for man. A stiff drink yes. A man, nope.

"Alright fine, peer pressure wins. But this is for fun only, not for a man. We clear?" I'm giving her my best stern face, which is total crap, I am a complete push over for Elise.

"Tell yourself whatever you need and meet us at The McKinnon Pub at seven o'clock."

"I promise I'll show, but only if you tell me more about how everything is going with Ryan. I love him, but you don't bring him around often, like four times, maybe and you've been together what, almost a year?" I keep my tone light, I don't want her to think that I'm angry with her just curious.

"I know, I simply want to keep him to myself. My mom and aunt can be so judgmental. I need my time with him before they try to sour everything. Make sense?"

"Jackson."

"See! You get it." We both burst out laughing. One word is all that's needed. My brother Jackson is the most protective older brother in history, always treating me like I'm still a ten-year-old little girl.

"Okay, stop stalling. I want the details."

"He's just Ryan."

"Wow, real articulate Elise. Just Ryan. What does that even mean?"

"Whatever. You'll understand when you meet your one." A soft sigh escapes her lips.

"Oh, so he's your one now?"

"It's only been nine months, but I think so." She shakes her head, then drops her voice to a whisper, "Is that crazy?"

"You look happy, genuinely happy. Don't overthink your relationship and just go where life takes you."

"Deal, if you promise me the same thing," she says with a wink.

"What do you mean, same thing?"

"I mean promise you will forget about Noah and just enjoy tonight. After all, it's your birthday." Elise holds out her hand. This seems monumental somehow, like if I say no I'll forever be the lonely, sad friend. Fuck that.

"Deal." I stick my tongue out at her like a five-year-old child. Please don't let this be a mistake.

I arrive home at six from running errands, and a quick check in at the bakery. I only have an hour before I need to leave. Shit. Walking up the steps to my condo a giant box of what can only be flowers sits on my porch. Peeking at the note, I forget all my troubles.

Happy Birthday Little Heart!
Love from far away,
Jackson

Flowers from my brother, and he is all the way on the other end of the world. My cheeks are hurting from grinning so hard. I can't believe my brother sent me flowers on my birthday.

I rush in my house, drop everything but the package in a large heap on the living room floor. Somehow I manage this while taking off my shoes, and kicking them into the pile by the front door without falling on my ass. I hurry to the kitchen, I place the box on the counter and search my drawers for scissors.

How is it that scissors never make it back to their spot...ah found them! With the scissors found, I cut the tape and peel open the lid and squeal.

My brother knows me better than most, of course he would never send me flowers. Oh, I got a bouquet but of donuts! Five glazed donuts and one chocolate glazed donut right in the middle. Jackson just won the awards for best brother.

How the hell did he pull this off? Only one donut shop around here does donut bouquets, but they don't make deliveries. That means someone local helped him. No way my mother would assist. She thinks I don't need donuts, that losing a few pounds will help me land a man, as she says.

Oh, well, either way, I am so grateful my brother remembered. I pull out my phone and use my favorites to dial him.

"*Little Heart.* Happy Birthday. Perfect timing too, I just woke up."

"For real? Where are you?" Jackson works in crazy places, but never talks about any of them because he signs non-disclosures for most of his clients. Working private security for celebrities has its perks and draw backs, like working overseas all the time. I swear he picks those assignments on purpose.

"How's your day going? That boyfriend treating you right?"

Who told him about Noah? Probably my mom. Jackson tends to be super protective of me and never approves of anyone I date. Hell, I didn't even date until he left home. Every guy was afraid of my brother. Our town isn't that small, and even with him away, a few guys cut and run after learning he we're related.

"My day is improving now after your donut delivery. Who helped you?" I don't answer about Noah, hoping Jackson won't bring it up again. Instead I take a bite of donut, let it melt on my tongue.

"That's my secret to keep, Little Heart. Now, what about your boyfriend? Where is he taking you for your birthday?" Jackson questions. Ughs, we always sticks his nose in.

"He better have reservations somewhere nice. Mom says he's a lawyer." He growls. I swallow.

"About that," I drag out the words, "we aren't together anymore. I'm going out with Elise and her boyfriend tonight and dinner with them tomorrow night." I hold my breath, waiting for the lecture. My parents and my overbearing brother always treat me like I can't do anything right.

"You broke up. When the fuck did this happen? I talked to mom this morning, sis." He's grilling me and in an instant I'm thrown back to a time when I'm Jackson's little sister who constantly disappoints him.

"Damn Jackson. This morning. Can you relax with the questions? The short story is he called this morning wanted me to change my plans. I said no. He pushed so I put my foot down and he dumped me. He said I'm too innocent for him."

The laugh that booms through my phone helps keep the tears from falling. I don't love Noah, but I gave him my virginity and being treated like nothing after hurts.

"Too innocent little sister, that's some bullshit. He must not understand you very well. I'm sure someone out there is way better for you. Now if you can only make better choices maybe you'll find him." He did not just say that.

Jackson's ability to make me feel good then turn the knife is only second to my mom's. I let the line go silent, the donut turns stale in my mouth. It's pretty obvious that that my family thinks I'm beyond naive, but on my fucking birthday. Nope, not happening.

"Wow. Okay, well I gotta go Jackson. I'll talk to you later."

I'm pissed and trying very hard not to let my anger come through my voice. I fight with my brother all the time, like all siblings do, but when he's working out of the country I try to keep everything civil.

"Don't be like that, Katy, I didn't mean it that way. Mom just told me Noah is a great guy. Then, less than a day later, you tell me that you're done with him. Your story seems a little nuts. Don't you think you were too rash?"

Too rash! "Jackson, I can't have this conversation right now. He dumped me. I only told Elise so far because it happened this morning and well, she's Elise. My best friend in the world. Honestly, now I'm glad he dumped me. He was treating me different after..." I clamp my hand over my mouth. *Dumb oh so dumb.*

"After what," he spits out on a growl. Oh, shit, how did I let that slip? I'm not stupid, Jackson is well aware of what I meant. His disapproval radiates through the phone. "Katy, answer me. After what? Did you sleep with him?"

"Okay Jackson so not your business, I'm twenty-five years old. My sex life is none of your concern." Geez, sometimes our five-year age difference blows.

"Heart, let's go! On time is late," someone calls in the background.

"Katy, I gotta go but this conversation isn't over."

"Yes, it is. Bye, Jackson. Be safe. See you soon Big Heart."

"Love you to pieces Little Heart." The screen flashes, alerting me to the ended call. Over-protectiveness aside, I miss Jackson so much, I haven't seen him in over eight years. It feels like a lifetime to me. Jackson drives me crazy and totally needs a lesson in boundaries but he's my brother and I wouldn't want any other.

Thirty minutes later, my brother forgotten, my makeup is magnificent and I finish my look off with a tight ponytail resting on the top of my head. My favorite Merlot colored dress reminds me of my dream. A shiver runs down my spine. This dress is sex on a hanger, with a low plunging neckline and open back. The hem rests just above my knee.

I can't remember the last time I pulled this baby out for a night. Noah always thought the dress was too revealing to be appropriate for anything. I shake thoughts of Noah from my head and get ready to head out. I'm not driving with the pub being so close to my house, I'll walk home or ride share if I'm out too late.

DING!

Thinking Elise is texting me I pull out my phone. Wrong, my screen flashes Noah. What could he want?

> ***Noah: Katy, I'm so sorry about earlier. I didn't even say Happy Birthday. Forgive me?***

What the fuck. Forgive him? He broke up with me on my birthday, and he wants me to forgive him less than twelve hours later, like it didn't shred me.

Did it really? No, but being dumped on your birthday and being told you suck has a way of fucking with a person. My gut churns with the intensity of my anger.

How can he think that I would take him back? Does he think I'm desperate, that I won't be able to replace him, if I want to.

Katy: No, this morning was unforgivable. I'm done.

Noah: Come on, baby, you don't mean that. I was upset. You know how hard I'm working towards this promotion.

Noah: This weekend is the key, and I overreacted.

Katy: Promotion plans or not, what you said crossed a line. WE ARE OVER!

Noah: You made your point. I was an ass. Can we move on now?

Noah: *I made plans to make this weekend special, even with being on a work function. Trust me, you'll never notice.*

Katy: *You're right. I won't...because I'm not going. We are over Noah, lose my number.*

Muting our conversation, I lock my phone and toss it in my purse. I secure my front door and head toward the bar before I change my mind. I will not let Noah ruin today any further. Tonight is my night and I plan to celebrate knowing I can always take a ride share if we finish too late.

Connor

CHAPTER THREE

"Alright boys, hit the showers!" My Uncle Casey yells through the megaphone. His jet black hair is slicked back under his ball cap.

"Why does he use that damn thing?" Grumbles my cousin Liam, grabbing his water bottle from the treadmill then douses his dark head and beard. Sweat fall off his arms and pants. Two hours running around doing drills will do that to you.

"No fucking clue. He's your dad, go ask him." My younger brother Graham says pushing back a loose pieces of red strands back into his bun.

"Didn't I tell you to cut your hair last week?" Our older brother Jameson grounds out. The redheaded behemoth folds his arms over his chest glaring at Graham.

Choosing to ignore my brothers, I pop the lid on my own water and chug two mouthfuls. Ahh, refreshing. Today's training session kicked my ass. I peel my shirt from my body and beads of sweat flick off. Shit, I need a shower.

"Mom says I don't." Graham snips pulling me back to their bickering. He pushes past a shirtless Liam who barely reacts to my brother walking into him. Graham has to check his balance, the gangly fucker. Man if he ate better and actually showed up to workouts he might fill out his thin frame.

Graham snatches his bag off the bench and is two steps from the door when Jameson calls out. "If you want long hair you ride a desk. Consult the dress code if you got a problem."

My little brother's face flares red. "Fuck you, bro. You don't run shit yet. Why can't you lay off for once?" He whines attempting to stretch his five foot tall frame closer to Jameson's over six feet stature.

"You know what, fuck it. Do what you want," Jameson says throwing up his hands. Giving us full view the scar that runs from his wrist to elbow. And there's his tell. Graham is walking a tight rope right now. Jameson always keeps that scar out of sight, hell he's had it since high school and I don't even know how he got it.

Graham perks right up ignoring the looks Liam and I are shooting at him. "Thanks bro," he replies coming back to the benches while we pack up for the day. His anger forgotten. Typical Graham gets his way and easy to handle but go against his wishes and you'll wish you never spoke.

"Don't thank me yet. I don't want a single complaint. One single issue and I'm buzzing your fucking head while you sleep. We clear?" Jameson orders.

"Crystal. Thanks bro you so get my style." Oh Graham. Jameson's lip curls and his eyes blaze. Will my baby brother ever learn to shut up. We all know Jameson only caved to avoid our mom not cause he get's Graham's laid back style.

My older brother shakes his head. "Whatever, but you better be here on time tomorrow to help set up. The family workouts are in the morning and Hadley Falls little league is using the field after for tryouts. Need you to handle setup and take down." Jameson orders.

"At least we can bust each other's balls if we get bored. Should be fun." Liam blurts breaking the tension. "Hey, Connor, did you hear your ex is back?"

"What?" My head snaps towards him, a mischievous grin is spread across his beard covered face. Asshole.

"Mom and dad ran into her yesterday. Rumor is she's back to stay, and her sights are set on you." He points his finger at me wiggling it like some child trying to give me coo-dies. The fuck. I narrow my eyes at him. My brothers chuckle. Dicks.

"Can you believe the nerve of her, treats you like dirt, takes off. Now she's back telling the whole town she's getting you back." Liam lets out on a hiss, rolling his eyes.

"This is the first I heard about it. Doesn't mean shit to me." A dull thumping builds at the base of my neck. Fucking hell, Kelly is a complication I don't want to deal with.

"Let's grab sandwiches on Main street for lunch? I'm starving and I got a meeting by the college. My treat." Offers Jameson.

Liam whistles. "Dang Jay, you hold more meetings than your dad. You working a corporate takeover?"

"What can I say? I'm a busy boy." Jameson counters with a wink.

"Don't get what makes you so special. What goes on at these lunches anyway?" Graham whines.

"None of your fucking business," Jameson blurts. A flicker of irritation goes through his eyes.

"Got some secret business brewing you don't want us knowing about?" Liam says, laughter in his eyes. My Jameson smirks.

"More like a deal completed, that doesn't concern you, unless you want to lose a limb." He lifts one eyebrow, looking like some carrot top version of the Rock, and we all laugh.

"Please don't be doing something stupid." Our cousin pleads.

"Relax Liam. I'm fucking with you, chill."

"Good, cause Cormac and I are still the oldest, and we'll kick your ass, little cousin."

All of us burst out in another round of laughter. The threat is bullshit, Jameson is a giant at 6'5. He's taller than any of us, and he's built like a stone wall. No way any one of us can take him down.

My big brother may not be the first born of our generation, but everyone my uncles included treat Jameson as if he is head of the family. He carries the weight of the universe on his shoulders. Everyone goes to him for advice and help. The dude is a fortress. He locks everything up tight.

"Can't. Gotta clean up and head to work. Friday night is always slammed."

"Do you ever take a day off?" Jameson asks.

"Do you?"

"Fair point. Jameson adds before turning to the others. "Who wants lunch on me?" Both nod their heads and all three head to the locker room. I collect my stuff and head home. Liam's words ring in my head the entire drive home.

The blaring alarm sounds from my pants pocket before I take one step past the threshold. Kicking the door shut, I pull out my phone to stop the noise before tossing it on the counter with a thud. Fuck. Three o'clock. Only gives me an hour to wash today's stink off, change, and head to McKinnon's before we open. The soft humming pain of a headache settling between my eyes hits. Every muscle in my body is aching. Shit, today was tough. Water is the only thing on my mind.

I head straight for the fridge and pound an entire bottle. Tonight is gonna be a long one. Why did I agree to training with Jameson on a Friday? The best perk of being a part-time employee is not having to attend all training days. Doesn't help my father owns the place, so I can decide not to show up but I'll leave the flaking to Graham.

I'm not a fan of the job, but committing a few hours a week to McKinnon Security is the only way Pops supported me leaving to open my pub. Thank god for Jameson to continue the family business.

By the time I gather all my clothes, take two aspirin and down another bottle my shower is hotter than shit. No time to enjoy it though so I scrub up and rinse quickly. The entire time I'm getting ready for work I can't get Liam's news out of my head. Kelly's back. Why? She left for a better life, more options. Why would she come back now, and for me?

Fuck, I don't need for her games or bullshit. I gave Kelly everything, and she threw every piece of information back in my face. She lied to me for months pretending to be happy when in reality she was just waiting for the perfect moment to play her hand.

Pain slams into my head behind my eyes. All thoughts of my ex evaporate. Shit. I pinch the bridge of my nose and rub my hand down my face then crack my neck to the side. The familiar cracking sound instantly eases the tension.

This shit is why I don't need a relationship. When I need to burn off steam I find someone to share my bed for a hard fuck. Keep it casual. Life taught me the hard way, there isn't anyone out there for me. The woman I'm looking for doesn't exist. So, no point dating. I have the pub, my friends and my family. Relationships they're overrated, anyway.

Connor

Chapter Four

Tonight is going to be long, but fun. McKinnon Pub is overflowing, every table and stool is occupied.

Nights like this excite everyone. The servers realize if they work hard they can make a killing on tips. My bar staff bust ass knowing they take home a percentage of them. Win win for everyone. I love nights like tonight, different people walking through the door. The hum of the crowd and the music fade into a collective signaling we are officially slammed.

Jamie signals for me to jump in. Two bartenders and three waitresses might not be enough staff for a night like this. Tonight is the busiest night since I bought the place. That knowledge helps make all the ache and tension from today fade away. The rush dies after an hour and I make a mental note to schedule a third bartender on Friday nights.

Thankfully everyone seems to be in less of a rush and making less mistakes. Good. Jamie and Grant confirm they are solid and don't need help so I finish my pass around the pub. Time for a drink of my own. I grab a lowball glass, and a bottle of my favorite Black Barrel Irish Whiskey. The smoky heat burns on the way down. Refreshing.

My body is still sore from workouts and all I want is a beautiful woman to lose myself in after my shift. Might as well start looking. Scanning the patrons for familiar faces I let my mind wander.

A pair of plump breasts catch my vision to my right. The woman is short, the only part of her visible is a gorgeous set of bigger than double Ds and a long mane of dark brown hair. No way she is older than eighteen with her size, I really should ask for ID. Our eyes meet. Pools of green with flecks of gold stare back at me and draw me in, making me forget my words. Catching myself I shake off the weird effect her gaze is having on me.

"What can I get you?" I reach for a hurricane glass expecting the overly sweet drink she is about to order. Girls her age are always order something trendy.

"I'll take what you're having, two fingers please." She gives me a smirk, biting down on the corner of her lip. Is she for real? Black Barrel Whiskey. Every woman I ever met hates the stuff.

I give her a questioning squint, but she only nods her head once in return. My hand hovers unsure what to do over the hurricane glasses for half a second before moving to swip a low ball glass off the shelf. *Don't stare at her mouth.* The woman licks her lips in anticipation. My eyes go straight to her lips. Damn, those lips are sexy as hell. The girl doesn't disappoint.

Pulling the crystal up to her nose, she takes a deep inhale. The scene is slightly erotic, she closes her eyes and lets out a satisfied groan. My eyebrow cocks in surprise and my dick twitches. *Get yourself under control, man.* Ignoring my stare she brings the glass to her mouth, tilts her head back finishing her drink in one swallow.

Fuck.

The only reaction she gives to the strong whiskey is a small hiss she lets escape through her teeth.

"Damn, I needed that, another, please." I hit her with another refill. This woman has spunk. Never in my life have I seen a woman take such a bitter drink so smooth. Watching her take a small sip while she savors the smokiness on her tongue is kind of erotic.

"Surprised you like Black Barrel, most can't stand the smokiness." She beams. Dang, her smile reaches her eyes and her entire face lights up like my personal ray of sunshine.

"I'm a huge whiskey fan. A friend of mine loved the stuff. Learned a lot from him," she chuckles. Must be more to the story. *Why do you care?*

"Well, they taught you well." I wink at her, pouring on as much charm as I can. "Welcome to The McKinnon Pub, I'm Connor the owner and your personal bartender this evening."

Her cheeks turn a beautiful shade of light pink as a blush sets in, the look turns me harder than stone. She's gorgeous.

"Hi, I'm Katy. Is this your..." A female screech high enough to break all the glass bottles in here cuts her off mid sentence.

"Katy! Oh, you came, you came!! And I see you met Connor." Elise comes barreling up to Katy, wrapping her arms around her giving her a squeeze. The woman is bouncing on the balls of her feet dripping with excitement.

"Hey sweetie! Of course, I'm here." The giant smile she gives her friend makes my cock jump in my pants. *What the fuck, you aren't a teenager,* I chastise my dick.

"Elise." I nod.

"Connor, this is my bestie, Katy. Today is her birthday and we need to celebrate. Since tonight is packed, can we make this a private party of four in your office." She bats her eyes at me.

"Only the two of you? Where's Ryan?" I search the crowd for my closest friend. No way his girlfriend is in here without him.

"He's parking. Please, Connor, only us." Elise points to me, her and Katy. I'm going to say yes. The girl always finds a way to victory, but this time I'm saying yes because something about this Katy woman is peeking my interest.

"You did call yourself my personal bartender this evening." The minx winks at me, and bites the inside of her lip. Game on.

"Well, I can't deny the Birthday girl, now, can I?" I wink at them, flashing my teeth with a giant grin. Katy lets out a giggle and Elise shakes her head, smirking at me in her knowing way. After a few seconds Ryan appears and I inform Jamie I'll be in the back and she's in charge the rest of the night. Perks of being the boss.

My back room doubles as my office and private meeting area. A two surface oak desk sits at one end of the room next to two filing cabinets and a small fridge. On the other side is where I meet with staff and vendors, giving the meetings a more laid back vibe.

A long sofa lines the wall. In the center sits a round table and four lounge chairs, all leather with Kelly Green stitching. They match the color scheme of the pub and give the space a business feel while still comfortable and not too uptight.

Everyone finds a seat and I head to the mini fridge to grab the drink tray and load us up on refreshments.

"One bottle of Irish Whiskey for the birthday girl and soda for those who mix." Katy's eyes light up at the sight.

"More Irish Whiskey! This day is finally turning around, thanks Connor." She beams at me, her smile turns smoldering, making my mouth water and my cock twitch. Traitor, we met her less than five seconds ago. Stop acting like a teenager with his first hard on. My dick jumps again in reply, refusing to stand down. Asshole.

"He's a prick," my friend blurts. Whose a prick?

"*Ryan.*" Elise smacks Ryan's arm, an audible whack resounding through the room.

He rubs this spot she hit him, pretending injury. His button down shirt stretches with each bend of his arm. "What? You said Noah dumped her over some bullshit this morning. That's fucked." Ryan raises his hand up in confusion. "I'm happy her day got better. Was I not supposed to say anything?" he looks so confused at both of the women.

Typical Ry, I chuckle to myself. Always too oblivious to realize when he says something insensitive. He's always been blunt, the man doesn't care about what you should or shouldn't discuss. If he's got something to say, he says it, simple.

"Elise, chill. I'm all good. Promise. He meant nothing by the comment. Noah is a dick and I'm not letting him ruin my birthday anymore."

"Wait, your boyfriend broke up with you this morning?" What kind of dude breaks up with a girl on her special day? *You could show her how a real man treats his girl.*

Where did those thoughts come from? I just met the girl, I'm not looking for anything with anyone, period.

"Yep, he ruined a splendid dream, probably did it on purpose to dig the knife in," she lets out a dark chuckle. "Thankfully, Elise is the greatest. She fed me chocolate and forced me to come out tonight." Katy smiles at her friend and gives her a hug before taking the glass of whiskey I poured her.

"A toast. Happy Birthday to Katy. May your day end better than your morning started," I say raising my glass. The sound of glass chiming rings through the office.

"To new friendships," Elise adds giving Katy and I goo-goo eyes, with a shit-eating grin on her face. What is she up to? "Let's play never have I ever."

Ryan scoffs first. "Elise, come on, we are adults." Uh oh here comes the puppy dog face. He stands zero chance.

"I know, but I can't think of a more perfect way to get acquainted. Come on, Katy, Connor, play. He can't refuse if you both agree," She whines.

"I'm in." Katy and I say in unison.

"Yes! Come on babe. I promise it'll be fun," Elise flirts.

"Fine, I'll start. Never have I ever had sex in public." Ryan utters gruffly, giving me a smug smirk. Payback for siding with his girl, I'm sure. I shake my head and take a sip, watching Katy to see if she takes one too, but I'm the only one.

"What! Sex in public? Where?" Katy asks her eyes shining bright with curiosity.

"Yep, in the bathroom at a baseball game. Almost got caught too. Thanks for saving the day Ry." We tip our glasses to each other and take giant swigs.

Hours later, we finish the entire bottle of whiskey while asking outrageous questions and getting further acquainted. The more I learn about Katy, the more I like. She speaks her mind, and doesn't wilt from harsh language or dirty words. Her boyfriend is an idiot to dump her this morning. Turd has no clue what he gave up.

"Wow, we finished the entire bottle." Elise giggles. Pulling me out of my thoughts. She turns to Katy. "Come with me to freshen up?"

"Sure," Katy replies as they both head out of the office and down the hall. I can't help but stare at Katy's very sexy ass as they do.

Ryan and I clear the trash from the table. He waits to make sure the girls are down the hall. "So, what do you think of Katy?"

"Where did you find this girl? You got lucky, by the way." I ground out.. The asshole is perfectly aware I hate blind dates of any kind. I should kick his ass for setting me up but this time I'm happy he ignored me. Katy is refreshing from all the chicks I normally hook up with.

"Yeah right you go a head and pretend to be angry. Katy is exactly what you need. The second Elise mentioned inviting her out tonight I knew she'd be perfect for you," Ryan chuckles.

"On the real though Katy got shit on today and in the past too. So if you hurt her I'll fuck you up as a favor to my girl." I think on Ryan's threat while he drinks the last bit of whiskey left in his glass. Acknowledging what he said with a nod, not sure how to answer.

I am insanely attracted to Katy, but relationships aren't my thing. *But you do hook ups.* No way am I going down that road with Elise's best friend.

The girls come giggling into the room, I'm not sure how, but Elise appears more drunk now than when they left for the restroom. Her cheeks are flushed, eyes are glossy. Ah, they had a little detour.

"Hey you cleaned up! What for?" Elise singsongs scrunching her face questioningly.

"Listen lady. You can't walk away from your tab. I don't care who you say you are." Nicole, a waitress comes barging in yelling, her eyes ablaze with fury. Before I can ask what the fuck is going on, Katy whirls around to face her squaring her shoulders.

"Like I told you out there. My purse is in here." Katy shoves her Visa into Nicole's face. "Here, close Elise's tab out." I snatch Katy's card out of the air before Nicole can grab it.

"Don't think so. The bill closed. Anything Elise or Katy ordered is comped." My tone is stern but not harsh. Nicole means well but I'm getting sick of having the same conversation over female customers.

This better not be anything more than her trying to collect payment. She is a terrific waitress, but her crush on me can sometimes effects her level of professionalism.

"You don't need to. Elise wanted to do a shot before we came back in and one turned into four and I forgot my card was in my purse. "We didn't mean to make a scene or cause an issue with your server." Katy rambles, it is the most adorable thing.

"Nicole, give me the receipt and a marker." She pulls the white paper out of her apron and hands them over. I write Connor Comp and throw the damn thing on my desk.

"The tab is closed. Like I said before if there is a problem when you close out tell Jamie to talk to me. You don't ever scream at a customer again. If someone is trying to leave without paying you call Grant or myself. Things can go wrong quicker than you realize," I say as my fist lands on the desk. "I don't want my employees at risk. Now, I won't write you up this time, but next time I will and it will be with three

Fridays off without pay. We clear." Nicole's eyes bug out at the mention of lost wages.

"Understood, boss," Nicole states, her voice defeated. She turns to Katy, "I'm sorry if I came off rude."

"No problem." Katy offers her hand with a soft smile. Nicole shakes her hand. I don't miss the glare she shoots Katy as she leaves. Fuck, I have a feeling her little crush is going to be an issue.

"Awkward." Ryan blurts, rubbing his hand over his neck and jaw. Elise lets out a high-pitched hiccup, giggling like a schoolgirl.

"And that's our cue to leave. Come on babe, you had way too much to drink tonight. Let's go home and I'll give you lots of water." Ryan kisses Elise's forehead before helping to lay her jacket over her shoulders.

"But I don't wanna go yet. Plus, Katy is the birthday girl she says when the night's over, not you," Elise whines, turning to Katy. "Do you want the night to be over?"

Katy glances over at her friend and Ryan. He is doing his best to shake his head yes without being seen.

"Didn't you promise Faye to help her tomorrow for Grayson's party? She is so going to text you to be at the park super early to set up."

"Shoot, I completely forgot about setting up tomorrow." Hiccup. "Crap, babe, we need to leave, NOW. I promised Faye I'd be at the park at like 8am, ugh." Elise's joys deflates like someone dumped an ice-cold bucket over her. She pouts while she grabs her things and gives Katy a hug bye.

"Connor, can you make sure Katy gets home safe, please?" Hiccup. I smirk.

"Of course I will." I assure her. Elise says a final goodbye to Katy before her and Ryan head out, leaving Katy and I alone in my office.

"You don't need to take me home." Katy says as soon they're gone. "I walked and I don't want to be a bother." She shifts her gaze to the floor. She's nervous, but I can't tell if they're because of me or something else.

How badly did her ex treat her? Taking two steps I put myself right in front of her. Hooking my finger under her chin, I force her eyes to mine. "No trouble, I plan on seeing you home." I smile warmly, grazing my thumb across the back of her hand.

All of a sudden I'm very aware how close I am to Katy and I can't help but stare at her mouth. Wonder how sweet her lips taste? *I bet you wanna know what her other lips are like.* I smirk inwardly, thankful as fuck Katy can't read my thoughts. Her eyes darken with desire, and her breathing deepens. She swallows, bitting the corner of her mouth then, nods.

I take the cue and press my mouth to hers; swiping my tongue across her lips before pushing inside and swallowing the groan trying to escape. She meets my kiss with the same need and intensity. I move my hand from her chin to behind her head and the other moves around her waist, pulling her closer to me.

Her nipples pebble to tight points under her dress, making my cock swell with need. Her hands roam my chest and shoulders, kneading at my shirt and muscles. My hard length presses into her stomach. She gasps as she pulls herself away.

"Does your office door lock?" She swallows, her voice raspy. Katy tries to even out her breathing, but she only manages to push her boobs out farther.

"Yes, but let's get outta here. You deserve better than a quick fuck in my office on your birthday." She lets out a squeak. Am I going too fast?

"My place is up the road and I live alone." She breathes before turning away and walking out to the bar.

Guess not. I'm about to make this birthday one she never forgets.

Katy

Chapter Five

Oh my gosh! The smoking hot bartender is walking me home. How did this happen? *Now you worry? You let him kiss you.* Shit, we did. Much dirtier thoughts cross my mind.

Can I do this? A one-night stand with a guy?

The front door creaks and Connor steps out on the sidewalk. He's wearing a dark button-down shirt, jeans and black boots. Damn, he reminds me of those McManus brothers from Boondock Saints. Yummy. I bite the inside of my lip. Well, question answered, I'm more than prepared to let Connor do whatever he wants with me.

"You ready?" Connor asks, rolling down his sleeves, covering his beautiful ink in the process. I'd love to get a closer look. *Umm you're taking him home!* Hush.

"Yep." I answer with more confidence than I expect.

The McKinnon Pub is in the center of Hadley Falls shops on Main Street. The building takes up the entire corner wrapping around both sides and is painted a beautiful shade of charcoal with dark green accents. Common Place Café sits a few stores up. I can't believe I never paid attention to Connor's pub. The girls and I need to come back during the day to try the food.

A slight breeze blows the fabric of my dress against my legs. I love this time of night. The streets are empty by one a.m. every night, mostly from the college campus curfew. Walking through the Historical District this late always puts me in a good mood. It calms my nerves down after a crazy day and occasionally a walk will knock free a new recipe idea.

"What are you thinking about?" Connor's gravely voice washes over me. My lady parts purr. *Chill out.* We are playing this cool.

"Thinking about how beautiful the city is at this hour. The silence is so peaceful." Connor stops and turns me to face him.

"Seriously, you know how dangerous walking home this late alone can be, right?" A hard edge fills his voice.

"Yes, my brother constantly tells me. But midnight strolls help me think. Plus, I only live two streets over." I point around the corner, smiling at him.

"So."

"Dislike me walking all you want. No way I'm driving my car three blocks every day. Talk about a waste of gas." Connor growls low and my jaw drops. Heat warms in my gut and spreads out through my body. Wow, that was sexy.

"How many nights do you walk home after midnight?"

"A couple times a week. Why?" Where's he going with this?

"Give me your phone." He holds out his hand and my eyebrows raise in question.

"Please." Smart man. I'm too curious to say no. I hand him my phone unlocked. He clicks one of my apps, I think messages I can't tell from my angle. A few seconds later his beeps, and he hands me mine back.

"Now you have my number. Next time you plan on walking home late text me and I'll meet you at your bakery." A protest is about to leave my lips, but Connor stops me with his mouth. Warmth ignites like wild fire in my belly causing my pussy to swell. Crap, how am I this aroused?

My arms wrap around Connor's neck as he smashes his body into mine. His soft thick hair feels silky on my fingers. Every time a surge of pleasure goes through me I pull and twist on his locks. The same needy sensation from earlier keeps rising inside me.

I want this man, all of him. For the first time in forever, I'm not thinking of anyone else but me and what I want, and right now I want Connor. A car driving by honks, shouting at us to get a room. We smile and Connor pulls me tighter against him. "Say yes," He growls.

"Yes," I breathe.

"Please tell me your place is close." His hands go around my waist cupping my butt and pulling my hips into him. The length of his erection grinds against my stomach. I lick my lips slightly before biting down.

Connor lets out a groan and an odd sense of power washes over me. I've never made a man do that before. An image of me on my knees gagging on his hard length enters my mind. He lets out a deeper groan this time it sounds almost painful. Can he read my thoughts? I wink, and touch my tongue to my top lip.

"Fucking minx. How far?"

"The next block."

"Perfect." He gives me another searing kiss before holding out his arm.

"Lead the way." All talk about him walking me home after my night shifts ends. Fine by me. I don't need to put anyone out over getting home. *Why are you a little bummed, he let the subject drop?* Oh shh. Tonight isn't about promises, it's about having fun and letting go.

The walk back to my condo is over in a few minutes. My palms are sweaty, I bet Connor can hear how fast my heart is beating.

"Want to come in?" I whisper. Oh crap, I asked him in. *You do realize, if he says yes, you are going to bang a stranger!* That thought should terrify me but it sends a thrill of excitement straight to my center.

"You know I do," Connor says through a clinched jaw, his eyes are dark with lust. My core tightens, goosebumps break out on my forearm. His hand finds mine and I lead us into my home.

Strong arms grip me, pushing me into the wall of the entry way. Rough hands brush my thighs, pulling them open and lifting me into his arms. Instinctively I lock my legs behind his back. Our mouths seal together in a bruising kiss.

Breathless and greedy he pulls away, for more. "Bedroom. Now." The deep tenor of his voice sends tiny quakes down my back. Pressure builds in my gut flowing right to that tight bundle of nerves above my opening.

"At the end of the hall." The words come out husky. Jeez, needy much, I sound as breathless as Connor. Somehow he maneuvers me over his shoulder and carries me to my bed.

"EEK" I squeal into Connor's ear, and he rewards me with a slap on my ass. His fingers squeeze and kneed my rounded cheeks. "Um," I groan.

He pushes my bedroom door open and tosses me on the bed. I pull at my dress, flinging the fabric into the corner.

"STOP." Connor commands.

My hands freeze above the hem of my underwear.

"Let me undress you." Connor leans over the bed, grabs the sides of my panties and pulls them down and off in one move. I pinch my knees together. He chuckles.

"Open up, I want to see you." Placing a hand on each knee he uses gravity to spread my legs inch by inch, keeping his eyes on my opening the entire time. My body heats under his gaze. He licks his lips and for a moment I think he is going to kiss my center.

"Beautiful. Next time, I'm going to feast on you. Tonight I need to fuck you. You ready?"

I swallow hard, shaking my head.

"You need to say the words baby."

"Yes, I want this Connor. Fuck me." For a second I'm stunned by how natural that felt.

Connor removes his shirt revealing his toned and muscular frame. Oh boy. Black ink in Celtic knot work wraps around his abdomen and biceps down to his forearms. The design is extremely beautiful and sexy.

His shirt hits the floor taking my mouth along with it revealing the infamous "V". Holy crap it's like a happy trail to his cock. Connor's belt moves and my eyes are fixated on his hand.

The movement of the leather strap is hypnotizing, drawing me in with each twitch of his fingers. Each button pop heats my body even more. He pulls his pants down with his boxers in one swoop.

Whoa he's big and hard as steel. There is a small drop of liquid is sitting on the tip. I wonder how he tastes.

"Never seen anything this enormous before?" The line is cocky and cheesy but makes me smile. I shake my head and wag my finger at him. He climbs on top of me, claims my mouth with his and moves one hand to unclasp my bra while cradling my head in the other. My breasts spill free and my nipples tighten into hard points.

"Fucking gorgeous," He growls, then drops his head sucking one tight bud into his mouth. My back bows and my breasts press further into his face.

"Ah! Connor, please fuck me." A hot itch crawls up my spine. The intense need to have him inside me, burns in my gut. He switches sides, sucking on my other nipple while his hand drops to my clit. My hips buck and I moan at the contact.

"Come for me now and I'll fuck you. Come." The pressure on those small bundle of nerves sears through my skin and I come undone. My entire body explodes and for a split-second my vision flashes white. I'm still riding my high as Connor covers me with his body. His thick length at my entrance. Warm arms envelop me, and he pushes into me with one thrust.

Holy crap, the fullness. My walls suck him deeper until he's seated in me. A second of pain and the fire is back. Flames rake my body and urge me to move. Connor rocks his body into me until the base of his shaft rests against my clit. The force increases with each stroke. His hands find my breasts, kneading and massaging, he flicks and pinches my nipple.

"Oh, Connor! I'm coming." I scream his name, urging him harder into me.

"Fuck yes, come again for me." My body explodes again, sending a tingling sensation all the way out to my fingers and toes. He roars loudly as my inner walls squeeze his length and my entire body pulses.

"That's it baby, watching you come is fucking hot." The friction of our bodies is driving me wild. I arch away from him with a scream.

"Connor. Right there." He pins my hands above my head, using the position of his body to drive deeper inside me. My thighs give way allowing Connor to hit the deepest part of me.

"Damn Katy. You are so tight. Squeeze my dick." His dirty words send more tingles through me.

"Yes!"

"Come for me one last time." His command sends me rocketing into ecstasy. My walls clamp down on his cock, he swells. Warm liquid spills into the condom. *Condom.* Thank god, he remembered. In my excitement, I forgot.

Dumb, lady. I know.

Our breathing is ragged. Real words won't form. "WOW! That was... Now I sound stupid." I'm glowing or floating. My face hurts at the edges from smiling so hard. "Magical. Your junk is um... Wow!" My face heats and I bury my face in my hair.

"Magical, don't think I've heard that before." I groan. "Hey, look at me." He leans over me, grabbing my chin to force my gaze to his. "Don't hide from me. You are fucking gorgeous. The face you make talking about my junk is sexy as fuck. I can listen to you say dirty things all night. Now, bathroom?" I tip my head towards the door to the right. He walks off and I'm left to float through my sexual high. Sex is totally a thing.

"Open your legs," Connor's deep voice filters through my fog. Huh? I furrow my brow at him. He moves between my thighs and uses the wet towel to clean me up; before placing a kiss right on my sex. Heat tingles all over my body ramping up for another round. Connor throws the dirty linen into the bathroom doorway while he climbs above me.

BEEP!BEEP!
BEEP!BEEP!
BEEP!BEEP!

The text alert hits me like a bucket of cold water. Ugh, no way. Only one person sends three texts back to back. Veronica, one of my best friends since high school. What the fuck does she want at this hour?!

Connor pulls back. "Do you need to answer?"

"Probably, I'm sorry."

"No, I understand."

"Thanks." I grab my phone off the night stand. Huh, a missed message from Noah too. Should I check? Nope, not tonight.

Veronica: OMG! Parker asked me out again!!!

Veronica: Do you think I can bring him tomorrow? To the park and your birthday dinner. Parker wants to go out tomorrow and I want him to meet everyone. This guy is so HOT!

Veronica: Almost forgot! Faye called and asked if we can all meet at 7am to help her set up. See you at 7! :)

Shit, V, maybe skip the espresso after dinner next time. She is the queen of long, multiple texts. I read her last text again checking the time. Almost two AM. Fuck! Coffee is going to be a must tomorrow.

Katy: See you then. Of course, you can bring Parker to dinner. Ask Faye about the party, but I'm sure she will say yes.

Damn it, I don't want this night to end. Connor is sitting at the edge of the bed, I walk in between his legs and wrap my arms around his neck.

"Sorry, where were we?" He grips my waist, and pulls me in for a kiss. This one differs from before, sweeter and gentle. It leaves a warm tingle in my belly, but he moves back sooner than I like and the feeling evaporates.

"Everything okay?"

"Yes, my friend wants me to be at the park at 7am. Total karma for giving Elise a hard time earlier." I whine, smiling at him. This is awkward. Now the passion and sex are over, I'm not sure what to do. What do you say to someone you just met and proceeded to give you the hottest orgasm of your life?

Connor speaks first. "Well shit, you got five hours," He says looking down at his watch. "Can I call you tomorrow?"

"Sure," my voice goes up, surprised. "My friend's son's birthday party is in the morning, and I have dinner with my friends for my birthday. Would you like to come? The party doesn't actually start until like 2 but its at a park. Friend duty means I need to spend all day setting up and holding the tables." *Word vomit much. Real smooth Katy, invite the Irish sex god to a little kid's party, I'm sure he can't wait.*

"Sounds like fun. I'm busy in the morning, but I'll text you when I'm done."

"Perfect. Let me walk you out."

Connor pulls on his clothes, while I grab my robe from my bathroom door. I'm tingling all over and my heart is a fluttering mess in my stomach.

"Happy Birthday Katy. I'll call you tomorrow." He places a kiss on my cheek.

"Promise?" A blush creeps up my neck. *Don't be lame.*

"You bet your ass I'm gonna call you." He turns back kissing my lips gently. "Goodnight Katy."

"Night Connor." Exhaustion hits me hard once the door is closed. My legs go weak and I lean into my door for support, my mind still racing. How did I go from this morning to this moment? Totally a question for another day. I'm too tired to think straight.

Every part of me wants to drift off to sleep wrapped in Connor's scent. But I know I'll be too tired to shower in the morning so I force myself to endure a quick shower.

Connor's promise to call is the only thought keeping my body upright. The warm spray helps soothe some of the ache settling in my inner thighs. I do a tiny happy dance excited from his promise to call tomorrow.

Don't be too excited.

As much as I want to scream shut the fuck up at my subconscious, she's right. I can't over think this, tonight was about fun. Guys do the whole one-night stand thing all the time. He probably won't call.

BEEP!BEEP!

What now, V.

Connor: Sweet dreams beautiful.

Oh, shit. A goodnight text. Be cool, be cool. *There's no one here, woman.* Oh, duh. My heart races. Maybe he likes me. Sleep takes me the second I hit the pillow and I welcome the darkness. Tonight's memory is going to play on repeat in my dreams.

Connor

CHAPTER SIX

Fucking hell Katy is something. She consumes my thoughts the entire walk back to the pub. I can't believe she slept with me, I adjust my growing erection. Damn just thinking about this girl is getting me worked up.

The parking lot is empty when I get back, I use my phone to double check the alarm is set. Then jump into my car and head home. I live about three miles from my shop so the drive goes by in a flash. My mind turns back to Katy and her sexy mouth as she shouted my name, before she came all over my cock.

Unfortunately, all thoughts of Katy disappear as I head down my street. My brother's black Audi R8 is sitting in my driveway, almost blocking all the parking.

"What the fuck." The clock on my dash shows two fifteen. Damn, this is bad. What happened now? Once again, I'm grateful I don't live on my family's property like my brothers do. They each have their own living space, but my mother gets nosy and demands her way, a lot.

Surprise, surprise, my older brother Jameson is sitting at my breakfast bar. Perfect, he's nursing a half a bottle with an empty glass of scotch. Guess it's better than finding him passed out drunk.

"That was unopened when I left for work." Jameson glances at the bottle, shrugs. Anger is rolling off him, the muscles in his forearm keep tightening. His knuckles whiten as he grips his glass to finish the scotch. He pours himself another.

Jameson reminds me of a Norse god, he's six-three and as broad as a door frame without a single piece of fat on him. His greenish blue eyes drive the girls wild, and at the moment his hair and beard are longer than usual. Well long for him.

The beard is all to piss off our mother. She hates beards, so of course us boys decided we would grow ours out. Tonight, Jameson is menacing sitting here alone drinking in the dimmed light of my home bar.

"You want one?" He grabs another glass and pours me a drink without waiting for my answer. I won't tell him no, not when he's pissed like this with things he needs to say.

"Help yourself. What does she want now? Or should I say demanding?" Jameson raises an eyebrow at me as I toss my keys down, and finish the drink in one gulp. Ahh, I love that stuff.

"Preparing?" He tips his head in approval. "Wait for this shit. Mom wants us to take Rhea, Kelly, and Miranda to Casino night. Says we can't say no because she promised Joy."

"Fucking hell. She didn't ask if I'm taking someone yet." The pleasure of the last few hours flees leaving a tightness in its place.

"Yeah, well, be glad she didn't ruin your night like mine. The woman lives on the same fucking property as me. Why call me while I'm on a date? All mom wants is for us to marry Joy's daughters, its annoying. Plus, I'm certain Bridget hates me now."

"Damn, bro she's fucked up. I don't care what she threatens, I'm not taking Kelly to Vegas night." Only my mother would push for me to take the girl who dumped me to a company event. "I'm sick of her matchmaking."

"Oh, you bitch now, but you will bow to her little brother. You always do. Hey, where the fuck where you, anyway? I called the bar around one but Jamie said you left around 12:30, and you're only now getting back?"

"Walked someone home."

"A female someone?" I don't answer, instead I pour myself another drink.

"Why would Bridget hate you? Did she overhear what mom said?" I ask in a lame attempt to change the subject, but I'm not ready to tell Jameson about Katy yet.

"Slick move little brother and this time I'll let this slip by, but you will tell me about this woman you're hiding and soon."

"Not hiding, I only met her tonight. Now tell me about Bridget."

"Alright, I'll lay off. For now." Jameson teases. Asshole.

"Thanks, now tell me about mom."

"Alright, I took Bridget to Ian's. Mom calls during dessert. Figured it must be important. Nope. She tells me I'm taking Rhea to Vegas night. I refused, she yelled, I hung up."

"Let me guess, Bridget had questions?"

"I told her the truth."

"So, what's the problem?"

"Joy. She sent a text telling me this will be the best night ever. Bridget threw a drink in my face, called me a dog, and stormed out."

"Fuck bro. Did you call her?" I take a sip of my drink letting the amber liquid coat and burn my throat on the way down.

Jameson's glass is empty and the bottle is almost done, so I pour him the rest.

"Thanks. She is refusing my calls."

"Give her space until tomorrow, she'll be easier to talk with. I thought you two are more like friends who hook up, anyway." He cares about Bridget but the feelings don't go deeper than friendship. Jameson runs a hand down his face.

"So, I'm not an asshole. I don't want her to think I'm hiding something. We both promised we would be up front if one of us starting dating someone. She thinks I broke my promise."

"Hate to tell you but, you are an asshole." Jameson snaps his gaze up, fire in his eyes before he catches the smile on my face. Prick thinks I'm serious. Fuck does our mom get to him. Shit, she gets to us all. Maggie's way or you got hell to pay was the motto in our home growing up.

"Lighten up, bro. Come on, don't let her bother you. Use my guest bedroom and do yourself a favor."

"Oh yea. What's that?" He snips back.

"Start house hunting next week. The best decision I ever made was leaving their property." My mom didn't like me moving out but my dad understood and supported my choice. He was a big part of me finding the perfect place.

A four bedroom house gives me with three extra bedrooms and way more space than I need, but works for when stuff like this happens and my brother's need room. They can escape and I still keep my privacy.

I'm positive that's why my dad insisted on using my trust fund for the down payment and mortgage for the first year. One secret I swear no one will ever learn. Although, I'm certain Jameson knows.

"You're right." He glances at his watch. "We need to leave in three hours. We should hit the sack. Morning will be here way too fast."

"Damn tomorrow or should I say today is going to blow. I'm gonna catch as much sleep as I can. Guest room should be ready for you." I turn and walk down the hallway to my bedroom, not waiting for a response from Jameson.

No point to change my clothes. I undo my belt, grab my phone out of my pocket before letting my pants drop to the floor. I send Katy a quick text but pass out before she can reply.

Six a.m. comes way too early. The bright morning light shines under my blinds and I wince. Ugh. Staying up past three a.m. is always a bad idea.

Sniff, sniff. I shudder catching a whiff of myself. The stench of sweat, scotch, and sex curls my nose. Damn, I reek, but I catch the faint smell of something sweet and buttery underneath the lingering liquor leaking from my pores. Katy. Yum, reminds me of fresh bread and homemade cookies.

"Wake the fuck up bro, we are gonna be late!" Dammit Jameson, I forgot he stayed the night. Damn brothers. Shit, mothers too with the bull my ma is pulling over casino night.

"Alright, I'm up". I make my way to the shower, throwing the water to boiling. The last thing I want is to wash the scent of Katy away but I stink. Wonder if her pussy tastes like her skin, sweet with a hint of salt, like chocolate chip cookies.

"Dickhead, hurry up! Dad called he needs us at the field now.." Jameson shouts as he comes barging through my bathroom door.

"Jameson, what? You here to hold my dick or something? We don't cross swords, bro. I'm quite capable of taking a leak without your help." He tosses my undershirt and company shirt at me. The clothes hit me in the chest giving me barely enough time to grab them before they hit me and end up in the toilet. He heads straight for the shower, turning off the water.

"What the fuck. Do I look like I showered yet?" I growl at him, I got to bed past three because of his ass. Now he wants to rob me of my shower. Fuck no.

"No time Connor. Dad called, Graham never showed up we need to be in now to set up before drills start."

Fucking Graham. I finish relieving my kidneys of last night's beverages and make my way to the sink. I give myself a splash of cold water hoping to help wake up. Grabbing my sweat pants off the counter I pull them up and tie them to my waist.

"Shit bro, I changed my mind. You should shower, like now. I cannot be around you smelling like this all day. You reek like liquor and sex. Mom will shit a brick if she catches one whiff of you."

"Fuck you. The two of you are the reason I'm tired and smell like shit. If either of you got a problem with my stench today, you can kiss my ass. Plus, if Graham didn't show mom's problems are way bigger than how I smell. Did you call him?"

"Voicemail," Jameson bites out. "Hurry up and meet me at the car in five minutes," He urges.

Jameson is taking on so many responsibilities at McKinnon Security; I can't remember the last time he didn't work a fifteen plus hour day. He needs a break, we all do.

I finish getting dressed and grab a fresh change of clothes for after training. If I'm lucky, I can meet Katy like I promised. Thoughts of her cause me to smile, damn I'm in trouble if the thought of her puts me in a better mood.

Checking my watch, I still got three minutes before Jameson will bitch. Perfect, I pull my phone off the charger and send a quick text off to Katy.

Connor: *Morning, beautiful. How you feeling?*

I grab my bag and head into the kitchen to fill my thermos with coffee. Jameson can wait. I unscrew the cap and take one sip of the dark, thick liquid. Ah. Best way to start the day. I take one more swig before heading outside.

DING! DING!

> ***Katy: Me too. I'm a little sore. Party set up will be slow today.***

I can't help but smirk. It's my pleasure to make her sore. I slip into Jameson's Audi and send a reply.

> ***Connor: Sorry. Next time I'll go easier on you.***

> ***Katy: You better not.***

> ***Connor: Oh really?!***

> ***Katy: Really, really.***

> ***Katy: Why are you up so early?***

> ***Connor: I'm headed into work at my family's company. You at the park yet?***

"Asshole, wanna join me?" Jameson snaps at me.

"Fuck, sorry what?"

"You talking to the girl from last night?" My head whips around to Jameson,

"Yes, her name is Katy. Happy?"

"You hooked up with her last night and you're texting now. This early? Damn bro. She must be something."

"She's got this way about her. Nicole came at her full attitude. This girl handled her with ease. She's got sass."

"Keep her from ma if you like her. She is hellbent on you making up with Kelly."

DING! DING!

Jameson Rolls his Eyes at me. "Better answer her."

Katy: On the way to pick up coffee for the girls before the park.

Connor: What are you doing later?

Jameson clears his throat. "Sorry, what did you say?"

"Graham. What the fuck is his problem? He's always late or calling in sick. No bullshit, how often is he coming in to the pub?"

"He isn't. Hasn't been in since right after the new year."

"Dammit, what is going on with him? Will you talk with him? He listens to you more." Jameson sighs heavily, exhaustion bleeding off him.

"Sure as shit can't be you. You'll kill him before he answers a single question. How long this bullshit been going on?" I hope Jameson is over-reacting. The alternative is my baby brother has a problem and my other brother is covering for him.

"About a month. I'm probably getting ruffled for nothing but Graham doesn't always make the wisest of choices." Relief washes over me. Typical Jameson. Most likely Graham is partying a little too hard somewhere neither of his older brothers will find out.

"Alright," I smirk at Jameson. "You know, sometimes you worry worse than ma." Jameson booms with laughter.

"He gets away with everything, he needs more people in his shit. Mom lets him slide on everything. She always gives an excuse why his behavior is acceptable and swears us to secrecy. Yet with us she airs our dirty laundry so often she could distribute a fucking newsletter."

"Be glad she doesn't send live text updates," I tease. Jameson rolls his eyes letting out a moan.

"Fuck that. Enough about Graham. Tell me about Katy. Do you like her?" Jameson's lifts his eyebrow like "the rock" and I shake my head and scoff.

"I met her last night but I can't stop thinking about her though. She can hold her own, and she likes whiskey as much as I do. I'm trying to see her tonight." Jameson grunts his approval.

"Any woman who enjoys whiskey is fine by me. Did you sleep with her?" Jameson tips his head like I'm supposed to dish like a school-girl about my hook up. In the past I told him about my one-night stands but Katy isn't one and I don't want to give him many details.

"Not going there, bro, so don't ask." Jameson pulls into the parking lot. I have never been happier to arrive at the office. We park, collect our gear and make our way inside.

BUZZ BUZZ.

> **Katy: I'll be at the park all day but call me when you're free.**

I smile, reading the message again. Today is looking up, I send a quick reply then slide my phone on vibrate and head into training.

> **Connor: Will do beautiful!**

Katy

Chapter Seven

Achy thighs and a growling stomach from my late night with Connor is a hell of a way to start the day. That man is devilish.

These feelings are new. Every movement makes me think of him. The morning text he sent blew my whole casual bull crap I told myself right out the window.

A morning text from the man made the whole casual crap I told myself last night fly right out the window. My cheeks hurt from my inability to stop smiling.

Unfortunately, my phone also had message from Noah too but I sent those puppies straight to trash. He showed his true colors yesterday. *Took you long enough. You didn't realize it either.*

Sometimes I swear, I'm crazy. I hope everyone talks to themselves as much as I do.

Rescue coffees at the ready. I pull into the spot next to Faye. She is hard to miss, thick dark brown almost black hair flows all the way down the middle of her back. Today her hair is up in a high ponytail, bouncing in the tiny breeze. Faye is amazing, but she doesn't drink coffee. Which means she forgets the rest of us need those magical beans to function, even more so after a night of drinking.

She is bending over the back of her van emptying firetrucks, red balloons and a host of party supplies into Grayson's wagon. Her rather plump ass is drawing attention from the few males out running the trail at this hour.

"Hey sweetie."

Faye turns around, a grin spreading across her face. "Katy, Happy Birthday. Didn't you and Noah stay out late?"

"Long story."

Clank

The sounds of car doors shutting draws my attention, sure enough Veronica is exiting her SUV with Elise and Lily in tow.

"Woman, how did you beat us here? Elise said no way you were getting up early, and she won't say why. Now pass out the coffee I know you're hiding in your car. Hand it over, then tell us all the secrets," Veronica demands. She is the silliest, one of us all and never lets anything get her down.

She's a bigger girl with wide hips and thick thighs. Her hair is the most beautiful shade of red. The fire engine color with a hint of wine that everyone willingly pays stupid amounts of money for. She is one hundred percent all natural and doesn't even see how many guys stare at her twice.

Did Elise blab? She shakes her head, reading my thoughts. Of course not, Elise is the secret keeper.

"Well, I stayed out late, but not with Noah. He dumped me yesterday." The girls collectively let loose a round of angry shouts and questions.

"He what!" Lily exclaims. "Why didn't you call us?"

I shrug. Who wants to tell their friends they got kicked to the curb for being a bad lay? Elise was enough. "Lets empty the van and I'll spill everything."

"Fine. You better not leave anything out," Lily states leveling her piercing blue eyes on me. She does her trademark hair flip making the sun bounce off her golden hair. The woman is a walking cliché, but I love her.

She has the biggest heart in the universe and always thinks the best of others.

"Shut up and move your butt, woman." Faye flashes me a gigantic smile.

"Thanks girl," She whispers. "They will talk all day and be no help if you don't give em a push."

"Anytime sweetie. Is Grayson excited about today?" Faye's face saddens for the briefest of moments before she plasters on a grin.

"Oh, you bet," she composes her self while grabbing a box of decorations to put out.

My heart breaks for them. She married a great man in Ray. A shame tragedy struck before he could meet Grayson. The little guy doesn't always understand his daddy can't be present.

Faye owns a tasting room, restaurant, and wine shop all part of a winery on the outskirts of town. Hands down she is the hardest working woman in the entire city and will do anything for her boy.

"Katy, hurry with the coffee," someone calls.

"Coming."

We work on covering the tables and adding the fire truck center pieces. The weather is beautiful. Warm but not sticky. Not a cloud in the sky and the slight breeze is keeping the heat away. A perfect April day.

"So spill," Lily urges and everyone turns to me.

"Fine." I reply. So I spend the next ten minutes filing them on my last twenty four hours. I skip right over the dream, some things my friends don't need to know.

"So what happened after Ryan and I went home last night?" Elise blurts.

"You two went out without us?" Hurt crosses Veronica's face. "Why didn't you invite us?" she whispers.

"Didn't you go on a date yesterday? Same for you Lily. I thought you and Isaac went out." Elise quips before I can say anything. Girl always has my back. Both girls nod. "There you go."

"We went to The McKinnon Pub, Ryan's friend owns the place," I toss out.

"You are missing the enormous detail here, woman. Will you hurry to the sweet stuff?" Whoa someone's feisty.

"The quick version. We kissed, he walked me home, he got my number, and he put his in my phone." I pause, knowing the suspense is driving Elise insane.

"Then." Faye chimes in. "Did you have sex? Come on, I live through you girls. There isn't enough time in the day for me to date. So tell us all the juicy details. Did you get it in?" she wiggles her eyebrows sending us all into a fit of laughter.

"Oh, my god. Yes, I got it in. Completely mind-blowing and everything you all proclaimed sex to be and more. We started round two, but Veronica text me about getting here at seven. He left after."

"Nothing else?" V shouts.

"Let me finish. He sent me a text last night after he left. We talked this morning too." Last night's experience shattered all my opinions of sex. Connor opened my eyes to something new and I like it.

"Holy shit you're blushing over a man. Well, damn. You never blushed over that asshole Noah." Lily drops.

"Oh, hush. I also never slept with someone after I met them the same day."

"Honey, I hate to break this to you but, you've only slept with one person before Connor. From what you told us, he sucked. Sex is supposed to leave you breathless. Intimacy with the right one leaves you in a cloud of euphoria you can't come down from. Like the world comes alive for the first time." Faye laments and her eyes glaze over as she stares off in the distance.

"Awe how sweet, auntie. Are you thinking about Ray?" Lily inquires. Her eyes go soft, feeling bad for her aunt. Hell, we all do.

"Huh? Oh, yep, I'm thinking about my man. Sorry, got lost." She blurts pointing to her head. The tiniest blush settles on her cheeks. Faye catches me staring. She shakes her head at me.

Okay, so not my business.

"So you like him sweetie?" Veronica pushes, hopeful.

"Nah, just wanted a hard fuck." I reply. Her face drains of all color and I let out a cackle. For as long as we've been friends she still can't tell when I'm screwing with her.

"Oh dammit, you're joking."

"Um, yes, I like to call it sarcasm. Guys, I'm scared because I don't like him, I like him, like him. He's hot and his voice is this deep tone that gives me butterflies. Am I crazy? We met yesterday, the same day I got dumped. Our one night can't go anywhere. Ugh, I'm over thinking this. Let's pick up the pace guys it's almost time for guests."

"Katy, always the manager and my hero." Faye mocks. "How would we ever finish set up if you didn't force us back to work?"

"Oh, that's enough sarcasm missy. This is your son's party, I'm trying to be helpful," I spit back.

"I'm teasing!" she sticks her tongue out at me. We all continue to finish decorating. Faye walks over to me and whispers, "I'm serious. Don't overthink him and let things happen. The universe doesn't let you pick when you fall in love." What's she getting at?

She doesn't wait for a response before walking away to put up more streamers. Her words stir something up in me. Could this be more than a hook up? I shake the thoughts from my head and decide to take Faye's advice. Let things happen.

The party is in full swing. We covered the entire seating area in all things red and firefighter. Veronica and Elise are freaking talented. They made these cool balloon streamers, they give the appearance of fire hoses wrapped around all the pillars. Two yellow, red and orange balloon towers are at each end of the patio. Mini fire hydrants and fire trucks as centerpieces on every table, topping off the decorations.

No cake for this party. Only the best cupcakes in town for the little man. The bakery made them exact to his request, red and orange frosting with yellow cake.

Of course, I made a dozen blood orange cupcakes with whipped cream frosting and filled with a chocolate ganache. I got the idea after eating one of those chocolate orange things. They've been a hit with my staff, I hope the adults love them.

A child squeals and I glance over at the children playing. Grayson having an amazing time running around with his friends from Pre-K. I never knew little boys could be as loud though, if not louder than girls. Ouch.

"Fuck! Those kids need a muzzle. Do they need to scream like that?" Isaac randomly shouts to no one.

Jerk much, we might all be thinking the same, but being so rude was not necessary. Shit like this, is why we can't stand Lily's boyfriend.

Dude has the worse case of small man syndrome. Isaac is only five foot five, he appears harmless. Key word appears, he was so charming at first but over the years he's become more of a jerk turning him ugly in my eyes. The striking jaw line used to make him seem mysterious now appears cold and calculating.

"Babe, they are being kids." Lily whines, trying to soothe his attitude.

"Did I ask you?" He snaps. Ugh, I cannot stand him. I'd love nothing more than to ask Jackson to rough him up. And since violence is never the answer I'll annoy him with my smart mouth.

"Chill out Isaac, or no drinky, drinky for you tonight." I say lightly, so he doesn't fly off the handle. Today is about celebrating Grayson. He scoffs shooting me a dirty grimace as he walks off to go by the other men.

"You didn't need to say anything," Lily, mumbles. "I can take care of my fiance."

"Yes, she did. Let him be mad at Katy for opening her mouth rather than you for contradicting him. He's an ass, he would have kept pushing." Elise raises her eyebrow, daring someone to say she's wrong. Lily shrugs.

"I don't like others fighting my battles. I can handle my shit." She tries to glare, but misses the mark, and we all bust out laughing at her attempt to be a hard ass.

"Oh sweetie. Of course, you're capable. We are comrades." Veronica fakes a Russian accents, "all for one and one for all kind of thing."

"Hey I thought I was the nerd in this group?" I jest.

V squints her eyes and continues, "On to happier topics. Katy where are we headed for dinner? Birthday girl's choice." Veronica states with a grin slowly splitting her face. No doubt thinking of her new man.

"Ian's Steakhouse. Now you owe us some information. Who is Parker?" Everyone's head turns. Her deer in headlight eyes are adorable. From the O her mouth is making I don't think she's told the others about him.

"Excuse me, who? You started dating someone and didn't tell us? I thought yesterday was your first one." Faye fakes a hurtful tone, then scoffs at her. I'm trying so hard not to giggle. My friends are ridiculous, but I love them to pieces.

"Yes. I'm horrible, but he's only taken me on two dates. I'm super nervous having him meet you guys so soon" Veronica confesses. "Be kind to him tonight, okay?" I'm pretty sure she gulped. Whoa she must more than like this guy. Good for her, she deserves some happiness.

RING! RING!

I pull out my phone and Connor's name lights up the screen. Holy shit, he's calling me. Um, crap.

"Hey you. I thought you were working?"

"Hey beautiful, I'm off now. You still at your friend's party?" His gruff voice sends shivers down to my lady parts.

"Yep, the kids are playing. We are doing cake and presents soon. I'll probably be here another hour. I need to go clean up for dinner with my friends and their boyfriends after we finish here."

"What about you?"

"What about me?" No way am I about to ask the guy I met last night to come out to meet my closest people. Nope, not putting myself out there. *Chicken.*

"So tell me did you purposely wear tight jeans and a low-cut top hoping you'd run into me? Or did you have them on display for someone else?" Interesting, I bite the corner of my lip.

"How do you know what I'm wearing? You jealous I might dress like this for someone other than you?" Who am I? I never talk like this with men. Desirable men too. They make me stumble and say the wrong words.

Is he here? A black Audi R8 pull into the lot. Uh oh, I'm not the only one who's seen the luxury car.

"Who the fuck is that?" Jared, Faye's brother-in-law barks. "This park area is rented for two more hours. The gate attendant shouldn't let anyone back here." Connor exits the black vehicle and heads my way before the car pulls off out of the park.

"Surprise beautiful." His gruff voice caresses me through the ear piece. Without speaking, I pocket my phone and head towards him.

The others are looking, whispering behind me. Questions about who pulled in are running wild. I approach Connor expecting him to be wearing workout clothes. Instead, he's in a tight black t-shirt it shows the outline of every muscle with dark jeans and shit kickers.

"You hung up on me gorgeous." He grumbles. "You gonna answer my question?"

"Which was?" I ask, sucking my bottom lip into my mouth and slowly dragging my teeth across the puffy flesh. "Oh, you mean if I dressed this way for a special someone? Only if that someone is you." I tease. He leans down and captures my lips with his.

"Right answer. I hope I'm not intruding. We finished early, and I wanted to see you." He flashes his teeth. My breath hitches. Connor is hot with his normal sullen look he sports but, this smile. It's electric.

A slight breeze blows by causing my nipples to pebble. His eyes go two shades darker the exact moment his gaze lands on them.

"I'll be your date. No woman should go stag to their own birthday dinner."

"You want to come to dinner with my friends. They will put you on trial with twenty questions. You ready?" I grimace, dreading what's to come.

He barks out a laugh. "I'm here aren't I. Won't they start the trial now?" He cocks his head towards the party and I swear about ten heads hard pivot in the other direction.

"You would think, but no. They will wait until dinner. The questions and answers aren't always kid appropriate."

"Well, let the firing squad begin." He brings my hand up to his mouth and places a soft kiss to my palm.

I introduce him to everyone except Faye because she is busy wrangling the kids up for presents and cake.

Connor pulls out an envelope and drops it over on the pile of other cards. "Oh, you didn't need to do that." I beam. This man is unreal and making my ovaries hurt with need. *You want his babies.* Hush.

"Least I could do."

"Connor, tell us what do you do?" Veronica questions sweeter than sugar. "Oh, and sorry for being a buzz kill last night. I didn't know Katy was busy." Oh, my god. She did not.

V's face goes so red I bet she wishes the earth would open up and swallow her whole right about now. Meanwhile, I'm frozen in place.

Connor's booming laughter pulls me out of my death stare. "Katy's talked about me? I hope I got rave reviews." He winks, giving my hip a little squeeze. Heat crawls up my neck. Naughty boy. I shrug, what else am I gonna say?

"Now that V gave us that bit of awkwardness, tell us what you do?" Faye asks appearing from no where. "I'm Faye by the way, Mom of the Birthday boy."

"Connor, it's a pleasure thanks for allowing me at such a personal event. To answer your question I own McKinnon Pub over on main street," he adds.

RING! RING!

"Damn, you are popular today." Elise teases. I pull out my phone. Weird, he never calls this often.

"Excuse me for a second, my brother."

"Hi Jackson." I answer once out of ear shot, still a little annoyed at his attitude yesterday.

"Hey little Heart. I'm short on time, but I wanted to apologize. I suck, okay. Call me big asshole Jacks."

I snort. "One could even call you a douche canoe."

"A douche canoe?"

"Yes douche canoe is the perfect name for your behavior."

He groans. "I'm sorry. I only want you to be happy. My ass went and stepped over the line. Forgive me?" His tone is soft and remorseful for once.

"Thanks. For real, you need to stop being over protective, okay? I can handle myself. I am grown enough to live with the choices I make. A lot like you have." I take a peek at Lily. My brother has a thing for her, but for whatever reason he keeps his distance. Stubborn people.

Sometimes I wish he made a move years ago. At least then none of us would know Isaac. Not like we do, anyway. Maybe the old, happy-go-lucky, wild friend would be here instead of the insecure woman she's become.

"I'm not going there, Katy. Stop. I'll be home in a few months. I love you, little Heart. We good."

"Love you too, Jackson. We're good. See you when I see you." Hanging up I force the tears behind my eyes to stay right where they are.

Connor, Ryan, and Elise are sharing about last night as I walk up. Connor wraps his arm around my waist, locking me in place against him. His warm hard body is comforting to lean into.

"How's Jackson?" Elise queries. "Is everything alright? He never calls you two days in a row."

"He's the same. Wanted to apologize for being an ass, and yet he still came off like an ass hat. The man needs a real lesson in people skills.

Jackson Heart is a fighter not a talker. An alpha male in every way, and sometimes his masculine need to protect spills over to me. My friends are used to witnessing his grouchiness firsthand. In high school they dealt with the same level of over protectiveness. Lily giggles with me knowing full well what I'm talking about.

"Oh you're funny babe. Your bro improving his friendliness. The man is all grunts and demands. I can't imagine the military or his current job made him any better at civilian interaction." Her eyes light up when she talks about my brother. They are both ridiculous. Neither can muster up the courage to admit they like the other, freaking maddening.

"How the hell are you so close with him, Lily?" Isaac sneers. "You fuck him or something?" The collective gasp is deafening. What the hell.

"N..No." She stammers. Trying to control of her voice. "Umm. He's Katy's older brother. He's always looked out for us."

"Some of us more than others," Veronica blurts. Fucking hell. Can she ever keep her mouth shut? The realization of what she said crosses her face, and she slaps her hand over her mouth. "Ignore me. I say stupid stuff." You think.

"No, tell me. What did you mean? Who did he give extra attention to? Bet it wasn't your fat ass." Isaac taunts. Veronica blanches. Hurt crossing her features.

"Watch your fucking mouth." I blurt. He whirls on me. Shit.

"You got something to say?" He snips. What is his problem? The dude is moodier than I am during my period.

"Yes. We're at a child's birthday party. The kids a few tables away opening presents. Shut up or leave. None of us need your bullshit today." I regret my outburst immediately.

Not because of what I said, but for Lily. Isaac is going to take this out on her. She's never admitted anything, but I fear he hits her.

"Fuck this shit. Lily grab your purse we're leaving, now." He storms off toward his car, red-faced and more than angry.

Ugh, why is my best friend engaged to such an asshole? My friend looks over at us apologetically.

"Later. Love you." She whispers before turning to follow Isaac.

"Sorry guys. I can't believe I did that." I wrap my arms around myself, forcing the nausea and bile back down.

"Why did I open my mouth? He's furious." Veronica is as white as a sheet.

"Don't worry sweetie. Katy showing her bigger pair did him in not you. Plus, you can't help yourself you lack a filter." Elise snickers.

"You do pack a rather enormous pair of balls there Katy. Connor, since when do you swing that way?" Ryan jests breaking the tension by getting us to laugh. Connor flips him the bird out of sight from the kids.

"I'll show you how I swing asshole." Connor swings his arm around my waist. He squeezes me close and plants a giant kiss on my lips, leaving me breathless. He leans to my ear and whispers. "You did the right thing. I'd never treat a woman like that." He leaves a peck on my temple before pulling away.

"Hey grownups. Cake. Come on, Happy Birthday time." Faye hollers at us from across the picnic area. The moment is broken be smile and head over to sing Happy Birthday.

Katy

Chapter Eight

We arrive to the restaurant five minutes past our reservation time. Ryan and Elise are the only ones waiting for us. No big surprise. Lily and Veronica are always late.

Ian's is one of my favorite places to go for a fancy dinner in Hadley Falls. An upscale establishment that welcomes families and large parties. The best kind of eating.

Outside the building is a dark brick painted black with massive oak front doors. The tables are lined white long linen table cloths decorated with shiny silverware. One wall shows off exposed brick, Ian's logo is hand drawn on the far wall, creating a massive statement piece. The other walls are cream colored with hints of deep red in the molding.

The food here is to die for. Most entrees can be ordered family style for big parties which is perfect for us. Only place in town who serves a more diverse menu where my friends will actually eat.

All three of them are picky about one type of food or another. It drives me mad. I will try anything as long as you don't tell me what it is before I take a bite. Exotic food tastes better than the name most of the time.

"Hey, finally." Elise calls to us dramatically. "What took you so long to get here?" I blush, my mind goes back to the blow job I gave Connor when we got back to his place. Connor must think the same thing because he drops his hand off my hip to squeeze my ass possessively. I squeak and give Connor a smoldering look.

"On second thought, I don't want to know." Elise blurts holding her hand out as a shield to stop me from answering the question.

"Oh, relax prude. We came from Connor's not my house, which is part of why we are running behind. Thankfully, I put all my stuff in my car this morning since I planned on getting ready with you." I snip at her. Like I'm really gonna tell her I was late because I blew my date. Please, I'm dirty, but not that bad.

Veronica walks in a few minutes later and holy cow knock out alert. Her vintage black dress flares at her hips. The white polka dots add a hint of fun. A slender man with a goatee and slicked back hair comes in behind her. This must be Parker. She grins at us, like a total nerd on her first date before wrapping her arm around his and dragging him over.

"Guys this is Parker."

"Hello. Nice to meet all of you." Wow, he is formal. *Be nice.*

This guy screams money, from his over pressed button down to his skin tight dress pants and loafers. Why loafers? Ugh, fingers crossed he's not like Isaac. Spoiled men and I don't play well together.

Relax. He hasn't even spoken yet. Fine. Okay, I might share my brother's protective streak. *Only a little.*

We exchange hellos. They take their seats, and we wait for Lily.

Five more minutes of waiting and two calls unanswered we decide to order our drinks.

"I don't think she's coming, and it's all my fault.". This totally blows.

"Sweetie, seriously, you can't blame yourself. Isaac was out of line." Elise states, reaching across the table to give my hand a squeeze. "Too bad my aunt and uncle can't see through his crap. They love him, which is part of the reason she stays." Elise's fists clench. Veronica and I both reach out to her.

"After witnessing your fiery nature last night, I'm not surprised you said something." Connor adds. "I kind of wanted to hit the guy. What's his deal anyway?"

"10 points for Connor. I like him already." Veronica blurts out.

"I'm glad." I respond before answering Connor. "Issac's issue is, he's a short asshole who grew up in the shadow of his older brothers who are all cops, or firefighters. He couldn't hack the academy. So he went to law school. He works at the same firm as my ex Noah. He's always been a dick but Lily's family adores him, and she loves him."

Elise continues the story. "Issac hates Jackson. One night when we were drinking with his soon to be sister-in-law Lily let slip that she crushed on Katy's brother in high school. Obviously she told her fiance, who told Isaac. He usually gets agitated when Jackson's name is brought up, but today's reaction was a bit nuts."

"Sorry to be a downer," I say before taking a sip from my drink. "We are usually more fun."

Normally we don't dish about Lily in front of anyone else. Her life is hers and private. Doesn't mean we can't worry and try to help somehow. This crap with her and Issac is getting worse.

"Hey, no complaints here. You girls are worried about your friend." Parker responds nodding at me. *See, he is sweet.*

"Thanks for understanding. I swear we aren't always this crazy and full of drama." Ryan clears his throat and I narrow my eyes at him.

"Okay, maybe some." He winks at me. "Parker, tell us what do you do?"

"I'm an investment banker for Myers International Group. My grandfather started the company several decades ago. Now my father runs things and in a few years I'll take over. All very exciting." The passion for his career is heavy in each word. "The traveling my job allows me to do is the best part."

"Oh, I've always wanted to travel." V says, a doe glassiness in her eyes.

Our drinks arrive, and we fall into a simple conversation, getting acquainted with the guys and me asking occasional grilling question to push some buttons. Parker seems like a great guy. A bit stuffy for my taste but sweet.

The food arrives and every item is beautiful. The first bites causes everyone to make small sounds of pleasure.

"This is so good. I'm so glad we came here. I know we didn't get to do your traditional dinner for you this year, but this meal is to die for." Veronica says. I smile in reply, my mouth being full of yummy food.

"What do you mean, traditional dinner?" Connor asks.

"Normally Katy invites us all over to a huge feast of food. She makes or orders all her favorites, and we gorge and drink lots of wine. We always have a blast and turn the night into a sleepover. It's a night of us acting like complete teenagers," Veronica giggles.

"Why the change? Sorry, just curious." Ryan inquires. My eyes narrow. *Don't be bitchy.* Truth, my friends made a ridiculous stink because they wanted their men to come and I only wanted us. I wouldn't budge, so we settled on dinner out. The girls turn to me and I shrug, not giving two shits what their response is.

Okay, so I might still be annoyed about not having my birthday plans I wanted.

"Things didn't work out this year." I blurt, then dive back into my food. Connor's hand lands on my knee under the table, and he gives it a tight squeeze. "It's no biggie. I plan on grabbing a few favorites for myself next month on my next day off."

Connor's fingers walk further up my leg. His thumb caresses back and forth on my thigh at the hem of my dress.

A slow burn in my gut ignites and moisture pools in my lacy thong. His hand continues to ascend up past my hem. The rough pad of his fingers play with the lace stitching of my panties.

At this rate, I can say goodbye to this pair by the end of the night. The others continue to talk and banter. I pretend to listen, but I'm only focused on Connor's touch and the delicious feelings they are brewing in me. He makes slow circles with his thumb on the outside of my thong.

His small brushes heat me all over, it gives me a rush that drops my walls and do daring things. Like be close to coming in a crowded restaurant. He pushes his finger against my button, more sparks fly inside my belly. I bite my lip to stop the moan from releasing.

"Katy, you're quiet. Is your dinner okay?" Elise pries. She kicks me under the table and shoots me a glare.

Oops, she caught me. I wonder if she is going to rat me out or give me the mom daggers. I peak. Ugh, her eyes go tight and I think she is willing whatever she thinks we are doing to end. Connor must catch her gaze because he stops, pulls his hand back to my thigh and chuckles.

"You don't miss much woman." Connor says to Elise. She smiles, scrunching her nose and eyes up in response. Everyone else is looking at us confused and I give her a kick back as a warning to change the subject.

"I don't. Katy's the talker of the group. There are only a few reasons she's ever silent. Enjoying her food is one cause hello she's a giant foodie and two she's or concentrating."

"Don't forget sometimes she plain spaces out," adds Veronica.

"How long have you known each other? You act more like sisters than friends." Connor asks.

"Lily, Elise and I grew up together on the same street until my parents had a cottage built on their B & B property. Then we moved, but always stayed close. We met Veronica her first day at Hadley Falls High. V and Lily were in the same classes, and she joined us at lunch. Been best friends ever since."

"Wait, I thought you are younger than everyone by a few years. Isn't that whole reason around your nickname 'The Baby'? How did you meet them in high school?" Ryan squints, puzzled.

"She's a wiz kid. Too smart for her own good. Katy was three years ahead of her age group, putting her in classes with me. We have always been her protectors because being a freshman at twelve sucks. Kids are jerks." Elise answers for me. "And we don't call her that anymore."

"Well, damn babe. I didn't realize you were super smart sexy nerd." Connor winks then kisses me on the cheek.

"Wait, what? My brain makes me sexy," I quip.

"You bet your ass it does." Connor leans down to my ear, his breath tickling my skin. "You can bet I'm gonna own that ass one day too." He whispers, sending shivers down my spine. I clench my thighs for the millionth time tonight. This man sets my skin on fire and I'll gladly burn forever.

Connor

Chapter Nine

One mention of ass play and Katy's skin heats beneath my hand.

"You like that?" I whisper her, making sure her friends can't hear. Goosebumps breakout on her flesh and her thighs clench under my palm. Katy nods her head in response, biting the edge of her lip seductively.

"Hey guys. Sorry I'm so late." The blonde from earlier announces, rushing over to our table.

"Yay. You made it. I'm so glad you came." Katy squeals, jumping out of her chair to wrap her arms around her. Katy says something, and she pulls away smiling before turning to greet the others.

"You must be Parker. Hi. I'm Lily." Piercing blue eyes land on me. "Connor, right? We didn't exactly meet earlier either. Sorry for my fiance, he's a bit of an ass sometimes."

"No need to apologize. It's nice to meet you." Connor says with a warm grin.

"Hello. Veronica talks about you a lot." Parker flashes her a bright smile.

"You missed dinner, but no worries. We haven't had dessert yet. Did you come alone?" Katy asks looking behind her friend.

"Yep, Isaac is still angry. I told him I'm not missing your night and left. He's a big boy he can deal." Lily says matter of factly, flipping her bright hair over her shoulder.

"Good now sit down and pick something for dessert. Order me anything. I'm going to use the ladies." Katy quietly announces.

My eyes are stapled to her ass as she walks away. One night did nothing to burn her from my system. I want more.

Scanning the crowd out of habit I notice a pair of eyes watching Katy's backside. Usually, I wouldn't care, she's here with me. There is something about his demeanor that isn't sitting right. He's looking at Katy like a kettle about to boil. The man keeps his eyes frozen on the bathroom door. Weird.

Katy exits a few minutes later. He excuses himself and heads over to her. What the? I tap Ryan on the shoulder discreetly. "Yo, who's that?" I don't want to attract anyone else's attention, especially if this is an old friend of Katy's.

"Awe man. That's Noah. Her ex. What the fuck is he doing here?" He growls, putting me on alert. Ryan likes everyone. If he doesn't like this guy, there's a problem. Excusing myself from the table I head over to Katy. A little back up never hurt anyone.

A little of the conversation hits my ears on my way over.

"Why are you here, Noah?" Katy snips.

"Priscilla and I. You remember her, don't you? Are having dinner before heading back to her place." He says. No denying what he's suggesting. Fucking prick is trying to make her jealous.

"From your office?" Her gaze turns to the woman seated at Noah's table. She's a leggy brunette with sleek hair down to her shoulders. Her tight-fitting dress suit reminds me of a damn corporate dude's wet dream. "Shouldn't you be at some couple's weekend with your potential client?" Katy throws at him. Not fazed at all by this woman who is falling out of her outfit.

"Yes, I should be, but because of your bitchy ass they picked someone else in my department to go. Being part of a couple was a mandatory aspect of the weekend," He spits at her. Noah isn't very tall maybe an inch or two taller than Katy, putting him around five eight. He's wearing the typical business suit minus the jacket with the sleeves of his white dress shirt rolled up.

"Oh, so now I'm at fault for your company outing being the weekend of my birthday. And you deciding not to tell me until the morning of? That's one hundred percent on you asshole."

"If you say so, but a woman worthy of a ring steps up for her man. You don't understand the first thing about being the woman I need. Bet your pathetic ass came here tonight stag while all your friends brought their dates," he snarls at her.

I've heard enough. Katy is handling this like a champ, but no one needs to speak to her like that. "Excuse me, the fuck did you say to my girl?" I snarl, wrapping my arm around Katy's waist. Making it clear she's here with me.

"Who the hell is this?" He addresses Katy, ignoring me.

"I'm Connor. Katy's date, and you are?"

"Katy, what the hell? One fight and you already picked up some neanderthal. Is this why you didn't answer my calls last night. Because of him?" He demands, waving his hand up and down dismissively at me.

Katy smirks at the fucker. And if it isn't the sexiest thing ever. "No, well maybe. We were together last night. But even if not, I wouldn't want to be with you. In fact, I owe you. Yesterday you showed me how much of a mistake our relationship is." Her teeth sink into her bottom lip. "I'm sorry let me start again." She pauses and Noah grins. "You taught me I'm worth so much more than you will ever be willing to give me. Have a wonderful life." His face falls and Katy turns away, dismissing him.

"Don't you dare walk away from me," he bellows. "Goddamn virgins. You were a complete waste of time." Noah aims his anger at me. "Trust me man, you'll regret ever jumping in bed with her. She's a horrible fuck." His voice booms across the restaurant. The collective gasp from the surrounding tables has every head in the house turning our way.

Katy's cheeks go bright red and her mouth hangs open.

I'm done holding my temper in check for polite sake. This asshole crossed a line. Dropping her hand I walk over to Noah and lean down in his face. "You're a piece of shit disrespecting a woman like that."

His eyes narrow. "Well, what are you going to do punk?" He's baiting me.

Katy comes up behind me and grabs my elbow. "He's not worth it babe."

Babe. That one word from her is like pouring ice over my anger. My dick twitches. Damn, even when I'm ready to fight, this woman gets me going. "Oh come on don't be a a pussy." Noah adds.

This ass thinks he's got me pissed enough to throw the first punch. Jokes on him though. "Hey Carter." I call to the manager. He turns to us immediately and I nod my head at Noah. "This guy is ruining Ms. Heart's birthday and insulting her. Mind escorting him out?"

"Right away Mr. McKinnon." Carter pushes a button and says something in his earpiece. The back door creeks open. Jerome and Carlos, Ian's on-site security team for this location step through the swinging doors. They head straight for us.

"Connor." The beast sized security guard nods to me. "Carter says we got a problem." Noah gulps. Don't blame him there, Ian's security is intense with tree stumps for legs and branches for arms. They train for MMA fighting at the local gym. You don't want to fuck with them.

"Oh good, security. Handle this thug, he's causing quite the scene." He utters in a huff, waving his hand at me like some limp napkin. Carlos heads over to us .

"Sir. I think it's time for you and your date to leave." He suggests pointing to the door.

"Excuse me. Why am I being removed? He's the one being rude here." Noah demands.

"Sir, you insulted the owner's best friend and his girl. We watched the whole thing on camera. You need to leave and please don't come back. If you can't follow the request, we'd be happy to help you out, or we can call the cops. Your call."

Both men cross their arms over their chests, making a solid wall of muscle in front of Noah. His mouth keeps opening and closing, but no sounds come out. He reminds me of a fish trying to breathe out of water. I'm glad I involved security over kicking his ass. Ian would kill me for fighting in his precious restaurant. This place is his baby.

"Bullshit! We are still waiting for our food. You can't kick us out. I'm a paying customer." Noah scoffs, his voice rising about five octaves. His date Priscilla gets up and heads our way.

"Katy, so nice to see you again." Her smile is anything but genuine. "Noah, let's head back to my place. We can order pizza like last week. Besides, my bed is way more fun." Noah's date leans into him and whispers something in his ear and a dark smile appears on his face.

Did Katy pick up on the bombshell this woman dropped? Fucking prick was cheating on her and he's sleeping with someone else while trying to win her back. What an asshole.

"Your date's idea sounds smart sir. Why don't you take your lady home and have a pleasant night?" Jerome adds.

"Fine. Priscilla, grab your things. We're leaving. Katy, this isn't over." He points at her and it takes every ounce of discipline I possess not to break his fucking finger.

"Yes, it is. If I'm not mistaken, your office buddy over there inferred you were with her last weekend when you said you were at work. We're done. I don't date cheaters." Katy turns on her heel and heads back to the table, dismissing Noah.

Her girls are on her before she can even sit down. She's lucky to have them. Katy may be over this asshole, but no one is ever okay finding out they got cheated on.

I head over to Carter and slip him a fifty. "Charge the card on file for everything, add a twenty percent tip." He pockets it. "Thanks for making the call. He was out of line." We turn to the door and Noah is huffing and puffing to his date while they exit.

"Thank you for not punching the guy. I knew you wanted to. Hell I wanted to. I'll make sure he's never allowed back in here." Carter pulls up the list Ian keeps of people who aren't welcome. It isn't very long but every place deals with assholes. Cause too many issues for Ian and he'll refuse to deal with you.

I head back to the table and pull Katy against my side when I sit back down and give her a kiss on the temple. She lets out a shaky breath. Noah had one mission, ruin her night and I'm not going to let that happen.

"Would you guys hate me if I want to go?" Katy asks, her bottom lip quivers.

"Katy don't let him upset you. He is a prick. Come on, let me take you home. Your friends can hang out here for as long as they like, drink and order as much as they want." I hold out my hand waiting for her answer.

"That sounds perfect sweetie, go." Elise pushes. I mouth thank you behind Katy's head.

"Okay, but I need to settle the bill first. I'm not sticking my friends with the check.

"Already taken care of."

"What. You handled it?" She screeches before wrapping her arms around me and kissing me sweetly on the mouth. It's a chaste kiss, she brushes her tongue to my lips before she is pulls away smiling. "No one has ever done something like this for me before."

"What? Buy you dinner?" I ask facetiously, chuckling to myself.

"Hilarious, but thank you." Katy kisses me again. My arms tighten around her, lifting her off the floor. She's almost jell-o in my hold so I keep one hand at her back.

Shel brings a bag of dessert out to us and we say a goodbye and head for the door.

"So." Katy claps her hands together. "How did you like meeting Noah, my ex?" Her calfs bounce off of the seat cushions, waiting for my response.

"He's the one?" I ask her, not taking my eyes off the road. We are on the way back to my place.

"Yes." She bites her lip. "I still can't figure out what he was doing there. Even if what he says is the truth, he wouldn't take a date to Ian's." Her teeth go right back to chewing her lip.

"No? The place is popular."

"Oh, I love Ian's. Hands down one of my favorite places, but Noah hates it. He says the cuisine is trying too hard. Personally he has bad taste. Which is why I'm confused about seeing him there. Oh, and that line about cheating on me, what a needle dick."

"Needle dick," I chuckle. "I like it. And I agree. Why bring that up?"

"It feels so weird. I don't feel anything knowing he cheated on me. I could have done without him throwing it in my face in a crowded restaurant. But the way he treated me yesterday proved I mean little to nothing to him." Katy lets out on a sigh.

"Did he really try to apologize yesterday?"

"Yep, he text me while I was walking out the door. He sent a few text and left two voicemails too. No clue what they say because I deleted them without looking. I don't care what he wants to tell me." Her hand flies to her mouth. "Shit. I'm rambling. This is probably too much info since we just met yesterday. But, I want nothing to do with him. Last night changed a lot for me. Like best night of my life amazing. I had no clue sex could be so...earth-shattering. Sex was awful before you. Wow that was a lot of word vomit. Can you pretend you didn't hear what I just said?"

The Best night of her life. *Earth shattering.* Fuck. I adjust myself so my zipper doesn't scrape my dick. Those words have me rock solid.

Katy notices the gesture. Fire warms her gaze, and she reaches over to rub my cock through my slacks.

"Fuuuck," I hiss. Damn. Katy has me keyed up with this insane need to be inside her, but first I have some dessert in mind. "Your hands feel fantastic." I grit out.

"Wait until I put my mouth around you again. The rushed blow job I gave you earlier was not enough." Pleasure shoots straight to my balls watching her teeth bite into her plump bottom lip.

"We are almost to my place, all I want is to spread you out and feast on you. Maybe if you behave, I'll let you suck my cock." Her eyes light with desire.

We pull into my driveway. My dick pulses when she pulls her hand away. I need to get her undressed and in my bed now. *Stick to the plan.* Right, the plan, I grab the dessert from the back seat, and we head in.

"Why did you get so many? You got six different desserts."

Six? Fucking Carter. The grin plastered on Katy's face is worth it. She's shaking the bags like a kid fresh out a candy store.

Katy is gorgeous. Her bright smile goes all they way to her eyes and the way the light is shining on her causes the copper bits of color in her hair to sparkle. Her eyes are hooded with desire and I can't help but pause to etch this moment into my memory.

This woman could make a paper bag sexy. The sweater dress never stood a chance. It hugs her in all the right places and the deep green stands out against her fair skin. The outline of her nipples are barely visible through the fabric. I bet if I pull it down her breasts would fall right out. The thought makes my dick thicken further.

We get inside and I lay out all six of the desserts.

"Wow! There are so many." Katy's eyes dance from each dish. "Oh man, which one should I pick?" She says bouncing her finger off her lip, trying to decide.

"Taste them all."

"No way. Lord knows my ass doesn't need anymore sweets."

"Hey, come here." I pull her into my hold. "You are the perfect size. And this ass is magical."

WHAP! I smack her meaty rear. Gripping her cheeks hard with both hands. She lets out a breathy moan and my dick twitches from the sound. "This ass is mine and I don't want you saying bad things about it. You are sexy as fuck."

She looks down, away from me. I grip her chin and force her gaze back to me. "I'm serious. You're hot. The second you walked up to my bar and asked for a glass of whiskey I wanted you. Elise being your friend has nothing to do with my interest in you."

I pull her harder against me, so she can understand how turned on she makes me. Her eyes light up as she smiles, reaching up for a kiss. I descend on her lips, forcing my mouth inside to claim every inch. She meets me with each thrust, pushing her tongue into mine and sucking hard.

Katy doesn't realize how amazing she is, I can't wait to show her in every way possible. I pull away first. Her lips are puffy and red, swollen.

"Take off the dress. Now," I command. She drags the fabric over her head, revealing a black lace thong. A few more pulls expose her breasts one by one confirming my earlier suspicion. "No fucking bra. Woman, you've had these beautiful tits free all night and I'm only now finding out." My palm is itching to smack her ass again.

"Not really? I had Elise sew a bra into the dress." Soft hands cup her breasts. Small pink buds poke through her fingers. The way her hair gathers over her chest is like something out of a dirty magazine.

I reach out and flick her nipple, covering it with my mouth, pulling and swirling. Katy pants. I move to the next one, licking and sucking while I pull on the other. A throaty moan falls from her lips. Soft skin clamps around my legs as Katy rocks her body against mine.

"Don't come yet." I command, popping her nipple from my mouth. I kiss up her neck to her ear landing at her lips. Katy pulls at my shoulders urging me to lift her. She wraps her legs around my waist locking her heels into my back. It sends the most delicious bite of pain shooting straight to my cock.

I push back, spreading her over my kitchen counter right next to the dessert. Her foot moves up my leg reaching for my balls. "I don't think so babe." A shiver runs over Katy's body and her eyes lock on mine.

My fingers reach out and skim the edge of her lace thong making goosebumps break out on her skin. One tug on the fabric pulls them to her feet exposing her pussy. She spreads her legs before me. Her cunt is glistening with arousal. Beautiful puffy lips, a tight swollen clit. Katy is the sexiest woman alive. I trace my finger over her opening before pushing inside. Her hips buck off the counter top, each time her tits sway with the movement. She's so responsive.

"Do you remember what I said I wanted to do next time I got you naked?" I ask her, placing a kiss right on top of her mound. She bites her lip again, applying extra pressure and shaking her head. "No. Well I'm eating this pussy. Feel free to squirm or scream. "

I grab the three mini cake dessert. Each is covered in frosting. Katy's eyes are glued to me watching my every move. I take each one, using the cake to spread the fluffy icing over her breasts and cover her sex.

"Have you ever had your pussy licked?" She shakes her head at me. "You're about too. Don't come until I say so. Got me?"

"Connor."

"Use your words baby."

"Yes, eat me." She whines. I smirk and reach for the hem of my shirt pulling it over my head to toss aside. I dive into her breasts, licking up all the frosting on one side before moving to the next.

Katy moans and pants.

"Yes, Connor, I love when you suck on my nipples."

Her words make me hungry, and I quicken my pace. I want the real prize. Wasting no time, I lick up the sugary globs dripping down her clit. I shove my face into her pussy and suck as hard as I can. Shoving my tongue into her entrance, her walls clamp down on me tight. Her hand grabs my hair and begins pulling and pushing me deeper into her pussy.

"Oh, my god. Connor, I'm going to come. Oh shit."

"Don't you come until I say."

"Please Connor, let me come. I need to." She's panting hard.

"Hold it," I growl at her. My sucking efforts turn to slow licks. Making my way from her ass to clit as Katy trembles beneath me.

She screams grinding her hips against my tongue, trying to fuck my face to get herself off. I chuckle against her pussy and she bucks.

"Fucking hell, Connor. Please."

Her pleas are the best fucking sound ever. She's moaning, wiggling her hips back and forth trying hard to push herself to orgasm but I won't let her, instead I suck harder on her clit.

"Come for me. Now."

"Connor." A flood of liquid squirts out of her and into my mouth. Holy shit that's hot. I keep licking and lapping up all her juices until she can't stop bucking.

Standing, I frantically undo my belt and shove my pants down to my ankles. I need to be inside this woman, now. Fisting my heavy cock in my hands I line my dick up at her drenched entrance. It slips in easily. Her walls grip and pull against me when I slide out. Katy's heels dig into my ass pulling me in deeper.

All my focus is on Katy, picking up speed until I'm pounding into her over and over. Her wet heat squeezes my dick trying to force my orgasm. I pull out, press my fingers to her clit flicking it in unison. The waves of her pleasure wash over her. I wait for her to be on the other side of the haze. Wasting no time I seat my cock with one swift strike. A scream rips from her lips.

"Connor, I'm coming."

"Yes baby, come with me." She does, gripping and milking my cock with her tight pussy. I come shooting hot ropes inside her. Claiming her as mine. Katy's eyes are glassy, dizzy on her endorphin rush.

"Uh Connor. Did you come in me?" Fuck, I look down where our bodies are attached and my release is leaking out around my length.

Shit, I always use condoms. We're tested for everything when we have check-ups, STDs included, so I'm not worried there. *What if she isn't on birth control?* We'll deal with it. *You say that now.*

"I'm on the pill." My gaze snaps to hers. "I'm clean Connor. But, I've never had sex without a condom before." A pink blush covers her skin. She lifts her torso off the counter to pull me to her. Katy kisses my cheek, I turn my head and take her mouth in a long demanding kiss.

"Hold on to me," I tell her through kisses. Her thighs tighten around me, and she wraps her arms tight around my neck. I pick her up cradling her ass in the palms of my hands.

"Ah! Connor, put me down."

Ignoring her I head straight for the bathroom, and set her down to turn on the shower. Katy sways on her feet, still dealing with the effects of her orgasm. I lead her under the water and let her sit on the bench built into the back.

The hot spray is a sweet balm on my back and sore muscles. I let the water run off me getting used to the heat, then I reach for Katy. I spin us angling her under the water and help wet her hair. The far off look on her face fades the more water washes over her face.

"Holy crap that was phenomenal. Did I squirt?" She's fucking adorable. I pull her lip into my mouth and plunder her with my tongue. "Hmm."

"Yea, you squirted." I wait before continuing. I'm wondering if this is new. Her head drops.

"I'm sorry if I did that all over you."

"I'm not. Katy you squirting was the fucking hottest shit I ever saw. Knowing I gave you so much pleasure you released in my mouth and all over my face makes me one happy man. No bullshit."

She peeks up at me from under her eyelashes. "You mean it?"

"Yes. Now let's shower then we can have more dessert."

"Deal." Now she's bouncing on the balls of her feet to kiss me. This girl loves sweets. I lean down to wrap my hand around her hair, pulling her head up to me and devour her mouth. I can't stop kissing this woman.

Katy changes the pace and starts sucking my tongue like it's my dick. My balls tighten. I reach for her nipples, rolling it between my fingers, alternating pressure.

"Fuck." A breathy curse from her lips. "I need you in me. Now." Katy wraps her hand around the base of me, barley covering half of it with her hand. . "Please, babe."

"Come here. Ride me." I lead Katy to the bench and she straddles me. My already thickening cock slides inside her. The warmth makes my dick and balls clinch so tight my ass flexes. She seats herself and I go straight for her breasts, sucking and pulling on her skin. I grab her nipple in between my teeth and bite down. Her cunt bounces up and down on my length as her moist walls squeeze around me, tightening with each thrust.

I let her control this rhythm. She picks up speed, slamming her hips down on my cock. Rocking herself forward she shoves her breasts into my mouth. I suck harder drawing a scream of pleasure from her.

My orgasm slams into me like a freight train while her pussy tightens like a vice grip on my dick and I free fall into bliss.

"Hell yes. Come." I growl. My cum shoots into her while she pulses hard three times around me. We stay like this, breathing for a few minutes until the water runs cold.

"More dessert now?" She cocks her eyebrows at me. Laughter erupts from my throat. Man she keeps me on my toes.

"Yep, more sweets for my Sweetness. For real this time. I'll leave something out for you to wear." I kiss her and head to grab Katy some clothes. Singing drifts out from the bathroom. Her voice is awful, but I don't mind. There is no denying it Katy Heart has put me under her spell.

Katy

Chapter Ten

Mondays suck. Three cups of coffee and exhaustion is winning the battle. With sex brain, all I can think about is Connor. How did he take my weekend from the worst to best one ever?

Talk about a complete surprise. The universe gave me two gifts Friday. A life lesson, and Connor, the Adonis and gentlemen wrapped in one. His gruff voice, rough hands and dirty mouth sends shivers down my spine. The way he handled Noah had me swooning. I was mortified when he showed up to my dinner.

The paper in my hand crinkles. Oh Shit. I unfold the paper trying to smooth out the creases.

I still don't understand why he was there. Talk about humiliating. All I wanted to do after was go home and let my house swallow me whole.

Instead, Connor made the night one I'll never forget for an entirely different reason. Who orders dessert to lick it off you? The way Connor's eyes got so dark they turned almost black when I told him he'd be the first guy to eat me out. Um, I'm getting wet in my office thinking about him.

Oh, does he have skills. He pulled on my clit so hard I saw stars and when I came he lapped me up, then proceeded to fuck the shit out of me. *Yea and with no condom!* Okay, that part was stupid, but thankfully I'm on the pill.

You're supposed to be working, not dreaming about dick. Well aware, thanks.

Ugh, this morning is more of the same. A vicious cycle of attempting to work. But thoughts of Connor creep in until I'm hot and bothered then the whole thing repeats. His pub being the inspiration for my new idea isn't helping. It's hard to avoid imagining someone when you're contemplating desserts themed after their business.

The Irish theme desserts are itching to go from my mind to the plate. A deconstructed Guinness cake with candied bacon and pecans. Irish mocha cream brownie served with apples caramelized in a brandy sauce, topped with ice cream. The new ideas keep coming, giving me more energy than the three cups of coffee I consumed.

To tie everything back to the bar everything will be served in small glasses. Rocks glass at the counter and offer the full dessert options at tables.

My sketches are complete and hopefully he doesn't get upset I used his business as my guinea pig. I couldn't help looking up his liquor list over the weekend and with the food choices they serve they should be getting more love.

RING! RING!
"Hello."

"Am I speaking with Ms. Heart?" Says a nasally woman.

"Yes, this is she."

"Hello, I'm calling from Bailey's Local Bank from the titles and loans department. This is your final notice. We are foreclosing the loan, you have sixty days to pay back the twenty-five thousand dollars remaining on the principal balance."

"I'm sorry, what." I choke out.

"Ms. Heart, are you okay?"

"Yes, but how is this possible? I don't have a loan from your branch."

"The business does and we can mail you a copy of the document. Your grandmother took a loan out against the bakery before she died. I can assure you this is real. Sixty days to pay off the twenty-five thousand dollar balance is more than generous. You cannot request any extensions."

"What that isn't possible." I squeak out.

"Our records show we sent several notices and all were ignored. Please call your loan officer if you have questions. Enjoy your day."

CLICK.

I'm frozen in my seat so I'm not sure how much time passes before my cell phone goes off. Dread fills me as the name Mom flashes on the screen. Shit, I swear the woman is equipped with radar for when my life blows up.

Gail Heart, my mother, is a fantastic mom. My parents always provided for us while growing up. I was just never enough.

Being smarter than my peers only made it worse because as my mother says it put me in situations I was too "young" to comprehend. She constantly forces Jackson to be my protector. A lump forms in my throat. I have to take a deep breath before I answer. No way she can know about the bank.

"Hi mom."

"Katy. I'm glad I caught you. How are you doing?"

"I'm fine, why?" This is odd. My mom isn't one to call randomly to ask how I am.

"You'll never guess who I ran into this morning."

"Who?"

"Noah, at the farmers market but I'm confused. He said you two broke up."

Fucking hell. She loves Noah. Thinks he's so perfect. My silence confirms her question.

"Katy, I don't understand you two were on track for a future. What happened?" Her voice goes up in pitch with each word. "He's a very sweet man from an amazing family," She scolds. "A future with Noah gives you choices, freedom, and comfort. You can sign the bakery over to your father and I. We can run the place properly and you can live your life." The phone slips from my hand and clanks to the desk. Crap. I scramble to pick it up.

"I'm not having this argument again mom."

"Who says we're arguing? Your grandmother didn't know what she was forcing on you at such a young age. We only want to help relieve the burden."

"Ease the burden? You hate that I own BreadLove. If you wanted to Ease my burden you would be offering to help.

Not always telling me to sign over the bakery to you."

"You're so young honey. You need to live your life. One day maybe not soon but in the future, you'll think back and wish you lived a different life. Experienced more."

The pencil tip breaks into my sketch sending a random line across the paper. Shit, I throw the pencil down with a sigh. Will my mom ever understand how much I love this place? Desserts, cakes, the fillings and doughs, baking isn't something I do it's apart of my soul. My mom however, thinks her way is best.

This is why she can't know about the loan. What the hell did my grandmother do with the money?

"Like I said, I'm not having this argument. Is Noah and selling the bakery the only reason why you called? So you forget my birthday but call to bitch me out over Noah. Did he tell you why we broke up?" The flames of my anger are boiling from the inside. I need water, air, anything to cool off.

"Katy, what are you going on about? Your birthday is Friday, I wouldn't forget something important. Why are you being dramatic?"

Oh Mom. I bet my life she forgot to turn her calendar over all last week. Usually my dad changes the day over every night, but the B&B is filled with guests in town looking over Summer School options at the college and spring weddings. Ugh.

"Noah told me you had a disagreement, and when he tried to make up, you were with another guy. Honestly Katy, how can you be so disrespectful? Why would you treat him like that?"

This conversation needs to end. There's a reason I keep my private life away from my parents and brother. Geez, I already yelled at Jackson.

"Mom, my birthday was Friday, as in the one that passed. And for the record, Noah broke up with me because I wouldn't go on a work trip with him. There was no disagreement. I even encouraged him to go. His response was to blow up at me and end our relationship."

"Honey, I think you misunderstood."

"Don't think so. But I'm okay." My shoulders release as soon as the words leave my mouth. Tension I didn't realize I was holding instantly washes away with my confession. Maybe my mom will see now, he's an asshole.

"Katy, he said you blew up over a trip away. Noah only wants to take you away for the weekend. Away from the stress. The bakery is taking its toll on you."

"Mom, I'm no more stressed than any business owner. How stressed are you?"

"Fine. I'll give you that, but sweetie, why were you on a date with someone else? Seems a little fast to me?"

My foot taps uncontrollably under the desk, while I think of a response.

"Gail, you talking to our baby girl? Put her on speaker." My dad yells from the background somewhere. Life saver as always. Thank god.

"Oh fine, maybe you can talk some sense into our daughter." Oh great the conversation never goes well when she uses our daughter.

"Hey honey! Happy late Birthday, did my text go through?" My father, Bill Heart, Mr. go with the flow. Unless he's trying to bake something. If you stick a mixer in front of him he curses like a sailor. It's what I love most about my dad, and the fact that he doesn't give me shit for cursing.

"Bill, what are you talking about? Today is the fifteenth her birthday isn't until Friday. You both are loosing your minds!"

My dad lets out a sigh. "Gail, you own a smartphone. Read the date. Today is the twenty-second. Katy's birthday was Friday. You didn't text her?" He grumbles.

Mom gets so lost in running their B&B she forgets everything else, including to check the day.

"Oh, my! Katy honey, I'm so sorry. You know how I am. Happy late birthday sweetheart. Forgive me? Let your father and I take you to dinner. We don't see you nearly enough." Her voice is back to her soothing octave.

"Mom, I'm okay. I'll see about dinner. There is a lot going on with the bakery, plus I took this past weekend off as a treat to myself." *Maybe dinner is a good idea.*

"Please, honey. We would love to see you and Noah. I'm sure you two will make up by the time we go for dinner." *On second thought, no to dinner.*

"No mom. No dinner, Noah and I are over. I forgive you for being busy and forgetting my birthday. But I won't forgive you for siding with him. I need to go." I'm not trying to punish my mom, but I can't deal with the issues she has with my life.

"Sweetie, please, I'm trying to help. Noah's..."

"A piece of shit who broke up with me on my birthday." My finger smashes into the red button ending the call. That is totally not satisfying enough of a way to end a call.

What am I going to do? Whatever it is I can't tell anyone. This is my problem and I'm going to fix it on my own.

A knock sounds at my door and I leap out of my desk. What could go wrong now? The door pops open and Meghan my assistant manager and morning baker, peeks her head in the door.

"Morning Boss, have a second?" Meghan is my favorite person at the bakery. She's ten years older than me but never treats me like I don't belong in the owners seat.

"Sure, what's up?"

"Oh, nothing. I'm taking my break and wanted to see how your weekend went. I brought coffee and I also heard you talking to your mom, thought you might need an excuse to hang up." She shrugs, not needing to say more. One reason I love Meghan, she knows how my mom is. She's been working here since she was in high school so she understands all the family drama.

"Thank you but you're too late, I already hung up on her. Not my finest moment." My nose scrunches. Add the call with the loan chick and the angst swimming inside my gut is enough to make me hurl.

"Eh moms make everyone crazy. It's what we do, go ask Baker if you don't believe me." A teasing smile crosses her face. "Anyway, how was your first weekend off?"

We move from my desk to the poufs to enjoy our caffeine break at small round coffee table I keep in my office for moments like this. "Don't worry, you don't need to explain Noah. Carter told me about what went down at Ian's. What a jerk."

"Wait. Did you say you heard from Carter? Is gossip about what happened at the restaurant spreading all over town?" All the blood rushes from my head, my skin breaks out in tiny beads of sweat. Please not the rumor mill. Hadley Falls isn't a tiny town, but when you live and work around Main street the closeness is as bad as living in the smallest town in the world. Everyone is up in your business.

"Katy, breathe. Rumors aren't spreading around town. The restaurant was close to empty Saturday. Carter made sure no one is gossiping about you. He only told me because I pushed when he asked how you are." Her hand reaches out to squeeze mine.

"Hold on, this happened Saturday. Did you finally go on a date with Carter?" Oh, this is awesome, Carter has been asking Meghan for a date for the last several months. Her cheeks flare pink. Awe, someone is blushing, how cute. She is such a no nonsense single mom. Always using her mom jeans and baseball tees to dumb down her gorgeous figure and beautiful long black hair.

"Nope, no subject changing missy. Carter told me who your date was Saturday so spill. What were you doing on a date with that hottie Connor McKinnon?" She wiggles her eyebrows, and we burst into laughter like we're back in second grade. After a few seconds of giggles, Meghan pulls us back on topic. "Okay okay, start at the beginning. What happened Friday?"

"Where do you want me to start? Noah dumping me or the hottie?"

"Screw Noah. Tell me about the hottie."

I cup my hand and whisper, "We slept together Friday night."

Meghan burst out laughing. "Why are you whispering? You had fun and did something for you for a change no big deal. And you did it with Connor Freaking McKinnon."

"Why are you saying his name like that? Is he some sort of celebrity?"

"Um Katy. You so need to get out more. Connor is only the owner and hottest bartender at McKinnon Pub. So did he sleep over?"

"Possibly."

"Tell me everything." Meghan demands. So I dive into all the details of my weekend. When I'm done we simultaneously take a sip of our coffees. Talks with Meg are always the perfect break in the day. She is like talking to a big sister I always wanted.

"Wow. A date the next day." Meghan nods her head. "He hasn't dated since Kelly broke up with him."

"Whose Kelly?"

"His ex, she dumped him a few years back. Never liked her."

A smile is spreading across her face.

"What?"

"Katy, I'm so happy for you."

"Megs, you're sweet, but it was only a weekend. Hell, the whole thing started with a one-night stand."

"Katy, you like him. Like really like him, don't try to deny it. What's wrong are you scared he's gonna hurt you?" Meghan questions while waving her finger at me, like I'm a child.

"Maybe I like him a little, but I can't get attached it was only a weekend. Look what happened with Noah. I gotta keep myself guarded." I take a sip of my coffee to give myself a second to think.

You like Connor. Yes, but I can't expect anything. Relationships don't form after a one-night stand, right? *You never know. Have faith.* Oh, so now you're optimistic. My mind is officially gone, having an argument with myself. Awesome, Katy. Letting out a big breath, I sip on my coffee. Such a needed distraction.

"Hey, don't worry." Meg says pulling out of my head while throwing back the last of her cup. "You may call it a one-night stand, but he called you the next day, right?"

I nod.

"And you saw him again?"

I nod again.

"See, that changes the game. I bet he likes you too. Connor hasn't slept with a girl more than once since he broke up with Kelly. That was almost two years ago." Meghan pinches her lips together. "Oh crap, don't repeat what I just told you. Carter let that slip yesterday." She turns her jade green eyes to me. I zip my lips and nod for her to keep going. "But my point is, don't sell yourself short Katy. You're a catch, any guy would be lucky to be your man." I squirm in my seat, speechless. Taking compliments is not my strong suit.

"A catch," I smirk, shaking my head. Meghan's phone beeps from her pocket.

"Looks like my break is over. We are running smooth as a baby's butt out front. Take the rest of the day off." She commands.

"I'll take the order under advisement, boss." We both chuckle.

"Never. This place is amazing, but I have no interest in the headaches running a shop comes with."

Meghan heads back out to the bakery, and I let what she said sink in. Don't overthink everything. My grandmother's words echo in my head. "Enjoy what comes, sweet girl." The memory of her words warm my heart. Being called an over thinker is nothing new. My friends always remind me to let go. But can I let go and guard my heart at the same time?

As much as I want to take Meghan up on her offer, I need to work on brining these ideas to life. Time to turn these sketches into real food. I'm so pumped over this new idea well not new, I've thought this passion project out for years. Funny how now with the bakery in trouble my dream could be the only thing that save us from the bank.

The next two hours fly by, getting the batter and frosting the perfect consistency. I taste one and it is to die for. The right amount of chocolate with a hint of bitterness. Now if I can score a meeting with Ian I might be able to make this idea take off. A meeting with him is close to impossible to schedule. The last months of trying came up empty. He is the key, the other local restaurant owners trust him and follow his lead with vendors.

Ian is the owner of three local restaurants in this city and four more in the surrounding cities, plus the owner of Side Car here in town. An exclusive club for members only. Local celebrities mostly, the member fee is over twenty grand. If we could land a contract for any of his businesses, it would be game changing for BreadLove.

What if I can't do this? All my employees depend on me. I could turn to my parents for help, but they would demand stipulations, like letting my mom take over. Nope, I'll never give up my bakery.

The loan needs to be kept a secret. I can do this. Ugh, I need a drink. My gaze travels to my desk clock. Five o'clock, wow the afternoon flew by. I think a visit to my favorite bartender sounds like a splendid idea.

McKinnon Pub is busy with the after-work crowd which makes it hard to spot Connor. So I make my way to the bar, setting the box of treats down with care.

Yay me, Nicole is working. "Excuse me, I'll take a double scotch neat." The woman glares over her shoulder in my direction but turns the other way to help the other patrons instead.

"Hello, can I order a drink, please?" She drags her gaze to mine.

"Oh sorry, I didn't see you." Her apology is as fake as her smile. "What can I get you?"

"Scotch neat, make it a double." I reply with a reciprocating grin. The busyness of the pub makes it hard to scan for Connor.

"Here you go." Nicole slides my drink across to me. "Connor isn't seeing anyone today, so you might want to leave after you finish your drink. Or set your sights on someone available." The bite of the scotch helps hide my shock.

"Does Connor know you talk to customers this way? I'm pretty sure I didn't ask your opinion." This chick and her bitchy attitude can fuck right off.

"I'm being helpful. Connor only sleeps with blondes, and he never goes back for seconds. You're wasting your time. You can think I'm being a bitch, but I'm saving you some embarrassment." She cocks her head at me resting her hip against the wood counter. Did the universe decide today is be a bitchy day?

Girls like her are all the same. They love to warn you, for your own good, of course. Why can't she say what she means? Stay away from the guy I like. Connor may not see it but Nicole is crushing on him, hard.

"Hey Jamie! How's it going?" I holler as Jamie appears from behind the bar. Ignoring Nicole's remarks. Her face brightens.

"Katy. You looking for Connor?"

"Yep brought him some goodies." Her eyes lock on the box.

"Are those from BreadLove?" Jamie asks, eyeing me suspiciously.

"Yep. Want one?" I wink shaking the box in my hand.

"Yasss. Thank you, you are so nice." She says licking her lips. "I pick up sweets from your shop all the time. Seriously the best. Connor's in his office. You're more than welcome to head back."

"Thanks," I reach inside my box of goodies and pull out an Irish Cream Cupcake.

They are beyond delicious, the cake is a chocolate stout topped with brown sugar frosting. The perfect duo. Subtle hints of chocolate with a bite of something you can't name. The Irish cream washes over your tongue finishing off with an explosion of sugary sweet alcohol. One of my new favorites by far.

"Here, this is for you. Irish Cream cupcake. It's a brand-new recipe. Let me know what you think."

"Girl, this looks delicious. Mind if I eat this now." Jamie peels back the cupcake wrapper not waiting for my response and sinks her teeth into the moist cake.

"Oh, my god. These are amazing. You made these?" An audible groan leaves her lips. I think she's having a foodgasm and nothing makes a baker happier than watching someone in pure joy eating their food.

"Yep. I'll bring more over later in the week so the whole staff can enjoy."

"You are the best. What are you drinking? I'll send another round back there in a few." She nods her head towards the back.

"Scotch neat. Thanks sweetie." I knock back the rest of my drink, grab my box and head for Connor's office.

The walk down the corridor feels a lot longer than it did Friday. My stomach flips, my palms are sweaty, and I'm feeling uncomfortable. What if Nicole is right, and he doesn't want more? Dammit, fuck her for making me feel insecure. No, fuck me for that shit. We are having fun, so there can be no hurt feelings if he's busy. Connor's booming voice calls from the other side of the door after one knock.

"Come in." Connor growls as I'm pushing the door open. "This better be important. I said no interruptions."

"I'm sorry, I can come back later." I stutter and attempt to turn around.

"Shit. Katy wait. I'm sorry I thought you were a staff member. We asked them for privacy. Come in." He gets up from his chair and wraps his arms around me. *See, he likes you.* He bends down taking my lips in a possessive kiss. Warmth fills me as his tongue pushes inside my mouth, dancing with mine.

"Ahem." Comes from someone in his office. We pull away from each other breathless.

"Sorry. Forgot we had an audience. Katy this is one of my good friends, Ian Dewitt. Ian, this is Katy the owner of BreadLove."

"I'm aware who she is Connor. You are the feisty baker who has been hounding my assistant for an appointment to see me for the last few months. Pleasure to meet you Katy." Light gray eyes stand out against rich golden brown skin.

He kisses the top of my hand like a classy gentleman and I use all my might not to giggle like a schoolgirl and fawn over his godlike physique. Ian is every girl's wet dream. Tall, and built with lean muscle on muscle. He's wearing black designer slacks, a salmon-colored dress shirt, and Gucci loafers. He's hot, but he's got nothing on Connor's scruffy jaw line and rugged appearance.

"Alright alright you can lay off the charm on my girl." Connor barks at him. My whole body warms at his use of my girl.

"I'm sorry if I'm interrupting but I was playing around with a new idea." I hold up my box of cupcakes.

"Hold up, you met her Friday, and she's already bringing you desserts. Damn, no wonder my staff date bakers." Ian quirks an eyebrow at me.

"She's mine." Connor says more rumble than words. He told his friend I'm his. My cheeks heat and my belly flips.

"Katy, I believe I owe you an apology. Carter informed me about the commotion during your birthday dinner. Please know I took care of him. He won't bother you in any establishment I own ever again." What does that even mean?

"Thank you. Would you like a cupcake?" I offer a little off my game.

"Yes, please." They say in unison.

"Here you go, an Irish Cream cupcake." Connor wastes no time digging in. Watching him devour the treat reminds me of Saturday night and heat creeps up my neck, my nipples pebble under my shirt. I have to shake the thoughts away.

Ian, however, studies the cupcake. He licks the icing rolling the fluffy texture around his mouth before he takes a large bite. The audible groans and moans coming from both men make this day a million times better. There is nothing I love more than the sound of people enjoying my creations.

"This shit is fucking amazing." Ian turns to me. "I'm sorry we haven't gotten a meeting on the books but if it has anything to do with these delicious cupcakes let's talk."

"Now? I don't want to interrupt." He waves me off.

"You aren't interrupting anything. We are old friends, busting each other's balls. Now, tell me why you want a meeting?" He points to the seat next to him and I sit. "Connor, have the bar send back a round of single malt. Anything for you, Katy?"

"The same, please." I reply reaching into my bag for my sketches. "Here is what I'm working on. Specialty desserts. I want to launch a division at BreadLove. Breads, cakes, and cookies are fun but my true passion is for plated desserts. So many restaurants, yours included are lacking in desserts that match the quality of their menus." Ian flips through the sketches before handing them to Connor.

"People love desserts, but owners give them no respect. Guests will order a beautiful dessert to say they ordered something different. I want to create a unique menu that caters to your restaurant's themes." They look them over.

"Katy, these desserts are all Irish themed." He caught me. Heat creeps up my neck. Connor's gaze moves from drawing to drawing, silent.

"I couldn't stop thinking about your pub, so I used it as my guinea pig. I hope I didn't overstep." I blurt ending the silence.

"Are you kidding? This idea is brilliant."

The worry falls away. Thank god. For a moment I thought I miscalculated using his business for inspiration.

"This has potential." Ian adds, handing me a piece of paper. "I'll tell you what. Here's my card, call Carter to set something up. Use Connor's place as the example. If I like what you come up with, we'll move forward. I assume you will also want a clause making BreadLove our bread vendor as well." He tips his chin to me.

"Yes, I would require that clause in our contract."

"Well Ms. Heart then I'll want to taste some samples of those when we meet. Bring the dessert ideas no need for more yet."

"Thank you so much. You won't be disappointed."

"I get the impress you never disappoint. Connor, where are our drinks? A toast of our new friendship is important."

Oh, my god. I got the meeting. Inside I'm dancing around air humping everything I see. On the outside, I keep cool and smile. This is the perfect chance I need to get us back on track and pay off the loan in time to save the bakery and my pride.

Connor

Chapter Eleven

I can't remember the last time I had so much fun hanging out with someone. Since Katy stopped by the pub last Monday, talk has been nothing but work.

Well, she wants to discuss work and I keep turning everything she says into innuendo. Watching her face scrunch any time I distract her is sexy as fuck. My girl is a dirty one, but she has nothing on my mouth.

Who knew someones temper could be so hot? Her cheeks flush and she gets this crease right above her nose. All I want to do is kiss her and fuck her.

Nothing I do distracts Katy for long. She is antsy and excited over her meeting with Ian next week. I'm happy for her, but she's keeping her ideas under lock and key until she talks to Ian and my curiosity is driving me nuts.

Her idea is brilliant. This could be the expansion I need to grow our revenue. There is no coincidence that he asked her to use my pub as the example for her pitch. Last month I told

Ian I need something to change for the better. Now things are definitely changing.

The scenario has the potential to make him a lot of money. Win win for him, he can test Katy's idea without risk having her try with my place over one of his restaurants.

BUZZ! BUZZ!

Ian: All set for tomorrow. Use the loft entrance.

Connor: I owe you one.

Ian: If the meeting with Katy goes as well as I think you'll owe me two. ;)

Connor: Fucker, always gotta have the upper hand don't you?

Ian: Always.

Fucking prick. He set this up because her idea has the possibility of helping us both. Plus he walks away with a favor in his pocket. Well, two favors.

RING! RING!

That should be Katy, unfortunately the caller id says Mom and not Sweetness, my nickname for Katy. I roll my shoulders back preparing for war. No way my brothers and I are going to take Joy's daughters to Casino night.

"Hey Ma."

"So your phone is working and you're still breathing?"

"Is that a joke? Cause you aren't funny."

"Sue me for worrying about you. Someone removed you from the schedule and I left two messages. What's wrong with missing my baby boy?" Step one in Maggie McKinnon's arsenal: guilt trip.

"Graham's your baby boy mom, we are all aware of that. Jameson took me off because a lot is going on at the pub. I requested the next three months off to give it my full attention."

"What are you talking about three months? Your father mentioned nothing to me." She screeches. "Is something wrong?" Her voice laced with concern. At the drop of a hat my mom goes from screeching banshee to a concerned parent.

"No. Things are right for a change. The business is exceeding projections. Interesting things are on the horizon that need my undivided attention."

"So this is about your pub? Fine. But I need you to take Kelly to Casino night. Joy and I set everything up. The Clarkes are picking her up from the airport tonight and coming over for dinner tomorrow. Be here at seven," she commands.

"Sorry mom I can't, made plans. You can forget about me taking Kelly to any event. She can find another date or go alone." My grip tightens around the closest whiskey bottle and I pour myself a glass. Arguing with my her sucks. I hate being in this position. Which is why Jameson accuses me of giving in. He doesn't understand, sometimes surrendering to mom is easier than fighting with her. Pops always sides with her and she never fights fair.

"Excuse me? What plans are more important than welcoming your girlfriend home?"

I clank my glass down hard on the counter. "Kelly isn't my girlfriend. We broke up almost two years ago. I'm not coming to dinner," I growl.

"*Connor McKinnon.*" Her shrill voice rings in my ear and I pull the phone back to preserve my hearing. "You will not speak to me like that. I am your mother, you will be at dinner tomorrow or you better have an excellent reason for missing. Your little bar isn't an excuse to miss."

"Mom, stop. Don't accuse me of being disrespectful when I didn't raise my voice or curse. Telling you no is not a crime. Let's try again. No, I will not take Kelly to Casino night and I'm not coming tomorrow. I hope you have a great time."

"I don't understand why you two can't work out your differences. She's the perfect girl for you. You were friends for so long and together for five years. I thought she was the one." So did I. *Until Katy.* The thought of Katy strengthens my resolve, I like her and won't jeopardize what we might be building for a woman who pushed me aside.

"She's back in town, why not try to rekindle something with her? Kelly regrets how your last conversation went. How many times has she tried to apologize? You keep shutting her out. Don't make her the bad guy. Come over tomorrow and talk with her then use casino night as a way to reconnect."

"No. I'm not rehashing anything with her. Dinner tomorrow is a no. I'm going on a date. Now you are up to speed on my business, happy?" I regret the words the second they leave my mouth. Never let mom find out about who you are dating, unless she's way beyond the realm of serious.

"A girl. Really? Well, if she is so important you are missing a dinner that mean a lot to me then you can bring her to family dinner next Saturday." She orders leaving no room for argument.

"Family only?"

"Yes. This one must be something if you are blowing off Kelly. After all she's the one you are meant to be with."

The fuck. What is my mom's obsession with Joy and her daughters? They cooked up this crazy plan of their kids marrying each other without ever consulting us. Thank god I don't live in a time when parents made marital decisions for their children.

"Mom, if I bring her to dinner you better behave."

"I'm always kind to people. See you next weekend, I'll give your regards to the Clarkes. I love you, son." There's my sweet ma.

"Love you too Mom. Tell pops I said hi."

"Sure thing. You would spend more time with everyone if you didn't take so much time off." Back to crazy mother.

"Goodbye Mom."

You got played. Fucking hell, she is sneaky. How did I not realize what she was doing? I rub my hands over my neck. Katy at a family dinner. What am I thinking?

I send a quick text off to Jameson telling him about the call with our mom. Now more than ever this idea of Katy's needs be the ticket to bringing more business into the bar. The business won't succeed if I keep stretching myself thin. McKinnon Pub must come first.

BUZZ! BUZZ!

My mood turns around when the read out says Katy instead of Jameson.

> **Katy: I can't wait for tomorrow. Where are we going again?**
>
> **Connor: Naughty girl. I think you deserve a spanking for trying to ruin your surprise.**
>
> **Katy: Connor, please what am I supposed to wear?**
>
> **Connor: Nothing works for me. ;) Kidding. Wear something semi-formal.**
>
> **Katy: Way to drop a hint. :***

My phone vibrates again.

> **Jameson: On the way. Graham is with me.**

A picture comes through. Katy. Fuck, she's wearing a black lace bra. The seam cuts right across her nipples pushing her luscious tits over the edge.

The smirk on her face tells me she's being very deliberate. My dick turns to steel in my jeans. Her pussy lips are on display and glistening with her juices, wet and ready for me.

Argh! I bite my fist, forcing myself to breathe rather than jump in my car and head to her house this instance. I want to fuck her until she can't walk a single step. My phone buzzes with another text from Katy.

Katy: Enjoy. I'll be wearing this all day tomorrow thinking of you.

Fuck, this woman is gonna kill me.

Connor

Chapter Twelve

A quarter to six. The light sheen of sweat forming on my skin is making me fidget at Katy's front door. *Calm down, this isn't your first date.* Easier said than done. I can't seem to relax. We are already having sex. Why am I so nervous? *Tonight is special.*

Setting the whole date up with Ian made me realize I like Katy more than anyone in my past. Kelly included. With her our relationship was easy, we were family friends, and our moms helped push us along.

With Katy everything is different, I want to spend time with her. I want her warming my bed, maybe forever. Whoa, where did that thought come from?

The front door opens cutting off my thoughts. Katy steps outside rendering me speechless. She's wearing a floral off the shoulder dress, the bodice is tight and hugs her chest. The skirt is short, cut like a v for a longer back. The outfit is sexy as shit. Her black heels accent the muscles in her legs.

It takes all my control to make sure I don't pop a spontaneous hard on. "Fucking breath taking." My voice sounds like I have gravel in my throat.

"Thank, you! You don't look too bad yourself." She bites the corner of her lip, her eyes heat with desire.

"Like what you see?"

"Well, I was wondering if we had time for you to have your way with me before dinner. What do you think?" The lust in her eyes is unmistakable. She wants me to take her right here. Fuck, this woman is amazing, she always keeps me on my toes.

"Trust me nothing sounds better than throwing you over my shoulder and burying my fingers in your pussy until you cum." My finger grazes her nipples. A moan slips from Katy's throat. The sound makes my balls pull up. "If I take one step into your house, We won't leave until morning, and we can't have that."

"Oh right, my surprise. Your dick could be my surprise." I bark out a laugh.

"You say the sweetest things."

The drive to Ian's private club is quick. Katy lives about ten blocks away from Side Car, the most exclusive member only club in Hadley Falls and the surrounding areas.

The place is legendary. Whispers are all over town about the place because only members are privy to what goes on inside. Even a membership doesn't guarantee all the secrets. You need to be a certain kind of member to experience different areas.

Tonight I reserved the loft area for a private dinner for Katy and me.

"Connor, what is this place?" She's looking around with wonder in her eyes, taking in all the fixtures and dark lighting.

"Side Car." My brows squint in question. I thought everyone had heard of this place.

"It's real? You hear rumors about the secret Side Car all the time."

"Well, welcome. Side Car was originally a bar and after time Ian started adding to the building and changing certain parts. About fix years ago he added the exclusive membership. He closed the whole place to the public not long after. Now Side Car is the hottest club around, if you can get in."

"Lucky for me you are a member, then." She chimes back.

We take the elevator up to the top floor. We enter the room and Katy gasps.

Ian did an amazing job. The room is perfect. Small candles are scattered around the room. The only light coming from their dancing flames. The floors are a dark cherry, adding a red hue to the glow of the room. In the center is a small table with a single booth attached. On the table sits a long stemmed rose in a small vase.

"You did all this for me?" Are those tears in her eyes?

"Babe, are you okay?" I squeeze her hand. "Here, sit." Katy takes her chair, looking around soaking up all the details.

"How in the world?" she whispers, astonished. Good. Tonight is only the beginning. Ian enters carrying an assortment of food.

"Ian. What are you doing here?"

"Who else would I allow to cook for a private event in my restaurant with such an honored guest, um?" He doesn't bother waiting for an answer before unloading his tray. "You are ravishing," he adds, winking at Katy.

A deep rumble escapes my throat. Katy giggles and Ian shakes his head with a smirk. "First up, fried mac n' cheese. These are fried mushroom risotto. Please dig in."

Katy's eyes brighten. "I love these. Thank you I can't wait." Her lips pull up in a giant grin. "Oh my gosh. These are delicious. So creamy and light. You are a genius."

"Thank you." Ian bows his head. "I cannot take credit for tonight's menu. All dishes are being prepared at Connor's request. The list of plates is lengthy." He hands us a printed list of the nights courses.

"The next plate will be fresh cheese and prosciutto tray served along side a mini caprese salad. Our soup course will be Italian wedding soup. And we finish the menu tonight with beef Wellington, potatoes au gratin, bacon sautéed green beans, and homemade baguettes."

Katy squeals, "Holy shit. Fresh bread? But you don't like to bake."

"You'd be correct. The bread is from your bakery, and the desserts Meghan made. I believe she works with you. Carter set that part up so I hope she is a talented baker."

"Meghan helped with this? She's amazing. I couldn't survive without her. How did you do all this?"

"I had nothing to do with tonight. Other than cooking that is. Mr. Silent and brooding over here takes all the credit." Ian waves over to me. "Now, enjoy and I'll be back with your next course." He disappears into the kitchen.

Katy turns to me, her face is so bright she's lighting up the room. "Connor, how in the world? How did you know?"

"How did I know what?" I ask playing with her is so much fun.

"This! All of these items I wanted to make for my birthday dinner. How did you know all my favorite foods?"

"Elise. I called her Tuesday to ask her about the dinner your friends mentioned. Found out the entire story. It bothered me you didn't get what you wanted on your day."

"So you made my wish happen?" She finishes for me. Her grin is stretching from ear to ear. "Thank you. No one has ever done something for me that was this romantic."

My chest puffs out. Katy is amazing, she puts her friends before herself and is a kind-hearted person. She deserves everything the world has to offer. "That's a shame. You're a catch babe. You don't need to believe me now, but you are." I lean into her and steal a quick kiss. "Can I ask a favor?"

"Anything."

"Will you come to dinner with me next weekend to meet my parents and brothers?"

"You want to introduce me to your family?" Her voice shakes slightly.

"I mentioned you to my mom. Now she wants to meet you. You up for dinner?" A moment of silence passes.

"Sounds fun." A smile tugs on her lips. Now the hard part; getting Maggie McKinnon's approval.

Katy

Chapter Thirteen

Connor and a glass of whiskey are the only thoughts on my mind as I step into McKinnon Pub but the second cool air washes over me everything fades. Agh this heat needs to end even a short walk has my shirt sticks to my skin in several places. Gross.

The place is empty, oh crap I'm early. My watch says it's only quarter to three. Connor won't be here for another fifteen minutes. McKinnon Pub opened little while ago giving the whole place to myself. I make my way to the bar and use the moment of silence to take the place in.

The oak table tops pop against the dark green interior. Odd fixtures in orange and white are placed along the pub. There is almost every Irish Sir Name hanging on the wall not to mention a small collection of police and fire department patches which will surely grow over time.

My favorite feature is the giant Irish flag fixed behind the bar against the glass. The flag is practically pristine, which must be impossible working around so much liquid. I'm so lost in thought looking around the pub I miss Nicole entering.

"Oh, you again. You didn't get the hint last time, sweetheart?" She sneers.

"Hint? Look, I don't know what your problem with me is, but you need to get over yourself."

"You're my problem. You and your lack of understanding for what you are." She turns to me cocking her hip out.

"Excuse me? What I am? Oh, yes, I'm Connor's girlfriend."

"You think... Damn, you are crazy. Sweetie, you are a one-night stand who is now Connor's go to booty call. Everyone can see it clear as day, but you aren't getting the message." Her words are like a slap across my face stunning me into speechlessness.

"Who the fuck do you think you are?"

"Who am I?" She opens her mouth to respond but instead snaps her lips shut tight.

"Don't let me stop you. I want to hear your answer." Connor's voice growls from behind me. Holy shit, my heart leaps in my chest and I launch out of my seat. How much did he overhear?

"Co..Connor, hi boss." Nicole stutters giving Connor a wave.

"You going to answer the lady?" His gaze furious gaze is locked on her.

"She's here all the time, always asking for you." Nicole waves to me.

The corner of the right side of my lip pulls up, I'm so over this girl and her obsession of what's mine. I strut to Connor pull him down for a kiss.

Every emotion from today pours out. My excitement, anger every bit drains from me as I smash my mouth into his. A deep purr rips out of Connor's throat as his arm locks around my waist, and he cups my head. He pulls away leaving us both breathless. Connor glares at Nicole, nothing but disgust in his eyes.

"Let me set the record. Katy is my girlfriend. Not some fuck and even if she were. That is my place to tell her not yours. You work for me Nicole, nothing more. This is your last warning. Any more attitude with Katy or any other female customers, and I'll let you go. I would fire you right now, but I know Katy would feel bad."

No I wouldn't. Connor peeks over at me before adding. "Eventually. Now get to work. Katy and I will be in my office. If you or anyone needs something ask Jamie."

Connor takes my hand and leads me to the back. The door slams shut. In the next instant I'm pressed up against the hard wood with his mouth claiming mine. A small moan escapes past our joined lips.

"I want you," he breathes while pulling down my top causing my breasts to spill out. Connor drops his head to my breast sucking my nipple between his teeth. His other hand keeps me pinned in place by my throat.

My core is weeping into my thong. Fuck, no one touches me like Connor. He bites down on my tight bud and I fall into oblivion. My whole body bows and a scream rips from me as the orgasm washes over me.

"Fuck me, please." The words are breathy. Connor pulls his hand from my neck to unzip his pants and pull himself out through his boxers. Whoa, that's hot.

A sudden urge to lick his dick hits me. I push Connor back. He squints questioning me but throws up his hands letting me have my way. My palm wraps around his cock, stroking him from base to tip.

He lets out a hiss. "Damn baby. I thought you wanted sex?"

"That was before I saw your hard dick. Now I want you in my mouth. Maybe if you're good, I'll let you fuck me," I smile taunting him.

"Oh, using my own words against me now, are we." His voice is strained. Good. My cheeks hollow, sucking the head deeper. My tongue laps around the tip, dipping into his slit. He lets out a strangled string of curses.

Connor uses his hand to push himself into the back of my throat. Pleasure blooms deep inside me at the loss of control. "Fuck baby, like that." He grounds out. My head bobs keeping up the pace and I use my hands to cup his balls. Saliva is dripping down my face. The knowledge that anyone could catch us is spurring me on.

Connor's head swells sliding deeper down until I gag. He wraps my hair around his fist and uses my ponytail to control his depth.

"Touch yourself while I fuck your face." He orders. I don't need to be told twice. My fingers find my clit puffy and swollen. One press and I'm bucking into my hand while I moan around his cock. "Does my dirty girl like playing with herself, while I fuck her throat?"

My reply is muffled around is engorged length. Connor builds up speed and I match him with strokes against my clit chasing my own climax in a rush.

"I'm right there." Connor grumbles. "Take all of me baby. I'm gonna come down that throat right now." The first rope of cum squirts down into my stomach and my orgasm rushes over me. My pussy clinches under my finger and my nub throbs relentlessly while I ride my wave of pleasure.

"Fuck woman." Connor smiles, placing a small kiss on my lips. He rights himself and grabs two waters from the fridge. "Are you good?"

"Huh?" My voice goes up. "With sucking your dick?" Water flies from where Connor's lips are touching the bottle. The deep chuckle from his belly fills the room. I swoon. His hand points towards the door.

"Damn, that mouth. Are you okay about earlier with Nicole? Her attitude was way out of line, but I'd be a liar if I didn't admit to how hot watching you stand your ground with her made me."

"Oh I'm aware. Her problem is, she wants you. You two never hooked up?" I cringe, not wanting to push and piss him off.

"Never. A about a year ago she kissed me but I turned her down. Explained that she isn't my type."

"So, I was going to forget about the whole thing, but last time she called me a booty call too. She implied, I didn't realize where we stood and today she said as much flat out." I let out a sigh, "You know what? Who cares about Nicole. You put her in her place, maybe now she'll lay off and act like your employee."

"Babe, I'll fire her if she doesn't. I'm not letting some employee's misplaced feelings mess with this, with us. You mean a lot to me." Connor grips my chin and forces my gaze to his. "You're mine, Katy Heart. Deal with it." He gives me a sweet kiss. "Now, how did it go this morning?"

"The meeting went fantastic. Let's sit down and I'll show you the ideas I created."

"Finally. Do you have any idea how funny Ian thought it was that you wouldn't show me." His lips are tight but I can see the laughter behind his eyes.

"You talked to Ian?"

"You swore you would wait?" I whine.

"Please don't be mad. He called to ask me what I thought of the desserts. The bastard wouldn't stop laughing after I explained your thinking." Connor says waving his hand around like he doesn't agree. "He told me to call back after you come by. Promise he didn't spoil anything. Can I see your portfolio?"

"Yes. Right here. Browse through and tell me what you think." I hand the book over and nervously bounce on the balls of my feet while Connor flips through the sketches I prepared. It shows final plates, breaks down cost for the establishment. There are price suggestions and lists of all complimentary combos available.

That binder is my baby. I am so proud of all the hard work I poured into it over the years. All those sacrifices are paying off, I hope you're watching Grandma.

Connor finishes flipping through the book, he jumps back and forth, looking at different ideas I showcased. "Babe, this is bad ass. What did Ian think?"

"He loved it. Connor, we are going ahead with a contract. He wants to inspect my kitchen first but do you know what this means? Now I can." I stop myself before finishing.

Fuck, I almost spilled about the loan fiasco. *Tell him, you trust him.* I'm not ready yet. He'll think I'm weak like my mom does and rush in to save the day. What if he tells Ian, I could lose the contract. Nope, can't tell him.

"Can what?" Oh shit balls, what do I tell him?

"Sorry, in my head. Expand our kitchen out. It needs it." My stomach rolls over the lie. I swallow it down and plaster a smile on my face. He pauses for a moment then shrugs grabbing a piece of paper off his desk.

"Well I think this belongs to you." Connor hands me a check for five thousand dollars. Five thousand dollars. The memo reads dessert contract.

"Connor, what is this?"

"What I'll owe for those desserts, I want them." He points to my portfolio. "The same deal you and Ian finalize. Draw me up a similar terms and I'll sign."

My eyes are glued to the check. My knees go weak, the ground rushes up at me. Connor reaches across to guide me to sofa in his office. My own superhero.

"Katy, are you okay? Your stuff is phenomenal and when Ian tells me to jump on something, I move. Before you ask that was the only detail he gave me."

"Connor, you don't have to do this. Five thousand dollars is a lot of money. You don't need to give this to me because I'm your girlfriend."

"Fuck that baby. Don't you ever put yourself down. You are amazing at what you do, phenomenal. You may be my girlfriend, but I wouldn't drop five thousand of my business's cash if I didn't think it was a smart decision." He leaves no room for arguing.

"Now, let's go celebrate. Elise and I arranged dinner with your friends. Three hours better be enough time to shower and meet everyone at Ian's."

"Wait, you got everyone together tonight. How?"

"Elise." We both state at the same time breaking out into laughter.

"Let's head to your place. I keep a change of dress clothes in my closet here. Mind if I use your shower?" He holds up the garment bag and I shake my head, he's like my own James Bond ready for anything.

"Fine, but you forgot one thing on our to do list."

Connor scrunches his brow. "Oh yeah, what?"

"More cunnilingus. There is plenty of time for some oral celebrations before dinner, don't you think?" His eyes darken and my thighs clinch. Moisture gathers in my panties, oh man that look makes me hot every time.

"Fuck woman, that mouth. I'm gonna make you scream my name before I let you up. Be careful what you wish for, baby girl."

The way he growls little girl sends prickles over my skin and stirs something inside me. Being with him is so easy.

Then let him in, tell him about the bank. No, I force that thought out of my mind. The loan default could ruin me, I can't risk telling anyone.

Katy

Chapter Fourteen

Sundays are glorious days. Especially the third Sunday of every month. Brunch day with the girls.

I'm the first to arrive at Corner Place. The line is almost to the door. Not surprising for this early on a weekend. What is surprising is the lack of pastries in their case. Yikes! I send off a quick text to Bridgette double checking her order quantity for tomorrow's delivery.

Bridgette catches my gaze while I'm in line and waves me out.

"Hey girl, busy today I see."

"A crap shoot. Someone came in right after open and bought half the bakery case."

"Wow. Need extra for tomorrow?"

"Yes. Anything puff pastry or croissant dough, and can you add two more of each please? Today is nuts and I'll probably forget to call." Bridgette wrings her hands. "Those extras bring Gran so much joy."

"Consider it handled," I give her a wink.

"Reason one million I love you." She blows me air kisses and tips her head to the back. "Your spot is free. I'll send your drinks over."

"You are the true angel. Thank you sweetie." I blow a kiss back and head to my table.

Elise and Veronica arrive a few minutes later and sit on the couch across from me.

"Hey, Girl, your man is so much fun. Parker is begging me to set up another night out next weekend." Veronica rambles smiling from ear to ear. She is happy and I'm glad given the crap she's been through.

"Can't. Connor invited me out for dinner to meet his parents and brothers." I raise my coffee cup to hide behind.

"Wow, meeting the rents so soon?" Elise says. I shrug not sure how I want to answer. This is quick, quicker than I was anticipating. *You thought it would go no where.* It still too early to say where we are going. Oh, my gosh, stop talking to yourself.

Ugh. These feelings are real but now is not the time. "I think this is great. Connor is perfect for you. Don't get in your head about this." She finishes with a wink.

Lily drops in the seat next to me. What the hell?

"Sweetie, what's with the sweatshirt it's like eighty out?" Elise questions.

"You know I'm always cold." Lily snips back. Oh, great. Something bitchy is on the tip of my tongue. Her eyes stop me. When did they become so sunken in?

For the first time in a while I take in my friends entire appearance. Her hair is dull instead of the glowing blonde shade it usually is, her clothes are hanging off her in several places. This isn't good. Lily has always been thicker in the thighs, but lately she's looking more like Elise and her ass is getting smaller too. I can't believe I didn't see sooner, I've been so wrapped up in me.

"What happened on Friday? I called you a bunch." I ask her.

"We ate dinner with Isaac's family. He didn't appreciate all the texting and calling." Lily replies affronted. What the fuck?

"Did he take your phone?" Yikes, I didn't mean to say that. Lily's eye heat and her cheeks flash red. Oh crap, I hit it right on the head. Rage simmers below the surface. No sane person does something like that.

"Don't be ridiculous." She scoffs.

"Not an answer." Veronica adds. "Something is going on with you. Is Isaac hurting you?" She places her hand on Lily's arms and Lil winces for a flash before schooling her features. Oh, fuck no. Using lighting speed I pull her sleeve up faster than she can stop me. An angry purplish bruise in the shape of Isaac's hand is right there on her forearm.

"What is that!" Elise exclaims.

Lily pulls at her sleeve. "Nothing, mind your own business. What was so important that you needed to blow me up, anyway?"

"Katy won a giant contract. We went celebrating." Veronica soothes, "We wanted you there. But right now you need to explain what's going on." Lily's face falls a fraction.

"I'm sick of you guys bagging on Isaac. The constant bitching is getting old. You always put me in a bad position. Like the other day, why did you mention Jackson?"

No way I'm gonna stop talking about my brother to my friends that grew up with him. Issac is spewing shit again.

"Where is this coming from?" I ask her.

"Don't act dumb. All of you hate Isaac but don't say it to his face. Why don't you want me to be happy? He's a catch." Lily balls her hands into fists. Her leaving out she loves him as a reason doesn't escape me.

"Is your mom pressuring you to stay with him?" Elise presses. "Please don't listen to her. Lil, she's enamored with his families' money. He can't do anything wrong in her eyes. If he's hurting you, tell us. We'll help."

Lily snatches her purse and stands up, almost knocking over our coffee. "I don't need your crap. Issac loves me and all you do is bash him. Anyone can see you hate him. If you can't respect my relationship I'm leaving." She storms out, bumping into the customers in line before flying out the door.

The silence drags on forever, no one wants to speak. There isn't much to say. Elise's bottom lip is quivering. Veronica rubs her back attempting to console her.

I'm not sure what will cheer her up. Lily and Elise are more like sisters, than cousins. Their moms shared a house for the first five years of Lily's life. We spent more nights than I can count at the Everette Estate once Sarah married Dean.

"She needs space. Whatever is going on with Issac and her is bad, but pushing her now could make it worse. You know she can't say no to her mom. All we can do is be there for her." I add.

"This sucks, can we discuss something else?" V and I share a look.

"Sure, how are you and Ryan doing?" Veronica adds.

"Really good." She perks up. "I met his parents last week, they are the nicest people. Even his sister was kind to me."

"Yay. Ryan is a sweet guy. A little buttoned up for my taste but right on the money for you," I tease.

"Hey, I can't help it if you like em, rough and foul-mouthed." Elise chimes back. "Why do you think I wanted you to meet Connor? He's perfect for you. Dirty mouth, plus I've heard the rumors about his you know." she wiggles her eyebrows it is the funniest and most disturbing thing ever.

We burst out in laughter, drawing the attention of the other patrons. Oops, I signal to Bridgette in apology for being loud, and she waves me off.

"Okay, wow, so not going there. Veronica, tell us more about Parker." Please catch on.

"Things are going well, but." She takes a sip of her coffee. Uh oh. "He's horrible in bed," she whispers. Shit.

Veronica goes see through. "Oh, my god." Red curls fly back and forth as her head darts around as if the man is going to jump out and yell surprise. My mouth contorts awkwardly trying not to giggle.

"Go on. Laugh. This is such a Veronica thing. Parker is clueless on how to please a woman. How can a man that amazing be so crappy in bed?"

"Let me guess, he thinks he's amazing in the sac, but he refuses to eat pussy?"

"*Katy*. We are in public." Elise scoffs.

"What," I ask looking around for any children, there are none. "Says the woman asking about my man's."

"Katy." Elise cuts me off turning a deeper shade than Veronica.

"Nope, there are no little ears to offend. Stop being a prude. V you gonna answer my question?"

She huffs, I cock my head at her waiting. "No, he doesn't. He's kind of snobbish about bedroom stuff." She finally admits. "He only likes missionary."

"Bet he enjoys blow jobs." Her gaze drops. "Hey, It really isn't a huge deal. Noah sucked in bed. You're the only one who can decide if the relationship is worth staying in." I shrug leaving it there. It is not in my place to tell someone to jump ship on someone they care about because of bad sex.

"Sex isn't everything, Katy. We aren't all obsessed like you are." Veronica turns on me.

What the hell? Lily and V are eating crazy pills. These women are the only people in my life I am one hundred percent honest with, sometimes to a fault. Like now, not one but two friends are agitated with my mouth.

"Katy only meant." Elise starts. I hold my hand up halting her.

"Sweetie, I'm sorry. I only mean for me sleeping with Noah was awful. Because I thought crappy sex was normal, I stayed. You guys were right. Sex is fucking supposed to be amazing. One thing I learned since dating Connor, if a man won't eat you he doesn't deserve you." My cheeks heat and my nipples tighten at the thought of Connor's head between my legs. *Focus.* Oops.

"She's not wrong honey." Elise whispers tossing before tossing me a shush.

"I'm not telling you to dump Parker, but be honest and open with him. Maybe he'll surprise you. We love you sweetie. All we want for you is to be happy."

"I love you guys too. I'm sorry for being bitchy." She leans forward, and we wrap our arms around each other in a group hug.

The embrace feels wrong with Lily missing. *She needs space.* Hopefully, she'll let us in soon. We'll give her space and time. Hopefully it fixes everything.

Connor

Chapter Fifteen

Mid month delivery day always sucks. Talk about a grueling work day. Days like this remind me I need to hire a stock boy soon. I'm too damn old for unloading shit, too many back injuries working for my dad. Alright, I'm done. Time for a night in with my girl. A knock sounds at my door interrupting my train of thought. Nicole walks in giving me zero chance to respond.

"Hey boss. Got a second?"

"I'm on my way out. Can Jamie handle this?"

"No, I want to apologize for the other day. I was rude."

"You were." I'm being a short with her, but my patience is growing thin. All I can think about is picking up Katy and getting her back home so I can bury myself in her until the world falls away.

"Can we talk about us?"

"Nicole, there is no us. You're an employee. That's it." My phone dings with an alert.

RIKER: *Emergency services requested at BreadLove. No other details. Chris and I are on the way.*

Fuck. "I need to go." Tiny fingers try to grip my arms as I pass but I shrug it off. All my thoughts are on Katy. My mind is running rampant with scenarios, none of the good.

I send a text to Jamie asking her to lock up my office.

A fire engine, two cop cars and several emergency vehicles are in the parking lot. My gaze searches the people milling around dead set on one. A brunette sitting at the back of an ambulance gets my attention.

Thank fuck Katy's okay, she's surrounded by Riker and two people I don't know. An EMT puts his hand on Katy's knee and gives her a friendly squeeze. Who the hell is this guy? Green eyes meet mine and she slips from his grasp. Good.

"Connor." She flings herself at me letting out a wince when I catch her.

"Sweetness, what the fuck happened?" I move away, checking her over for any major injury. There is only a piece of gauze covering a minor cut. Everyone's eyes are on us, but I don't give a shit. Katy's safety is all that matters.

"Wait, how did you? Nope. Don't care, I'm just glad you're here." She tilts her head up lips puckered. *Keep cool.* I repeat the mantra, so I our lips touch as soft and sweet as possible.

In reality, I want to throw her over my shoulder and scream Katy is mine.

"A friend gave me a heads up." Riker lets out a small cough into his fist.

"Ma'am I'm sorry to interrupt, but do you think you can finish answering my questions?" Riker asks helping me lead her back to the ambulance.

"Sure."

"Hold on Riker, she's got cuts and bruises plus a swollen wrist. Katy needs to be checked out. You can interview her at the hospital." Says the EMT. He places a hand on Katy's arm and helps her put on a brace.

"Cam, I'm not going to the hospital. I'm fine." Katy leaves no room for argument in her tone.

"Katy, do what Cameron says. He wants to take care of you." I inspect the woman's features; she must be Katy's mom. They share a nose, eyes and jawline. Where Katy's hair is dark brown with chestnut with amber colored highlights, this woman's hair is blonde with golden under tones and cut into a simple bob.

Unlike Katy whose curves go on for days with her luscious ass and glorious rack. The woman next to her is more straight lines. "I'm fine mom." Knew it.

"Sweetie, your mom and Cam are looking out for you." The older gentleman adds.

"Babe, I can take you to the office in the morning for a check up if you're still sore. Doc gets in at six a.m. tomorrow." Her entire face brightens.

"Who are you?" Her mom inquires.

"This is Connor, my boyfriend. Connor this is Bill and Gail Heart my parents. The friendly EMT is Cameron, a friend." Katy introduces us all, and we shake hands. Cameron gives my hand a hard squeeze. I squeeze back harder hoping he gets my message. Katy is off limits.

"Again, sorry to intrude Ms.Heart, but I need your statement. I'd rather not ruin your day tomorrow. Connor is right about waiting to see Doc. She's better than the folks at the hospital and faster." Riker informs.

"You two know each other?" Katy waves the question off. "Never mind. I'm sorry officer there isn't much to tell. We were locking up for the day. The phone rang for the bakery counter. Some kid making a prank call."

"What did they say?" Riker inquires. A shadow passes over Katy's face for half a second before she hides it away. No one else noticed, hell I only saw because I'm staring at her so hard.

"Their voices were muffled. Then out of nowhere a lit bottle crashed through the front window. The loud bang knocked me back in surprise and I landed on my butt, which is how I got this." She waves her braced arm in the air. I'm positive Katy is holding something back but now isn't the time to ask.

"You're lucky the fire was small, and you got it out fast. Is there anything else you can remember?"

"Nope, if I do I'll call you. Can I go now? I'm tired and starving." Katy states.

Fifteen more minutes of questions, and we are given clearance to leave. Katy had to sign a paper for refusing to go to the hospital. The EMT was rather insistent. Thankfully Katy got him to back down.

"Now that we are free to leave I'm hungry. Katy, you and Connor should join us." Gail suggests.

"Actually, today has been long and I'm sure Connor wants to get home too. Rain check?"

"Let me rephrase. Dinner on us. Little Italy is around the corner." Her mom shoots Katy a look that says don't fuck with me. Katy and I gulp, damn she is tough. *And you're the one dating her daughter.* This should be interesting.

Little Italy is a small homey place. The tables are covered in white and red checkered tablecloths. A bottle of Chianti and candles being held up in wine bottles are scattered throughout the entire restaurant. The kitchen is open, giving guests a full view of the chefs at work.

We are seated quickly by the hostess and place our order within minutes of sitting down. The Hearts must eat here as often as me.

"Connor, how long have you known our daughter?" Gail kicks off the questions. Let the inquisition begin.

"Since her birthday. Elise set us up, she's dating my friend, Ryan."

"You mean Ryan Sellers? Such a sweet young man. We're friends with his parents, they are season regulars at our B&B. Good people the Sellers." Bill adds.

"Do you work with him?" Gail tosses out another question.

"Mom. Slow down. We are here for dinner not an interrogation." Katy sighs.

"All good babe, I can handle a few questions," I reassure her giving the back of her hand a kiss.

"Oh good. So do you work with Ryan?" Her mother presses.

"No, construction isn't my thing. I own The McKinnon Pub."

"Oh a business man. When did you open?" Mr. Heart inquires.

"Three years ago. You two should stop in some time."

"Three years, not bad for a bar. What did you do before?" Gail continues.

"Worked for my family's business. Still do when they need me, but I'm transitioning away from there to work at my place full time." I'm puffing out my chest a bit. The pub is my baby.

"So you left an established job to start a bar. Following your dreams is admirable, however, the restaurant industry isn't easy and the liquor one is even worse." Bar is uttered like some dirty word.

"Yes. This is a dream for me. My place allows me to work on two of my passions building community and drinks."

"Still, bars aren't reliable."

"Gail." Bill warns his wife.

"A pub differs from a bar. McKinnon's is a neighborhood spot the everyday person can enjoy. We strive to be somewhere you can order quality food and indulge in genuine conversation with friends or other patrons.

Wednesdays and Sundays are family nights. With our new dessert offerings coming soon, business should continue to go up."

I give Katy's hand a reassuring squeeze. Gail's questions don't bother me, they remind me of my mom. I'm sure they will grill Katy the same way this weekend.

"After being in the service industry my whole life, I can tell you it isn't all fun, and the work is demanding. A career without job security places a lot of tension on a couple and later on a family. Dreams are fine, but if you want your household to thrive, something will have to give."

"The stress is fun," Katy whispers.

She ignores Katy's statement and keeps pushing. "A lawyer. Now they have an upstanding place in the community, people respect them, and they aren't subject to the whims of others. Take Noah for instance, he's an amazing young man with a high-paying job, and he's about to make partner at his firm. He is the kind of man you need."

Her hand waves at me dismissively. "Not someone who will continue to drag you deeper into this craziness of restaurants and high stress. Didn't you learn anything from us or your grandparents? Food Service is hard. Look at today. You could have lost everything."

"But I didn't." Katy bites back. "Today was some freak accident. Most days I don't battle flaming jars coming through my window. And I told you last time we spoke, Noah and I are over. Stop bringing him up. Plus no one here is talking about marriage so quit with the toll on the family crap."

"Don't be so sensitive. We ran into him and his parents the other day. The man is miserable without you. He told me so himself honey. How can you throw your relationship away over one fight? Honestly Katy, I don't understand you half the time."

"Mom." Gail puts her hand up stopping her.

"Don't mom me. Your father and I decided. Tomorrow you will sign the bakery over to your father and I. We will own and manage the place from now on. You are welcome to stay on as a baker, although I don't see why you would. Now you'll be free to go to college and go after a more secure career."

Gail crosses her arms and drops her chin. She's daring Katy to challenge her. Katy's shoulders are trembling and tears are gathering in her eyes.

"No." Katy grits out.

"Did you tell me no?" Her mom questions.

"Now, honey. We need-" Bills starts.

"Don't you now honey me. This is a long time coming. My mother never should have left her the business, it was a mistake. She can't handle the pressure. Look, she threw Noah away for a bartender." She turns on Katy. "You got lucky the only damage done today was a table and a small scorch mark."

Oh, Gail Heart is cut from the same cloth as my mother. I'm seething in my seat. Nothing is ever good enough for women like them. Never giving you enough slack to do anything with but always judging you for your choices.

Nothing Katy does will ever make her happy. Two tears roll down Katy's cheek. Fuck first impressions.

"Katy, you don't need this. Let's go." I toss my napkin down on the table. Gail's face lights up like a teakettle about to go off.

"You're what? Our food hasn't even arrived yet. Sit down and don't make a scene. We are having a chat." Gail takes a drink.

"No, the only one here making a scene is you. Your daughter graduated from high school early and became one of the best bakers in this city. Katy is following her dreams. Do you realize how much heart and balls that takes? I can't sit here and listen to you tare her down."

"Your choice babe, but I'm leaving." I stand, reach for my money clip, pull out three hundred-dollar bills and throw down. "This should cover everything. Please enjoy your meal."

"That man is rude, don't you dare follow him." Gail snaps.

"You don't even know him, but he's right. I don't deserve to be treated like this." Katy then walks to the door.

"For the record Mrs. Heart, the man who isn't good for her is Noah. He's a man who dumped your daughter on her birthday. So what if I'm not what or who you want for Katy. I will always treat her with respect."

I turn to her father. "Mr. Heart, it was a pleasure getting to meet you." With a nod I give them my back. Marcella, the owner's daughter, is waiting at the hostess stand with a bag of food. Great job reading the situation. McKinnon's needs a girl like her.

We walk out the door and get around the corner. Katy stops in her tracks. "Connor, what you did back there..." She chokes on her words. There are tears streaming down her face. Fuck, I hope I didn't overstep. Maybe I overreacted, but Gail was breaking her and I couldn't stand by.

"Thank you. No one has ever done that for me except my grandma, and I think you beat her too. Thanks." I bend down kissing her softly and wrap her into my arms. The food bag swings into her hip accidentally, and she pulls away with a small grin.

"Thank god Marcella boxed up our order. I'm starving, let's head back to my place." We slide into my car and head off toward Katy's house.

"Sweetness, I'm sorry if I overstepped. Your mom tearing you down was not cool. Help me understand. Your parents followed their dreams why doesn't your mom want you to follow yours?"

"Long story, but my mom loves my father so much she made his passion hers. My parents' and grandparents' owned businesses in the service industry my whole life. I'm aware of hardships and pitfalls but all I want to do is bake . She's always seen me as too immature or too young to understand the sacrifice."

"I'm sorry, babe. Families especially mother's can be rough."

"You sound like you understand from experience."

"Let's talk over dinner."

"Only if you agree to Netflix and chill after." She chuckles behind her hand and I bark out a laugh. Fuck, this girl always gets me.

"Deal princess. Wait, isn't Nexflix and chill code for sex?"

"Duh," she teases and a cackle slip out, the sound warms me. Her mom upset her, but she won't let their argument ruin her night.

We arrive at Katy's, set out our food and dig in. Katy wastes zero time getting me to handle my part of our bargain.

"Deals a deal. Tell me about your family. You haven't met Jackson, but you just witnessed the shit show called dinner with my rents." She sucks her bottom lip into her mouth and shrugs at me with big eyes. I can't help but laugh at her word choice, tonight was definitely some kinda hell.

"Okay, shoot?"

"What was it like growing up with all brothers? I have a big brother, but I'm a girl."

"Thank god you told me you're a girl. Those giant tits you got make it hard to tell the difference." A pillow flies at me almost spilling my plate off the table.

"Damn Sweetness, you're gonna make a mess."

"Oh, stop and answer the question." She reaches behind her for another pillow. I grab her wrist and drag her into me smashing my mouth to hers. Her teeth graze my lip snagging flesh in her bite.

"Fuck woman, you make me crazy. Forget the walk down memory lane, I want you naked now." Grabbing her rear in my hands I move her on top of me and grind her pussy against my prick.

"Are you trying to distract me with intercourse Mr. McKinnon?"

"You bet your ass I am."

"Come on Connor, give me something. Please." The breathless plea is sexy as hell.

"Okay. I yield, but sex first." Fuck waiting for a response. I wind her ponytail around my fist, pull her head back and dive for the crook of her neck. She squeals with delight sending pleasure straight to my balls.

Her hands grip into my shoulders as she grinds against me. I take my free hand and release her breasts to the cool night air. Her nipples pebble and her skin flushes a light pink. A look of pure bliss is on her face.

"You're fucking gorgeous, all exposed and needy for me." I'm loosing my handle on my self-control.

"More, please." Katy whines. "Connor, I need you. Now."

"Take off your pants before I rip them off." I command. She moves to wiggle out of them but I'm too impatient. "Not fast enough." The seams above her waist rips away with one tug, splitting the fabric in two. Katy gasps, lifting herself off me enough, so I can pull her torn bottoms free from her legs.

"Don't ruin another pair of panties. These are pricey."

"Fuck that, I'll buy you all the expensive underwear you want, so I can shred them." A blush spreads across her body at my words which only makes my erection harder. She pulls her shirt over her head, giving me easier access to her breasts.

Light pink tips peek through her lace bra. Saliva coats my mouth. I reach for her and suck her nipple into my mouth.

"Fuck Connor, yes. Right there." The louder her moans grow the harder I suck. "In me, now. Please," Katy withers.

Reaching behind herself, she unclasps her bra and lets the lace fall to the floor. I reach for my belt buckle, but she swipes my hand out of the way to pull my zipper down and release my cock.

Katy gets on her knees and pulls the head into her mouth sliding her tongue around the slit and slowly working down my length. My dick hits home, and she gags but continues bobbing up and down. Saliva is dripping everywhere.

"If you keep this up I won't make it in you, Sweetness." I hiss through clinched teeth. Big green eyes full of lust and power stare up at me.

"So, that's what second times are for." The little minx. Her pace picks up, and she slams me into the back of her throat. A moan pierces through her stuffed lips.

Her tongue touches the underside of my head, I'm done for. "I'm coming. Don't stop baby." My release rushes into me, making the hairs on my body stand at attention. "Katy! Fuuuck." My hips buck and I push her further down my length, filling her mouth with my release.

Katy swallows every last drop taking care not to miss anything. A giant smile is on Katy's face as she finally comes up for air. Her teeth scrape against her bottom lip. It's sexy as hell.

"Yum." Her eyes are hooded with lust. "You ready for round two?" No need to ask. I pull her on top of my still hard length. Katy slides down until she's seated against my pelvis.

"Fuck baby, sucking me off gets you that wet?"

"What can I say. Your pecker and I have a connection," she teases with wink. A laugh bursts from my throat.

"You say the sexiest things." She moves, gyrating her hips against me. Her walls stretch to accommodate me. Holy hell her cunt is tight squeezing me like a vice working and pulsing along my vein. I buck up into her, and she moans pushing down to meet me with each thrust.

She controls the pace slow at first, only moving in small circles then getting bigger and deeper. Katy leans forward dangling her luscious rack in my face. My tongue laves over her sensitive flesh again and again biting down on the tip. Her pussy clinches and moisture floods her slit. An organismic scream rips from her lips on a curse.

"*Connor. I love you inside me.*"

"Yes babe ride my cock." Her cheeks flex tightening her pussy's grip on me. She's making me wild, and ready to bust as quick as a fucking teenager.

Katy lifts herself off me, keeping herself hovering above my dick.

"Fuck me hard." Not wanting to disappoint I grip her hips holding her up in place and slam my cock into her over and over. The way her walls grip my length controlling exactly how deep she wants me.

The familiar sensation brews in my balls and I slide home, putting pressure on Katy's clit. My balls strain shooting rope after rope of liquid heat straight to her core. Her walls tighten, and she screams her release into the night, her own juices flooding out all over my jeans.

We stay connected together breathing heavily. Giving each other tender kisses.

"Oh my gosh, you're amazing. Your pants are ruined though." She giggles to herself and swings her leg off me to stand. A few seconds later she appears with sweats I left here last time and a towel.

"Thanks Sweetness," I say and head off to clean up.

I exit the bathroom to find Katy laying in her bed, hair fanned out completely naked. "Come here. You owe me a story," she arches her brow like she's trying to scold me.

"You never give up when you want something, huh?"

"Nope I'm like a dog looking for a bone. I'll bug the crap out of you until I get what I want."

"Alright but will you put a shirt on? No way I can talk with you naked. All I can think about is getting back inside you." Like magic she produces an oversized shirt and shrugs it on.

"Better?"

"No, but at least I'm not thinking of sliding back into you right this second."

"Stop talking about fucking me or I'll abandon my quest for knowledge and spread myself for you." I cocky my at her in question. Dear god be serious.

"Kidding well, maybe not, I will totally cave if you touch me but I want to know more about your family before I meet them."

"Valid point. My Pops is similar to yours; laid back and always the one to keep my mom in check when she goes a bit off the cliff. She means well but damn is she over bearing."

"Totally sounds like my parents. It is why I never stay mad at her. My mom drives me nuts but at the end of the day she only wants what is best for me. The problem is she doesn't understand me enough to realize I am where I want to be." Katy shrugs, what else can you do. "Continue."

"My brothers and I are only about a year apart each, so we've always been close. My older brother and I are closer, mostly because our younger one gets away with everything." I let out a sigh and rub my hands over my face. All the recent crap with Graham runs through my mind.

"Hey, you don't need to continue. We can do something more fun." Katy wiggles her eyebrows while fidgeting in the edge of her shirt.

"Thanks." I pull her in for a kiss. "I'm okay," I say taking a long breath. "It's just my mom demands perfection and blind obedience. It's frustrating as hell. My brothers and her butt heads most of the time."

"Yet you were the one who struck out on your own. Are you still working at the family business?"

"Yea." Pain radiates from my jaw.

"Face the wall." Katy commands pointing to her left.

"For what?"

"Cause your shoulders are about to cave in you look so tense. If talking about this is making you uncomfortable, I'm good. You shared plenty to prepare me for Saturday."

"You think that now." I tease, swooping her into my arms.

"Connor." Katy lets out on a giggle. It's light, carefree and infectious. I squeeze her hip, and she flails. "Don't do that."

"Don't do what?" I squeeze again. She bucks. Oh, she's ticklish.

"That. Don't do that." My fingers flex again skimming lower she stops, her breath hitches. "Connor." The word comes out breathless.

"Yeah." Her ass rubs against my growing erection. Jesus, woman. Katy jukes and somehow wrestles out of my grasp. Damnit.

"Victory. Now, I want some whiskey," Katy declares and skips out of the bedroom.

I swipe my boxers off the floor, chuckling at her antics. Following the noise I find Katy in the kitchen pouring two glasses of amber liquid.

"Here you go." Picking up my drink, I narrow my eyes at her.

"That easy?"

"What?"

"Subject change. You closed the topic because I looked uncomfortable. This isn't some ploy to force me to talk?"

Katy's lip pulls up in a quick snarl. "Um, no but I do have one question."

Damn, I really thought she was different. "Go ahead."

"How did you go from working with your family to owning a pub? Oh, and how did you meet Ian? So two questions."

"Ian and the pub?" Is she fucking with me?

"Yep," Katy states taking another swig of her drink. Her teeth bite into her bottom lip, fucking cute as hell, and she does some little flick with her foot. She'll kill me for thinking it but damn she's adorable. "Come on, spill."

"Okay, a few years ago he needed someone on site for security for a whole month. Reluctantly I took to job. Less than a week later he was teaching me about food and how to make drinks. I fell in love with every aspect, but I'm not the best cook. Liqueur concoctions are where I found my passion. He taught me anything I was willing to learn. At some point we became close friends."

"You're lucky, the man isn't known for taking people under his wing." Katy refills her glass.

"You're telling me. One day, Ian asked me if I ever considered a pub. Thought it was something Hadley Falls lacked. He showed me how keeping a small menu would increase revenue but not cost too much. Every night from then we worked on a plan and Ian became my investor. The rest is history. In a few years I'll own McKinnon Pub out right."

I wait for her reaction. Kelly hated my business and her disdain was what split us up. Fuck why I am thinking about my ex? *Because she's back in town.*

"That's brave. How did your parents take the changes?" A warm sensation builds in my gut at the look of pride on her face. I'm not sure what to call it. Happy, content, no clue but I like it.

"My dad understands," I shrug. "My mom. Not so much."

"I'm proud of you. The pub is gorgeous." She fiddles with the rim of her glass. "You did an amazing job on the ambiance, the food. Everything is perfect. Don't even get me started on the whiskey selection."

"You like my place?" Not sure why I care so much about her answer but my palms are sweating.

"More like love it. You stock labels I never seen before. You deserve a toast." Katy throws out her hands. "Cheers to you Connor McKinnon for following your dreams and refusing to bend to the will of others."

We clink glasses and finish our drinks. The warm whiskey burns my throat on the way down.

"Ah. You keep nice shit, Sweetness. How do you know so much about whiskey? An old boyfriend or something?" The teasing tone helps hide the tinge of jealousy I'm feeling.

"A friend from high school."

"The EMT?" I grind out.

"Why Connor McKinnon are you jealous?"

"Not an answer."

"Awe are you jealous" She's teases.

"You still didn't answer the question."

Who cares she was with Noah before you. Her past doesn't matter. "Awe babe now you're pouty. Come here and kiss me," She pleads. I step around the counter and swing her into my arms, kissing her with everything I have. Katy Heart is all mine.

Katy

Chapter Sixteen

Oh my gosh his parent's home is stunning. Tall trees line a vast lawn and a small fountain sit in the front yard surrounded by flowers. The house itself is huge, built like a log cabin, but all the stone gives it an appearance of a castle in the mountains. The house is homey and charming with enormous windows all around the face.

My gaze lands on the driveway, what the? This can't be right, there are at least 6 cars here. Shit, I thought he said his parents and brothers, not his whole family.

Crap, I swallow and take a deep breath, willing the butterflies in my stomach back into their jar. This is simple, I love people and a few more is nothing. Easy, charm the pants off em. Hey my little pep talk worked, the flutters are settling, and my mind is calming. I send a quick text to Connor and climb out of the car.

One last check of my outfit in the reflection of my car. At least I feel hot if I'm meeting all these people. I'm wearing my favorite knee-length navy colored dress accented with gold and teal feathers. It hugs my curves in all the right spots and the halter-neck line shows off the perfect amount of cleavage without being inappropriate for meeting the parents. Connor exits out the front door and makes his way down the steps.

Whoa, he is one sexy man. His biceps ripple as he takes each step. My body ignites remembering those strong arms wrapped around me yesterday. Wet heat pools between my legs and my nipples tighten and scrape on the fabric of my bra. A tingle flows through me.

From the dark, heated stare on Connor's face, I think he knows where my thoughts are right now. I shake my head trying to clear images of Connor and me.

"Damn, you are gorgeous Sweetness." He growls the words out through his teeth. His arms wrap around me and he crushes his mouth to mine, sweeping his tongue across my lips before pulling back flashing a fiery smile.

"Thanks, you clean up good yourself."

"Want to tell me what you are thinking about. Something dirty, maybe?"

"You above me last night and how much I want to be back in your bed right now." Warmth rises up my spine at my confession. Connor smirks pleased with the admission.

"We can. Say the word and we'll go to my place." Something about his tone is off, cold almost.

"As amazing as that sounds, aren't your parents expecting us? Are you unsure about me meeting them?"

"Fuck no." Ouch, I can't help my flinch. "I'm sorry that came out wrong. Of course I want you to meet my family, but

I don't want you to be overwhelmed. Tonight isn't only my parents and brothers. My mom is throwing a birthday party for my uncle, and everyone is inside. She swears she told me about it and I forgot."

He says forgot with air quotes. "Tonight is one hundred percent up to you. We can go in and I'll introduce you to everyone, or we can leave if this is too much."

"Um let's stay. I can handle your family but only if you want this." Fake confidence, I got this. On the inside though I'm freaking out, second guessing my decision and wondering if he truly wants this or is making the best of the situation. *Stop over thinking.*

Connor lifts my chin to meet his eyes. "Let me set the record on something first. I fucking like you a lot. If I didn't want you to know my family I would have called you when I got here." I blush at his admission. He likes me!

"And don't think I didn't read your face when I came outside." He drops his head to my neck, whispering against my ear, "I will be fucking you all night long." He takes my mouth, taking everything I have to give. The deep kiss bruises my lips, and brings back my earlier thoughts. We pull apart breathless. "Now, let's head in before my mom comes out. She will bring all my aunts with her if she does."

All thoughts of sexy time disappear at the mention of this mother.

"Yes please let's avoid a scene out here." I plead and Connor chuckles.

Connor leads me into his parent's home. Two tall men are standing in the entry way. There is no mistaking them for anything but McKinnon men.

"About time you came inside, son. Any longer and your mother was talking about sending a search party." He chuckles, looking around his son right at me.

"You must be Katy, I'm Jameson Sr. Please call me James." Wow, Connor's dad a total fox. Tall like Connor and the other man, who I think is his younger brother. His father's hair is jet black with a dusting of gray that carries down to the five o'clock shadow he's sporting.

"Hi. Thank you for inviting me into your home, sir."

"Connor, Cormac is looking for you, he's out back." A woman, all red hair, and mama bear attitude comes in from the kitchen. A huge smile is spreading across her face while she makes her way to us. She throws her arms around Connor placing an over the top smooch on his cheek. Her lipstick presses into his skin leaving a lip stain behind.

"Mom, come on. That shit is nasty." Connor takes a swipe at his face. "Yuck". He's turning red but I can't blame him I'm not a fan of lipstick either, it can be suffocating and the waxy film, ick.

He's wiping at his cheek so hard though he reminds me of a five-year-old boy who got kissed by Great Aunt Mildred. I can't stop the giggles from escaping my mouth, which brings everyone's attention right to me.

"Oh, hello. I'm Maggie, Connor's mother, and you are?"

"Mom, this is Katy, my girlfriend."

"So you're the new girl. I'm glad Connor brought you." Her words are kind, and she's smiling but something about her demeanor is odd.

From what Connor told me, calling her overprotective is an understatement. And she can be a force when she is unsure of someone. Especially if the person in question is dating one of her "baby boys" as he put it. He gives her a weird glance.

"A pleasure to meet you, Mrs. McKinnon. You have a lovely home."

"Katy, this is my little brother Graham." One point for me on guessing family members. *Wow, nerdy much.*

His baby brother is adorable. A mini version of Connor. Same style of clothes and their hair color is almost the same too. Where Connor has hints of red, Graham's hair is brown with touches of gold and rust. His eyes are a lighter shade of green than mine, and a few freckles dot his face.

The only actual difference is their overall style Graham is clean-shaven with long hair unlike Connor and that amazing beard and tight cut. My body tingles again thinking about the way it scratches my thighs when he goes down on me. Wow, so not appropriate time for those thoughts.

"Hi. The similarities are unreal. You two could almost be twins."

"Wait until our other brother gets here, him and Connor share more in common. Except for the fact that he is about as wide as a brick house and always growly." Graham says.

"Don't be silly, Jameson is nothing but polite." Maggie scolds him.

"Notice she didn't say nice." Connor whispers. His mother glares at him and James lets out a laugh.

"The boy makes a good point, love." Senior adds. His wife gives him a gentle smack.

Connor's father ushers us outside. Holy crap. The McKinnon family must car pool because I'm counting at least thirty people here. *You got this, don't freak out. They won't judge you.* I peek over at Maggie, okay maybe she will, but the rest appear friendly. As if they heard my thoughts everyone glances our way. Four men and a woman approach us.

"Connor, who is this beautiful creature?" A man around similar height as Connor but built broader asks. His eyes are kind like Grahams.

"Back off Liam, she's mine." Connor snarls, startling me, but then he laughs and wraps his arm around my waist.

"This is my girlfriend, Katy Heart. Katy, these are my cousins. This one is Liam. Those are the twins Keegan and Teagan, their brother Micheal and this tall Irish lass is Bryna."

"Hey," I say with a wave. "Forgive me if I mix up your names. There are a lot of you."

They all chuckle. Connor is looking around, scanning the crowd. "Where's Jameson?" He asks the crowd just as the back door creaks on its hinges.

"Right here little brother, I went on a beer and whiskey run. Ma got Jack Daniels for some nasty fucking reason." The crowd of cousins bursts out in laughter. Connor's brother puts the beverages down next to the ice chest and heads to us on the porch. Holy shit, no way that can be...

"What the fuck, Little Heart. What are you doing in my backyard?" Time slows and I turn to find Jameson, my brother's best friend with the biggest smile ever spreading across his face. I squeal as the giant picks me up and twirls around. Then he gently sets me back on my feet, placing a quick peck on the top of my head. Ugh, still acting like my big brother. Some things never change.

"Jameson, what are you? Oh, my gosh, I can't believe I didn't put two and two together. Duh, how many Jamesons can there be in this town? Connor mentioned his brother's name was Jameson the other night, but I didn't think in a million years it was you."

"How the fuck do you know Katy? She's five years younger than you?" Connor bites out.

"She's Jackson Heart's, little sister, that's how. Plus, who do you think introduced her to her whiskey?" He smiles the goofy grin I remember from high school.

Jameson is as hot as ever but boy he is bigger than before, which doesn't surprise me given what he does for a living. Same firm jaw and dark blue eyes, but now he has a beard, it's sexy as shit too. Elise is going to flip.

"Jackson Heart, as in your best friend? The one I keep trying to recruit with no luck?" Jameson Sr. asks.

"Wait, you want to hire my brother, and he turned you down?" I let out a slow whistle. "Don't let my mom find out. She's been scheming to get him to take a job in town for years."

"Do you think you could talk to him for me?" Mr. McKinnon urges hopeful.

"Sure, I can't say he'll agree, he tends to do the opposite of anything I ask, but I'll chat with him." The older McKinnon smiles at my reply, and heads off to the aunts and uncles in the corner.

Connor tenses at my side, his eyes are cold and fixated on the side gate. Following his gaze I see three leggy blondes walking in with a couple. He heads over to the family who arrived without me and I follow in his wake. Something is definitely off.

"Look what the cat drug in." Maggie says to the woman, then turns to the younger one. "Oh, my god. Kelly, your outfit is stunning." She embraces the blonde in a motherly embrace. The other two woman say hello as they walk past us and bee line for the drinks. Connor nods is head in hello back, not giving them much attention or introducing us.

Nope. His attention is glued to the thin busty woman with slick blonde hair. The woman his mom called Kelly. Something about her name is bothering me but I can't place it.

The woman is a good four inches taller than me. Her yellow green sundress is light and gives her a sophisticated air about her. Maggie pulls away and practically pushes her towards Connor. What the hell?

"Connor, doesn't Kelly look beautiful?" His mother presses.

"Sure. Hey Kel, been a long time." She wraps herself around Connor and it hits me. This is the ex-girlfriend. Why is she here?

They continue to their conversation, but I don't hear a single thing. My palms are clammy and I fidget from foot to foot. Why would he bring me tonight if his ex was going to be here?

He said he didn't know about the party. Fine but why would his mom ask me over and invite his old girlfriend? I'm so lost in my head I don't even realize Connor isn't standing here anymore and it's me, Maggie, the older woman and Kelly.

"Oh Joy, this is, I'm sorry, what was your name again? No worries, she is the new girl Connor is dating." She is so dismissive of me my skin crawls. *Stop, you are over thinking this.*

"I didn't realize Connor was seeing someone, he didn't mention it." Kelly says to Maggie. She turns to me. "Hi, I'm Kelly, Connor's ex and well best friend too. I'm sure he's mentioned me." Her mouth curls up, reminding me of a cheshire cat.

"Katy." We shake hands and I feel like I'm on a roller coaster where you hit the drop and your stomach flies into your throat.

Bile rolls in my gut. I confided so much in Connor. *He confided in you too.* But he is best friends with his ex-girlfriend, and he never told me. What else is he hiding?

You need to let him explain. Meghan told you about her. Don't freak out. Yes but he never said shit, and she's right in front of me not some random person I can put out of my head. Oh my god, why am I talking to myself?

Someone says something to me pulling me out of my inner crap. "Hello, Kitty, was it?" Says Joy I think, she is older than Kelly, long blonde hair the same piercing silver eyes.

"No, my name is Katy." I respond through my tightening jaw.

"My apologies." She throws Maggie a pointed gaze. Awesome, I'm sure that was intentional.

What a bitch.

"Come on, let's sit down and catch up. I missed you so much. Connor will be back with our drinks soon. There is so much to fill you up on. We are all so glad you're back."

Maggie wraps her arms around the women effectively excluding me and walks over to a table to sit down. Kelly throws a smirk over her shoulder at me and I'm thrown right back to high school.

My stomach contorts on itself, I need water and quiet or I might puke for real. Now I'm smirking. I bet that would bother Maggie and perfect Kelly, but I refuse to make a scene or ruin anyone's party. I pick up an ice water from the tub of drinks and down half.

I roll my shoulders back and head for a small group of Connor's cousins and dive right into conversation. They are discussing whiskey and which desserts go best. Someone mentions a caramel brownie and the rest goes by in a blur.

I'm having fun. His cousins' knowledge on liquor is impressive and before I realize it almost an hour passes. But I haven't seen Connor since his mom sent him for drinks. Why hasn't he come to find me? Shit, I sound needy. *Don't be that girl, no drama, no scenes.* I scan the crowd for Connor twice and come up empty. Where is he?

A boom of laughter catches my ears. I turn around with a grin on my face only to spot Kelly with her hand on Connor's arm, both are laughing. She is giggling and sticking her rather large chest out at him. My face falls. Why is this happening? Fuck, why am I still standing here? Screw this.

I fumble with my purse getting out my phone, pretend a call came through and excuse myself from the conversation. Without looking around I head straight for the side exit. Hoping with everything in me he is looking for me as I glance back to find Connor. He is in a conversation with Kelly. She is sitting next to him and her face is dipped into Connor's neck making appear like he is whispering to her.

Anger light in my gut, I should be an adult and walk over there but I can't make my feet move. I'm done with confrontations and public fights with people this month. All my fight is gone. My inner warrior is too tired.

I turn away from them. My heart cracks into pieces I try to clear my head and lungs but the air gets stuck turning to ash. Fuck, is this a panic attack? My hands are sweaty, my blood is rushing in my ears and I can't catch my breath. Sobs are working to break free, but I swallow them down and force myself to breathe. The pounding in my chest is making it hard to focus. *Don't cry yet, don't cry yet.* I repeat to myself and slip out the side gate unnoticed. Tears fall in a rush as soon as I'm clear from view. In my haste my foot catches on the small stone fountain in front and I land on the hard seat. Ouch.

"What the hell you doing crying on my lawn, Little Heart?" Jameson's deep vibrato rumbles through me. His use of my old nick name makes the corners of my mouth turn up involuntarily. I wipe at my eyes trying to hide my pain, but there is no hiding from Jameson.

The skin beneath my eyes swells, the drying sensation behind my lids feels even heavier and pronounced.

"I'm fine Jameson, needed some fresh air is all."

"Bullshit. What did my dumb ass brother do? No wait, let me guess. Kelly." I let out a snort so hard it gets caught in my throat and I cough hard. The force of the cough throws me off balance and my footing slips on the damp ground.

Air rushes around me and I brace myself for the rush of water. The water never comes, instead Jameson swoops me off my feet saving me. He places me down tenderly and I use his warmth to catch my breath and my barrings.

"Always trying to hurt yourself. Some things never change."

"Who says I didn't want to go for a swim? Show your mom how classy I really am." I throw all my anger in the statement and purse my lips. The hard expression holds for about two seconds before belly laughter erupts and I'm laughing hysterically. It must be infectious because Jameson joins in.

"The fuck is going on here?" Connor booms.

Connor

Chapter Seventeen

15 minutes prior...

I'm an asshole and I prove myself right the second I walk out of the house with everyone's drinks and head straight for the table my mom and Kelly are seated at instead of looking for Katy. I'm not ready to talk yet. Watching Jameson lift my girlfriend up and twirl her affectionately is bringing up a lot of old shit. Did they have a fling, or some sort of relationship in high school?

Jameson doesn't keep friendships with woman only hook ups. The worse possible scenarios are running in my mind. Katy played me to get to my brother. Wouldn't be the first time. Jameson is only two years older than me so we fought over girls we. I had a few girlfriends back then use me to gain access to him.

I should grow up and talk to her, ask about their history. We were never close with each other's friends growing up. In high school Jameson was a player no girl was off limits to him. His best friend's little sister wouldn't have been any different. But like I said, I'm an asshole so I choose the easier route my mother, Joy and Kelly.

"Connor, what took so long? All this gabbing makes me thirsty." My mom states, taking a sip of her drink dramatically. "Sit, sit. You two talk. Did you know Kelly visited Rome while in Europe. What a romantic city."

"Rome, cool. You've always wanted to visit there." She appears the same but different from the last time I saw her. Same blonde hair, and long legs but the lines around her face and mouth are deeper like she's seen a fair share of trouble too.

"The city is beautiful. I was missing you the whole time though." Kelly's cheeks flush. "Oops, I didn't mean to share that. But I do miss you. Can we still be friends now that I'm home?"

"We will always be friends Kel. After all our moms are like sisters so if we aren't friendly it could be awkward." She laughs and reaches out to touch my arm. She dips her head down to whisper in my ear.

"I miss you." Her breath tickles my neck and my hair stands on end. A shiver rolls down my spine. I shake off the sensation and turn the conversation back to her trip to Europe and the last two years.

Kelly fills me in on her trip while the chatter and noises of the gathering fill in as buffer. My cousins are chatting in the corner by the ice chests making crude jokes. The random burn being yelled by someone followed by hyena laughter. My aunts are huddled up at the table next to us talking about the latest family gossip or who is going to make what for our Memorial Day gathering.

"What are you up to? Still hitting the gym hard, you are bigger than I remember." Kelly flirts, batting her eyelashes at me. She reaches out and gives my arm a squeeze. "We should grab dinner sometime and get reacquainted. It's been forever." She licks her lips and cocks one eyebrow leaving no room for misunderstandings.

My gut turns cold. Seriously, she met my girlfriend two seconds ago. *The girlfriend you're ignoring?* I glance away looking for Katy, instead I notice the smug glare on my mother's face. She thinks Kelly's words are affecting me. A few months ago my mother would have been right. Now, sitting here feels wrong.

"Kelly, you can drop the act." I say under my breath, no way I'm causing a scene today. Her face turns into sad puppy dog eyes.

"Huh, what are you talking about. This isn't an act. I meant what I said, I miss you." She sputters batting her eyes. Enough.

How did I not realize the entire night was a setup? I need to find Katy. My mom calls my name to come back but I ignore her calls and search for my date.

I stop and ask the group of cousins she was talking to but they aren't sure. Cormac, my eldest cousin is grabbing a water. "Your girl took off out the side gate, she seamed upset." He points his water at me.

Fuck I hope she didn't take off. *If she did, you can only blame yourself.* Damn why did I have to be a dick? None of it matters, ifs and buts won't help me now.

I make my way outside and stop short when I spot Katy wrapped in my brother's arms and she's laughing? Jameson follows right behind. My heart is racing. All the feelings of jealous brewing from before are back. I'm ending this shit now.

"What the fuck is going on here?" Katy jumps at the sound of my voice. Her eyes go wide like a deer in headlights. In the next second her jaw sets.

The hell, she's out here in my brother's arms and is upset with me. No fucking way.

"Connor. Finally remember your girlfriend was at this party?" She snaps. My anger is bubbling inside.

"Don't throw your attitude back at me. Was this your ploy all along? Did you crush on Jameson back in the day and when you found out my last name. You what, decided you'd try me out first?" I'm being a tad irrational, my train of thought doesn't even make sense to me but I can't see through my anger. Katy gapes at me, mouth open, cheeks heated, I think I spot tears building in her eyes. Good.

"You really believe that don't you. Well, fuck you Connor McKinnon!" She roars at me. "I came here for a family dinner to meet your parents. Instead, there's a giant birthday party where your ex girlfriend. An ex girlfriend who you never even told me about, shows up with her family like she belongs here. Oh, and the important fact that your moms are best friends. Did it ever occur to you to warn me."

"Warn you about what?"

"Oh, I don't know. You have an ex girlfriend who will always be more than an ex because of your past. That your families are as close as family and she calls you her best friend." A sob breaks through.

"Katy..."

"I confided in you. Told you all about my life, my ex. Fuck, you witnessed firsthand how he treated me. I broke down in front of you." A high pierced cry leaves her throat. "You are the one who deserted me. And now you're accusing me of wanting your brother. News flash asshole if I wanted Jameson, I could have had him years ago."

Katy's body is shaking and tears are streaming down her face. Her words run back in my head, she could have had Jameson years ago. What does that mean? My rage is still too fresh blinding me from understanding.

"Oh Connor, there you are." My mother's voice calls from the front porch. Great. More fuel to add to the fire. She is the last person I need out here right now. "We need you inside sweetie. The event next month is important. we want to finalize some details."

Chancing a glimpse back at my mother, damnit she isn't alone. Kelly and Joy are standing on the porch behind her. Their eyes are bouncing between the three of us.

All three women are wearing disgusted frowns. Fuck, I don't need them seeing this. My love life is none of their business. They will only run back inside and ignite the gossip with my aunts. I ignore her request turning my attention back to Katy.

"Just fucking go. Seems like they need your assistance." She sighs and turns to Jameson cutting me off. Ending our fight in one move and stalking to her car.

"Katy, wait." Jameson calls. She only shakes her head in response. Then climbs in her car and pulls out the driveway. What the hell just happened?

"The fuck did you do?" Jameson bellows at me.

"Jameson. Calm down or everyone will hear you." My mom screeches at him from behind me.

"Go back inside, mom! Your precious angel will be in soon."

"Fine. But hurry, we need to speak with Connor." My mother clips before shutting the front door with a click.

"You are a fucking idiot, little brother. That girl is gold, fuck that she is more precious and rare as a red diamond. You only get one shot at a woman as amazing as her and you fucking blew it. Over what? Me catching her so she didn't end up soaking wet in the fountain?" My mouth hangs open like a damn carp. "I hope you feel as stupid as you look asshat. What is your problem?" Jameson balls his fists at me. "Let me guess, you came out here and saw her in my arms?"

Geez am pissing off everyone? "Connor you're an idiot. We were laughing because Katy is still the clumsiest girl I ever met. She tripped and almost fell in the fountain." He shakes his head at me. "You fucked up brother. Mom set you up, and you fell for her bullshit. She threw this party together last minute so she could invite Kelly. She wants you two together." Jameson pauses.

Did I overreact? No, I glimpsed something, a spark between them. They have a history. "I don't believe you." I blurt.

"Fine, call Elise. She can tell you everything that went on between Katy and me. After you speak with her, call Ryan. Maybe he will help you salvage your relationship because I sure as hell won't. Katy's a fantastic fucking woman and you need to fucking decide who you want more, her or Kelly."

"The fuck you talking about. I don't want Kelly." I spit at him. Jameson has lost his mind.

"Oh yeah? Why do you think she was crying out here when I found her? She was bawling her eyes out when I came outside."

The air leaves my lungs as if someone landed a punch in my stomach. Hurting Katy was the last thing I wanted to do and I hurt her anyway. Why didn't I ask her?

"Here, I can see you still don't trust me. Which is bullshit, I never stole a girl from you. Never touched any of the girls who used you to get to me either. In case you thought different." Jameson thrusts his phone up to my ear.

"Hello."

"Connor? Why are you calling me from Jameson's phone?" My brows knit together. What the fuck, he knows Elise too?

"How do you know Jameson?"

"None of your business." Ryan mumbles something in the background.

"Okay. How does Katy know my brother?" I say through gritted teeth. I'm trying not to be a complete dick here.

"Long story, but. Oh shit. I assumed Katy knew, but I bet it never crossed her mind."

"Knew what?"

"Hold on. Explain what you did. Jameson doesn't call me. Where is Katy and how much did you screw up?" She snaps at me, her protective side coming out in full force.

"Royally. My mother invited my ex. And I kind of ignored Katy when I realized she knew Jameson because I was jealous. The night only got worse from there." Bile rises in my throat. "Basically, I'm an asshole. Now please tell me how Katy and him are so close." I plead.

"No. That's Katy's story to tell. But they were never more than friends. Making you a jerk. Did you make her cry? You did, didn't you. Katy needs me. You messed up, big time." The phone beeps ending the call. For a second I stare at Elise's name on the screen. How do I fix this?

"Jameson, what do I do?" I ask, handing him back his phone.

"Not sure, but like I said, I'm not helping you. Call Ryan, maybe he can save you." He says Ryan's name like a curse. What's that about? Nope, I don't need any more drama right now.

"You're my brother, come on. I'm sorry for assuming the worst, I jumped to conclusions after what happened inside with mom and Kelly. Help me."

"No." He pauses. "Shit, okay. I'll throw you a bone. Grab her favorites, pepperoni pizza, a two litter of cherry soda and a cinnamon roll from her favorite spot might save your ass. Might wanna add a fire and coffee to the list too."

"You think so? Wait, what. Fire? And how..."

"Don't worry about how. She likes you a lot and after tonight I'm not sure why. Do yourself a favor and don't go back inside. It will go over better if you go after her now, not after you went back to talk with Kelly."

Jameson checks his watch. "Shit I'm late. I need to go. Fix this bro."

"Okay. thanks and I'm sorry Jameson. I'm an asshole." Jameson grips my hand in return.

"We're good. Bro stop over thinking." Jameson heads off and I pull out my phone to call Ryan. I'm gonna need some help.

Katy

Chapter Eighteen

The trip home feels like the longest drive of my life. I'm an idiot. Am I doomed to always be second choice? A sob rips from my throat, hot tears sting my eyes while falling down my cheeks by the bucket full.

My best friend is waiting on my porch with not one but two bottles of wine. Thank god I love this woman. How did she know? My lip curls up, Jameson, who else? I exit the car and head right for Elise's out stretched arms.

"Oh Katy." She wraps me in a tight hug. The tears flow like a river pooling on her sweater. My heart is cracking. She rubs my back to help ease my pain. "You guys will be alright. Let's go inside, open this bottle and you can tell me what happened."

We start with the red. I pour two full glasses and take a seat on the couch. For a few minutes I say nothing, I'm not sure where to begin. The thought of retelling the whole mess means replaying tonight in my mind, and I can't.

"Katy, talk to me. Jameson called me so obviously something bad happened."

"*No way.* He called you. I assumed he sent a text or a carrier pigeon." We snort in unison. "Hold on, how did he have your number? You dropped the high school one years ago."

"It's Jameson the man trades in knowledge. You are right though, we don't talk." Is that pain in her voice?

"Elise, are you okay?"

"Yep. Tonight isn't about me. I'm here for you." She takes a long sip from her glass. "Now, tell me what happened. Start at the beginning."

Thirty minutes later I lay out every detail. From my kiss with Connor to him telling me he likes me all the way to the gigantic ending with my dramatic fuck off exit.

"Is it horrible that I still want him?" I shrug rolling my neck to help mellow the tension building. It doesn't work. "Ugh, the whole thing is dumb. Elise, I think I'm falling for him. How is that possible?"

"Katy, your feelings don't come with a recipe. You can't control how long feelings take to brew or how long they stay with you after the relationship ends. Even when you move on to someone new."

She stares inside her glass. I can't help but wonder if she is speaking from experience? She and Jameson fell for each other hard and quick in high school. To a teenager everything is life or death and the greatest thing ever until it isn't.

"Connor's ex, she has two sisters? One older one younger. Mom's name is Joy?"

"Yes. You met her?"

"No, Joy is Maggie's best friend. From what Jameson told me and remember this is old intel. It's their dream for one or all three of their kids to marry so they can become family. The whole thing is a little sick if you ask me. Jameson's never liked Rhea, but Connor and Kelly are the same age and grew up as best friends. They started dating in high school or right after I think. Ryan told me she broke up with him because he opened the pub."

"Wait, what do you mean because of the pub?"

"I think she and everyone thought Connor would follow the same path as Jameson."

"He told me, how he came to open the place and Ian's investment. Why did Kelly dump him for that?"

"Money, sweetie. After a year of running the business, she gave him an ultimatum. Her or his dream. Connor dumped her in the middle of lunch, according to Ryan."

"She wants him back." The rising sob gets stuck in my windpipe. "The worst part is I think he wants her back too."

The gravity of my statement sets in. Did he ever want me? Was I something different he was trying on? Kelly and I are nowhere near the same. She's a tall legging blonde, I'm a short, plump brunette.

"Stop. He likes you. Don't question everything because of one misunderstanding that turned into a fight."

"Doesn't let him off the hook for being a dick. Jameson was comforting me and he blew up at us. He's the one who left me."

"Katy, I talked to Connor. He told me he acted jealous. I'll tell you what I told him. Nothing. You need to open up to each other."

I open my mouth to interrupt her and she holds up her finger. "They are not excusable, but I think you both need to talk before you write the relationship off. Don't take this the wrong way but we aren't in high school anymore. Relationships don't end because of one fight. Real relationships don't work that way. Not if you care for the other person."

"You're right. But what do I say? He hurt me."

"Give him time."

"Ok, time and more wine."

"Stop." Elise narrows her eyes.

"Buzz kill. This one is dead, want to open another?"

"Sure. Hey, let's order some food though. I'm starving and you know I'm a lightweight."

"Deal, I'll bring the takeout menus."

"Umm they make apps for that now. They even deliver your meal to you."

"Not getting your point," I quip, scrunching up my nose. "I'll be right back." I take my time uncorking another red before I return to the living room with our glasses and the liquid previsions tucked under my arm. I stop in my tracks at the big bearded man standing in my living room.

"What are you doing here?"

"Can we talk, I brought food. Please." He points to the pizza box on my coffee table. Saliva coats my mouth, shit I'm hungry.

"Babe you okay? Say the word and I'll tell him to kick rocks." Elise declares pulling my attention away from the yummy, delicious slices of heaven sitting on my table.

"I'm good Elise."

"Call me tomorrow."

"Wait, you can't drive."

Ryan waves Elise's keys. "Oh, Hi Ry."

"We planned for all contingencies." He says, wrapping his arms around Elise and helping her to the door. She giggles, protesting that she isn't drunk.

"You hurt her and I'll send Ryan and Jameson on your ass so fast. We clear?" My bestie threatens as she passes Connor poking him with her finger. The threat is so unlike her, I think my eyes bulge out of their sockets.

"Swear." Connor says, shutting the door behind them.

We stand in silence forever. I'm not one to lose my voice over anything but I have no clue what to say.

"Hey." Hey, did I really say hey? Ugh my mouth is refusing to work. Fear of saying something wrong, or horrible and making everything worse keeps me silent.

Sometimes I escalate things even when I don't mean to. "Hungry?" He stares at the glasses and wine I'm holding on to. "If that is your second bottle, we should eat. You didn't eat anything at the party." The petty part of me says to lash out, tell him I didn't eat because of him, but I don't. I keep my mouth shut and head for the couch to dig into the pizza.

The explosion of flavor in my mouth is heavenly. My stomach gurgles after one bite confirming how hungry I am.

Connor smirks, heading to the kitchen he comes back with two plates, napkins and a jar of parmesan cheese. Crazy how in our short time together he knows where my things are. He sits down on the other couch, hands me a plate. I drop my pizza down and load up the cheese. Connor takes a gulp from Elise's glass. The look of utter disgust that crosses his face makes me burst with laughter.

"Don't like wine, Mr. McKinnon?"

"No, how you woman enjoy that shit baffles me. The crap is horrible."

"You own a pub, you don't taste before you buy?"

"Jamie or Ian handle the non spirit orders. Too much time in church while growing up." He shutters. "Side effect of being from an Irish Catholic family." His grin makes my insides melt. *No, don't cave because of that sexy smile.*

"Let me grab something stronger." I say heading over to my liquor cabinet for something more to his liking.

"This better?" I ask dropping a bottle of Irish whiskey and a glass in front of him. He smirks. My lady parts flutter, this man is hot. *Stop.* I shake off the feelings and watch Connor serve himself two fingers and take a sip from his glass.

"Ah, much better. Thank you." He refills his glass but sips the liquid this time. "I'm sorry. I was an asshole." His words are what I want but I'm still at a loss for what to say. "I won't spoil the apology trying to excuse my behavior."

"Connor I need an explanation though. You coming here to apologize is a great gesture but you're right, it isn't enough. I poured my heart out to you about my family, my past with Noah. You never told me about Kelly. Hell, my friends have told me more about her than you. The giant family get together I could have handled no problem." I take a sip of wine. "Your mom dismissing me so she could talk with your ex was awkward. Still, I was okay until you left me too. I'm not blind, I saw how hard she was flirting with you. Is there still something between you two?"

"No, Sweetness." He reaches for my arm, pulling me to sit on the couch next to him. My legs drape across his lap. "You're the only woman I want."

Connor wants me. "Then why did you leave me?"

"Jealousy."

"Jealous of who?" He purses his lips, quirking his eyebrow at the same time. It clicks. "You can't mean Jameson. Don't get me wrong your brother is hot but we're friends."

"Watch it." Connor growls his deep voice sends shivers down my spine and heat pools in my belly. Treacherous body. I can't help but giggle at him. This big burly man of mine is jealous of his older brother. The cackle takes over and I hunch into myself laughing.

"What's so funny? You called Jameson hot, after earlier. Not funny."

"Oh, but it is." A fit of laughter takes me. One glance at Connor tells me he isn't amused. "Fine. I'm done laughing. I'll make you a deal. You tell me the full story on Kelly and I'll tell you everything about Jameson and I. You can't repeat anything I tell you though."

Connor scrunches his eyebrows together. "Fine, but no promises I don't go punch Jameson after."

"Deal." I use the moment to slide off Connor I need more pizza. "Jameson was the only one of Jackson's friends to be nice to me. We hung out a lot during parties. He taught me about whiskey while I played around in the kitchen."

"If it was so innocent, why wouldn't Elise tell me?"

"Was Ryan with her?"

"Not following."

"This is the promise not to repeat part."

"Okay. Promise."

"Jameson practically lived at my house during sophomore year. We became easy friends. Then he met Elise and he was constantly trying to pump me for information. After they went out, and broke up we stayed friends. His only rule was never mention their relationship. Neither of them will tell me what happened. One day they were a couple the next they weren't. Both of them keep secrets tighter than a damn vault so good luck finding out more."

"Wait, are you saying I have nothing to worry about between you and Jameson because of him and Elise?"

"Yep, he still wants her too. Why do you look so stunned?"

"Beside feeling like a bigger jackass than before? Fuck, I'm so sorry. I should have asked you how you knew him."

"Yea, why didn't you? We would have told you."

"You have no idea how many ex girlfriends tried to use me to get Jameson, the star corner of Hadley Falls High."

"Well, they're stupid and so are you if you can't see how much I care about you. I..."

"You what?"

"Nothing. Your turn. Why didn't you ever say anything about Kelly? And what is up with her and your mom?"

"Her and my mom are, odd. I'm not keeping a big bad secret or anything I just don't like to think about her. We grew up together. Started dating after high school. Then in the blink of an eye she went from normal to behaving like my mother. I'm sure Elise told you, but I dumped her at Ian's during lunch. She gave me an ultimatum, the pub or her. So, I picked my pub."

"Wow, what a bitch. I knew I didn't like her." The edge of Connor's mouth lifts up.

"That was about a year and a half ago. After I got over the pain I promised myself to never get caught off guard like that." He takes a long drink from his glass.

"Not that I'm not grateful, but I heard the rumors about how you are Mr. one and done. Why did you decide I would be different. Because I don't look like Kelly?" Connor's gaze locks on me.

"Truth. Looks had everything to do with what drew me to you. You are stunning and when you laid those green eyes on me I wanted you." His confession has my inner me jumping up and down inside.

"No way."

"Once I got to know you a bit I realized how different you were from not only Kelly but all the girls I dated before."

"Then you fucked me and my tight pussy got you hooked." My cheeks fill with air and I clamp my hand over my mouth. Connor lets out a deep chuckle.

"Pretty much. Once I had you I was hooked but I wanted this to go farther, I wanted to claim every piece of you."

"Well there is one piece of me you haven't claimed. Yet." His length thickens against my thigh. My words are turning him on and giving me a sort of head rush.

"I'm aware but before we go there-"

"Go where? Anal?"

Amber liquid sprays out the side of Connor's mouth. Sending him into a coughing fit. "Geez woman, warn a guy next time."

"So, next time warn you before I mention anal. Sure." I wink taking a sip of my wine.

"Jokes aside are you okay?"

"Yes, but if you ever have questions come talk to me. Please." We seal our deal with a kiss. A quick one at first, light and sweet. It quickly turns needy. I attack his mouth showing him with each kiss and sweep of my tongue how deeply I need him. He does the same, pushing his into my mouth so forcefully I can't help but suck and pull.

"Fuck Katy. Bedroom now." Connor slides me off him with his command. My feet go out from under me and I'm being thrown over his shoulder.

"Hey! Put me down. I'm too fat." Connor pulls my dress up then slaps my ass three times. Each time harder than the last. I'm panting from anticipation.

"Don't you ever say that again. This ass." Strong hands grope my plump flesh. A flood of desire fills me. "This pussy." Warm fingers slide my panties over and one slides into me. Oh fuck. "Damn Sweetness, already? That's so fucking sexy."

Katy

Chapter Nineteen

We enter my bedroom. Connor tosses me on the bed and pounces on top of me pinning me in place. He leans down to take my mouth, all gentleness from earlier gone replaced by the same raw need I am feeling for him.

I need this man. Every touch sends my inner muscles tightening more and more. My entire body hums underneath him. He pulls away, leaving me to wither.

"Damn Katy, you are so beautiful like this. Loose the dress before I rip it off, but don't take off your bra, pull it down far enough so your nipples stick out and touch yourself."

A rush of fluid runs down my lips, dripping off my ass cheeks at his words. I do as he asks and skim my finger over my wet folds, rubbing the wetness over my clit.

"Fuck, baby. Do you have any idea how sexy you are?" I shake my head. He points to his growing erection which is straining against the front of his pants.

"You gonna watch me all night or are you going to come takes what's yours?"

"Mine. Dip your fingers inside of yourself, and spread your pussy for me. I wanna see all of you." Spreading myself with one hand I show my pussy off to him and dip my fingers into my wet heat. Using my other hand to squeeze and tease my nipples until a groan slips past my lips.

"Like this baby?"

"Fuck yes, look at what you do to me." He orders, cupping his balls and cock in one hand through his pants. "You want me in you, don't you?"

"Yes." My voice is breathy my body is tightening like a coil. I'm going to cream all over his the second he slides in me.

"What you're thinking about? Naughty girl." Connor drops his trousers. His erection bobs free, smacking against his belly. Fuck waiting for Connor, I slide myself forwards sitting up and taking him into my mouth in one swift movement.

He's musky scent fills my nostrils, making my pussy drip further. Every bit of him turns me on, his voice, touch and most of all his taste. His cock slides down my throat until he bounces off the back of me.

My lips stretch wide to take his entire length. There's a power coursing through me as I glance up at him. His eyes are rolling back into his head.

"Connor, fuck my mouth." The command spurs him on and he pushes himself deeper with each thrust, causing me to gag around his length.

"I'd rather fuck something else. On your back. Now." There is no room for argument in his tone. I crawl backwards, sliding across my bed. My legs raise into the air, falling open to showoff my wet opening. A growl comes from his throat sending shivers all over me. He puts his hand over my sex and one finger slips through my wetness.

"This is mine." He says, laying kisses on my heat. "You belong to me."

"Yes. Please fuck me."

Connor's reply is to spear me with one thrust. "Fuck yes, baby. Take this long dick." My walls squeeze him deeper and deeper. He keeps up his pounding pace, branding my insides, and claiming every inch of me. Rough fingers dig into my hips and turn me over.

"Up on your knees, babe, arch your back." His grip anchors me in place, so he can surge forward slamming into me. My breath to catches.

"Oh, god."

The sensations are over whelming. I'm so tight like he's fucking me for the first time. He pulls out leaving me empty and needed for more. In the next instant he dips his fingers into my wetness sliding it up to my untouched hole. My thighs twitch and my stomach jumps.

"Relax, baby. I won't hurt you. I'm not fucking you here tonight. You need to be ready first." Connor swipes his finger over my back entrance slowly, barely pushing at the tender flesh. His other hand rubs circles around my clit igniting a new heat inside me. Connor picks then to breech my tight ring of muscle with his thumb.

"So fucking tight. Your little ass is gonna grip me like a goddamn vice. You like that, baby?" His dirty words and pressure on my nub have me drunk with lust.

"Yes, it's so different."

"You want me to put my dick back in you?" I'm flying way too high to speak, only shaking my head in response. He stops the circles on the small bundles of nerves and lines himself up with my slit.

Thick flesh pierces me with his thumb still seated in my ass. The sensation sends shock waves throughout my body.

Oh my god! I'm buzzing, every nerve ending is coming to life. I'm so stuffed. He starts moving in and out of my tight hole in time with his fucking of me. I am lost to the sensations going on inside me, my nipples tighten, sweat breaks out across my skin. A scream rips from my throat as he pounds into me.

"Connor."

"Fuck yes, I'm going to come." Connor shouts, emptying himself into my aching body, covering my walls with him, claiming me all over again.

We lay in each others arms until Connor cleans us up. After he wipes me up, he trails kisses up the back of my thighs before moving to my center to place a kiss on my button.

"You are so damn sexy baby."

My body relaxes into his tenderness. "Wow I didn't realize .."

"Babe that was only the beginning." Connor kneads my muscles as I let my body slide forward, turning onto my back at the same time. He doesn't stop kissing my tender flesh, flicking it and sucking my hard little nub into his mouth.

Connor slips two fingers into me. My body arches off the bed. I can't control the sounds leaving my lips. Neediness is in full force and I'm ready for him to take me again. He removes his fingers, replacing it with his tongue, lapping up every bit of my cream. My screams fill the room as I float into oblivion.

Connor

Chapter Twenty

Damn it's warm and my skin is clammy. I crack open my eyes to find Katy draped across my chest. Shit she is so beautiful like this. Her curls are splayed over her face, like an angle at rest. Last night must have taken a lot out of her if she's still asleep. Her body is so responsive the way she pushed against my thumb in her ass. Fucking gorgeous, I couldn't quench my need for her.

Fuck, I'm one lucky man. I still can't believe I almost blew us up yesterday. I was a prick. Nothing brings out your best like family. And here I thought I was over all those old feelings and issues I had with Jameson.

I'm falling for this girl, hard. Something is off with her though. Gotta be the Bakery. Shit I'm a hypocrite, but after Kelly I refuse to put myself in the same situation. We both need to be open for this to work. Okay, enough deep thought for the morning. I need some coffee.

Sliding out from under Katy I grab my pants and head towards the kitchen. I start the coffee, and swipe my phone from the counter. Oh man, six missed calls from my mother. Two from Kelly, plus several text messages from them both.

> **MOM: Where are you?**

> **MOM: Connor this isn't funny. We are waiting.**

> **KELLY: Where did you go? I thought we were gonna catch up.**

> **KELLY: Your mom told me you're taking me to Vegas Night. ;)**

Fuck, I forgot all about Vegas night. My mom can forget those plans, no way am I taking Kelly to anything. Katy can be my date or I'm not attending. My phone buzzes. The read out says pops so I answer.

"Morning."

"Connor you got a second? Sorry I'm calling so early on a Sunday but I don't want to have this talk at the office."

"Is something wrong?"

"No, nothing serious. Your mother is out with Joy and Kelly having coffee and I don't want Delores listening in to our conversation. Found out she reports everything back to your mother."

"Jameson and I caught on about a month ago. Katy's still asleep, so I got time now. What's up?"

"You aren't happy." I pull the phone away confused. This isn't normal talk from my dad.

"Dad, what are you talking about I'm happy."

"You hate working at the office. You're not as content at McKinnon Security as you used to be. I appreciate your loyalty and more so after you opened your place. You always come in when we need the help."

Is that pride in his voice? Jameson McKinnon Senior has always been an amazing father, but telling us he's proud isn't something he does. At a boys are not why I help out, helping family is what McKinnons do.

"Pops, you know I'm always there for you."

"I'm proud of you son, but at some point you need to do what's best for you. Follow your dreams or you'll regret your whole fucking life. Connor, I can't give you an answer on when I won't need your help anymore, especially with Graham screwing up left and right recently. I swear your mother babied him way too fucking much for his own good."

"Everything is fine. I'm here for you when you need. If something conflicts with the Pub, I tell you. Since we are trading secrets, don't tell mom but I'm actually working on something with the potential to increase revenue."

"Terrific news Connor. About last night." Here comes the lecture for going against Maggie McKinnon's wishes. "I'm sorry."

"Huh?"

"You heard me. Your mother was out of line throwing a family party but telling you different. The stunt she pulled with the surprise guests was uncalled-for.

"Thanks dad."

"Don't mention it. I approve of Katy. Firm head on her shoulders, sweet girl."

"She's great considering she accepted my apology for being a complete prick at the party."

"Sounds like a keeper. You two are okay?"

"Yea."

"Good. Hey, your mother just pulled up. I'll talk to you later." The phone clicks before I can reply. Fuck, this is an odd turn. My mom always made it seem like they both don't approve of my pub. Turns out she is the only one with the problem.

The conversation with my pops plays on repeat. Pops is okay with me leaving McKinnon Security. My heart is rejoicing. The end date isn't written in stone but I'll take it. Damn, my blood is pumping, I wish Katy was awake.

"Hey." Katy greets, stepping into the kitchen like an angel, her voice is husky, and her hair is a tangled mess. She looks sated and a little ginger in her movements.

Pride fills me knowing I'm the one who did that to her. My eyes take her in, one of my t-shirts hangs off her curvy body. Thick legs peek out from under the hem which stops mid thigh and I wonder if she is wearing any panties. Fucking hope not. Katy for breakfast sounds perfect to me.

"Morning Sweetness. How d'you sleep?"

"Fantastic, this super hot guy fucked me so hard last night. Knocked me right out after the third time. Although, I think passed out is a better term." She smiles, my cock thickens in my boxers. Katy winks, ah she caught sight of our morning guest. Katy walks over and gives me a chaste kiss.

Oh hell no. I grab her wrist with one hand. My other grips the back of her head and pushes her back down to me thrusting my tongue into her mouth leaving no question of what I want.

I let her pull away, thinking she is going to head to the coffee pot. Instead, she surprises me, dropping to her knees and dragging my underwear down to expose my throbbing member.

Katy teasingly licks the head, darting her tongue over the slit before sliding her whole mouth around me and sucking deep. She drags me out across her warm, wet lips and sucks me back in. Katy makes the most amazing gurgling sound.

"Baby, I'm going to come if you keep this up." Big green eyes gaze up at me from under her lashes. I watch Katy make every inch of me disappear. She bobs her head up and down my length, covering me in saliva.

Katy doesn't stop she picks up her pace, sucking and slurping over and over. My balls tighten. "Fuck baby, you ready?" She shakes her head and takes all of me. I put my hand on the back of her head, guiding her up and down on my shaft.

My body jerks as my orgasm washes over me and my skin draws tight. A deep growl rumbles my chest and I watch fixated on her mouth as she laps up every drop of my release.

Katy beams up from between my legs. "You like?"

"You're amazing come here." Our tongues intertwine and I taste my saltiness on her tongue.

"Fuuck, now that was hot, mm." She bites her lip. Is she getting turned on from my kiss?

"What, me kissing you after the blowjob. You deserve a hell of a lot more. Don't tell me no one ever kissed you after." My hands caress her thighs.

"Nope, my ex wouldn't kiss me the rest of the night after." Geez, her ex put her through some shit. Her phone interrupts us going off from the living room.

"Don't answer." I tell her. She shrugs, kissing me instead. My phone goes off this time. Katy steps away.

"Check whose calling, could be important." I lean around her to check the call. .

"Ryan."

"Answer."

"Hey Ry. I'm a little busy."

"Well, if your girl would pick up hers I wouldn't be calling you. She is still your girl, right? You didn't fuck up the apology?"

"Thanks for the faith, asshole. No, I didn't fuck it up she's right here, but we're a little in dispose." Katy scoffs, snatching the phone from me.

"Ryan, I'm here, what's up? Is Elise okay?" Katy questions. I pull the phone from her ear and put it on speaker.

"She's fine. I'm calling cause. I want to propose. Help?" My woman is frozen to her spot.

"Are you serious?"

"Yep, I love her and I want her forever, but I need both of you. Can I count on you?" Ryan's normally calm voice goes up an octave.

"You sound like you're gonna shit your pants Ry." I say teasing him and earning a glare from Katy. Oops.

"Of course. What do you need?" Katy squeaks way too perky for this early in the morning.

Ryan and Katy take half an hour to go over every detail of his proposal. Two weeks until his big day, and they already planned the event down to the last detail. They're crazy.

I catch a glimpse of Katy while refilling my cup. She has the biggest smile on her face, its beautiful. An image of Katy naked, belly growing round with child passes through my thoughts. Whoa, hold up. Where did that come from? We haven't exchanged I love yous yet. My brain needs to slow down.

Katy is a ball of energy, full of happiness and cheer for her friend. "Oh, my god. How sweet is Ryan? Elise is gonna freak."

"So, talk to you about weddings and you turn into an energizer bunny?" I tease, dragging her onto my lap.

"You can always put a giant smile on my face, Connor. You make me happy."

"Do I?" My hand brushes over the skin on her stomach. Little bumps break out over Katy's flesh, and she shivers. Her eyes go dark and again I'm struck by how beautiful she is.

"Spread em for me, baby." I command. She complies opening her knees, giving me full access to her core. My fingers slip into her molten heat. "Fuck. You aren't wearing any underwear."

She sucks her bottom lip into her mouth, shaking her head. My middle finger sinks deep inside her. Katy hisses as I pump in and out, grazing her clit with my thumb. "Umm, Connor."

"You want more?" A nod is the only answer I receive. I add another finger stretching her walls. Her body moves back and forth on my hand. "That's it baby fuck my hand."

Her moans fill my kitchen as I insert a third, her movements are becoming jerky. Her orgasm is so close. I withdraw my fingers as she whimpers in protest. My dick is poking her ass and rubbing against her.

"A girl could get used to mornings like this." She maneuvers to face me and slides her hand between us. In one swift move her hand reaches into my boxers exposing my throbbing cock. I'm rock hard and the vein running along my length is pulsing. A clear drop of liquid is leaking from the slit. Katy rubs the moisture over my tender flesh until I hiss.

She pops her finger into her mouth licking me, "Yum." The copper specks in her eyes are dancing with desire, her cheeks are flushed and her breathing is heavy causing her breasts to rise and fall.

She raises herself off me enough to slide my dick underneath her. But she doesn't seat herself, instead she holds her body above me so only the tip of my thick flesh is touching her wetness.

"Fucking hell woman, you trying to kill me. I need to be in you." Katy slowly lowers herself down on my length. The heat of her slick sheath drives me wild and I use all my control to let her determine the depth.

The descent takes an eternity, finally her pelvis is flush with mine. My hips buck into her, enjoying the ragged screams coming out of her throat.

"Connor, hmm. You're so deep. Don't move baby, let me ride you." What guy is gonna turn down such a request. I immediately stop moving and let my hands fall to her sides.

"Hey! What are you...? Touch me. I said don't move, not quit touching me."

"If you insist." My hand encloses over breasts and I squeeze and roll her nipples while she rides me.

"Oh, this is amazing." She rocks her hips into me and I massage and caress her in time with her movements.

"*Connor.*" Her words send a shiver and jolt straight to my balls. I'm close to coming.

Orders be damn I meet each of her thrusts wanting her to cream all over my cock before I fill her. Katy throws her head back, screaming for me to give her more. I keep my strokes slow but deep, bottoming out inside her then letting her pull up. We both come in a rush, and she shouts my name over and over.

My phone buzzes, reminding me about my workout with Jameson in an hour. Fuck. Neither of us attempt to move. My release mixes with hers, leaking into my boxers.

"Oh crap." She bites her bottom lip, chuckling to herself.

"You weren't kidding. Thanks for marking me. Damn, girl." Thankfully, I can go commando.

Katy's face flushes, and she turns away. Shit.

"Sweetness, don't, I was joking with you. I don't give a shit about these boxers. You and us are my only concern. We okay?"

"Do you even need to ask after?" Her arm waves in the air.

"I guess not. Come here." Katy slips from my grasp.

"Nope, you need to go, and we both know you won't go anywhere if I let you touch me."

"Oh, we do, do we." I reach out and catch her arms, pulling her into me for a soft kiss.

"Umm. That is nice. I like kissing you." She leaves ginger kisses on my lips. My phone buzzes again, alerting me to my second alarm set to get me moving.

"Fuck."

"You need to go, it's okay. Call me later?" She says as she walks to her bedroom. My eyes are fixed to her back side. Her ass barely visible under my t-shirt which is now bunched up at her hip on the one side. In the hallway she pulls my shirt over her head and catches me gawking. "Don't ever stop."

"Stop what?"

"Starring at me like you want to devour me. I love it, you make me feel like the sexiest woman alive."

"Sweetness I promise. No way I'll ever tire of looking at you naked." This time she blushes, making her entire body flush pink. I adjust myself to stop from getting hard all over again.

"You say the sweetest things." Katy calls while exiting her bedroom. This time wearing a white robe and holding a pile of neatly folded clothes. "Here, put these on before I call

Jameson and tell him you'll be late to your training or whatever you're doing today."

"Tempting but I'd never hear the end of it."

"Exactly why you should get dressed." I do as she commands, throwing my jeans on and carefully pulling up my zipper to avoid giving myself a metal tattoo. My watch beeps, shit ten minutes before I'll be late.

"Go." Katy giggles tossing a fresh shirt at me.

Warmth fills me as I climb in my car. This feels so domestic but so normal and right. Maybe Ryan is on to something.

Connor

Chapter Twenty-One

I've been on the treadmill for half an hour, thoughts of Katy still running through my head. Am I considering the long haul after only a month of dating? I can't wrap my head around these feelings. Kelly and I dated for five years and marriage never crossed my mind. Not unless my mother mentioned something, but I always shrugged her off with excuses of being too young.

Deep down I knew we weren't meant for forever. Banging sounds draw my attention and realize I'm so in my head I never saw my uncles file in for their workout. By the stench of sweat filled clothes assaulting my senses, they started a while ago.

"Finally noticed us, boy?" My Uncle Casey asks, throwing me a wink. Both of them have the same dark hair as my dad. All of my uncles sport a dusting of salt and pepper around their hairline too. Must be a family trait.

"I guess so."

"Tell me what's got you thinking so much the crease above your brow looks stuck." He points to my forehead and I instinctively wipe my the center like I can make the line go away. "You got girl trouble? The beauty you brought to the party last night kick you to the curb?"

Shit. My face falls, I hadn't realized my uncles paying attention to us yesterday.

"You saw or does my brother have a big mouth?"

"Your mama and her annoying friend does." Injects my Uncle Dorian. He's the oldest of my uncle and the bluntest. He loves my mom like a baby sister, but he can't stand Joy. "Plus you never bring girls around. So when you do, we take notice, even if we don't say anything." He gives me a knowing nod. "If you didn't beg your girl for forgiveness I'll kick your rear myself." A collective chuckle fills the room. "You laugh but I'm serious."

"I apologized and explained everything. It's why I disappeared from the party. Sorry Uncle Casey for bailing on your birthday."

"Forget about that shit, kid. If cancer taught me anything it's you only live once. That girl is a keeper you won't get a second chance at someone like her. Shit the boys are still talking about her this morning."

"What? No way."

"Yep. They like her, even Bryna thinks she's something." My uncle grins. "If you're square, what on earth are you contemplating so hard about?"

"Can you be in love with someone after less than a month?"

They toss each other a knowing smirk. "There isn't a time limit on love, kid." Dorian injects. "Sometimes you fall fast, other times you need to work at it. Katy seems pretty special though."

"You didn't say a word to her." I protest.

"Didn't need to. See any woman who makes my nephew look as happy as you gets my vote. Plus, this is the most relaxed we've seen you in years."

"Like you did when you first announced your pub. I don't care what your mama says, Kelly isn't good for you. We never liked her." Casey admits, and Dorian nods in agreement.

"You don't like Joy, so that doesn't surprise me much, Uncle Casey." The only response either of them give me is a grunt. We all get back to our workouts and I'm left to my thoughts again.

The door to the gym flies open and in walks my older brother with our dad. "Hey Pops, at least Connor shows on time." Jameson says to him, throwing his chin in my direction. They jump on the two available treadmills to start their workouts.

"Uh, did I miss something?" I ask.

"Let me guess, Graham is late. Again." My uncle Dorian states, jumping off the stair stepper, giant globs of sweat dot his shirt. His graying brown hair with a red tint appears blacker from all the sweat. He takes a deep pull from his water bottle before continuing, not waiting for a response from Jameson. "Fucking fourth time this month, at least. Shit needs to stop, boy. You want the reigns one day Junior better step up." Dorian tsks. My pops lifts his brow in question and Jameson's jaw locks into place. Fuck.

"You think I'm not aware." Jameson snaps. "I tried to talk to him privately. He won't open up, always gets mad and goes around Mom. The ass knows I won't say shit in front of her. He's being a little shit lately if you ask me." Jameson slams his fist down on the rail of the treadmill. His face is red and I don't think it's from his workout. Anger is rolling off him in waves.

"What do you plan on doing about it?" My father demands.

Whoa. My father makes all personnel decisions. No one interferes or gives input. His word is final and law around here. "You want to show me you can handle more without me. Here's your chance. When Graham arrives, I want you to handle him. Prove to me you can."

My gaze shoots over to Jameson, his chest puffed out preening like a peacock. He's waited years to show our father he can take over the personnel side as well as he handles every other aspect of running the company.

"No interference from you?" He asks skeptically.

"None. But if I feel the need to speak up or add something I will." My father leaves no room for argument and continues his workout. Jameson nods his head.

"You got a deal, pops."

Ten minutes pass and Graham walks with blood shot eyes. Fuck he's hung over. The smell of liquor rolling off him is so strong it wipes out the dirty sweat of the gym. Damn.

"Glad to see you could join us." Jameson adds.

"Whatever, I'm here." Graham sneers.

"Not whatever, this is the fourth time this week you're late. You are over two hours late for your four-hour workday. Care to explain? We can do it here or in my office." I'm impressed Jameson is keeping his cool, I can see he wants to shake the shit out of our little brother.

"Shut the fuck up Jr. I don't answer to you and I got clearance from Mom to come in late." Everyone stops in their tracks. I almost slip off the machine I'm using.

"The fuck did you say boy?!" Our father roars. "You're done." My father points his finger at my younger brother. "Let's get some things straight right fucking now. One, you never talk to anyone like that in this building ever again. Two, you will stop being late and for the four times you came in late this month."

Graham opens his mouth to speak. "Don't." My father gives him a venomous glare.

"You are late, I told you before you need my permission or consider it late. Your mother handles the administration shit. She doesn't know what I planned for the schedule. So for the four times you were tardy, I'm docking you for a day's pay. Three, this one goes for everyone so listen up."

"All non admin personnel will answer to Jameson Jr. from now on, everyone in this room included. If you or anyone else has a problem with that, I'm sure Maggie can find a place for you behind a desk. Do I my make myself clear?" The silence is deafening. My father scans the room daring someone to disagree. Not a single one of us dares to speak. "I asked you a question, Graham. I expect a response."

"Yes, sir." he grinds out.

"Perfect, so we're clear you ever show up to work this late or this hung over again, I'll fire you on the spot. Now go take a shower and clean that disgusting stench off you then go the fuck home. The last thing I need is you getting injured."

My brother drops his head turning to leave. "One other thing, you will stop going to your mom for anything related to work. Jameson or HR are the only places you go for work issues. If I hear you ran to your mother about anything, dog house be damned I will fire you."

Fury fills Graham's face. For a split-second I think he is going to tell dad off. The stare down lasts seconds but feels like hours, Graham makes the smart decision and stalks off to the showers without a word.

Pops walks over to the stereo system, turns on his Pandora station. Eighties hard rock blas into the room. My Pops only does this when he wants silence. No one speaks. Even my uncles, who normally raze each other are silent. I give Jameson a look trying to ask what the hell happened. My phone buzzes a few seconds later.

JAMESON: Tonight.

Damn things are changing.

Katy

Chapter Twenty-Two

"I have an idea, well, more like a request." Ian states from across the table. We are at BreadLove going over details for Ian's first order. We've been here almost two hours and his ideas have been nothing short of amazing. I understand why a lot of the restaurant owners in this city turn to him for advice the man definitely has a knack for business.

"You mean a demand." I tease. "Shoot. Whatcha thinking?"

"I want to take your theme idea and expand on it. What do you think of exclusive desserts? Now before you say anything, let me explain. All locations can stock brownies, for example, but I want each to carry a different kind. No repeated dessert or plate design at any restaurant. Build this into your contracts and I'm confident I can bring a few other restaurants on board."

"Nothing replicated." The ideas are firing in my head. "You think this will grab the attention of the other owners?"

"Yes. Everyone buys from the same handful of vendors. Exclusive options at different places will help drive new business to them." I take a sip of my water, turning his suggestion over in my head.

"So, say you, Sally Sue, and Connor all request chocolate cake. Connor would receive a Guinness cake with bailey icing and whiskey caramel drizzle. You would get a triple chocolate cake with ganache filling and a dessert wine infused chocolate frosting. Leaving Sally Sue with a fudge cake, raspberry center and dark glace finished with gold leaf."

"Exactly. Damn, no wonder Connor is infatuated with you, beautiful, smart and your food brain." Ian rumbles in his deep vibrato. "Every meeting we have gives me more confidence you can do this job."

"Baking is my life and platted desserts are something I've always been in love with. Anything you throw at me, I can handle."

"It shows. We covered enough for today. Have my first order ready for delivery by June fifth and I'll give you the remaining fifteen thousand instead of waiting until the end of next month. I want to lock my orders in at top priority before everyone finds out about you." He winks at me.

Holy crap. Fifteen thousand upfront, I can pay off the debt. Oh, shit, I can save the bakery. Inside I am doing back flips and a happy dance. Antsy to see Connor I grab my bag to pack my things.

"Don't break his heart."

My bag bangs the floor, the sound reverberates in the silence. Thankfully, the place is empty this close to closing time. Only my staff are here in the back. My head snaps towards Ian.

"Excuse me?"

"Connor, he's in to you."

Saliva coats my mouth, I'm not sure what to say. On one hand, I'm pissed he thinks he can inject himself into our personal business. On the other, I'm happy Connor has someone other than a family member to cover his back.

"Same for me."

"Good, because Kelly did a number on him. She's lied and manipulated him. Connor is all about trust and honesty. She never trusted him with her feelings or issues. It drove him mad." His meaning isn't lost on me. Does he know about the loan? Damn, he might. The man is connected with everyone in this town but shit. I haven't told Connor because my bakery isn't his business. *Liar. You don't trust him to stay.* Where the fuck did that come from?

Unsure how to respond I stand in silence. Ian speaks first.

"I'm aware of your troubles and I understand why you are keeping them close to the vest. My advice, lean on him. He won't think less of you. I don't." I'm again stunned from Ian's words. He holds up his hand to stop me from speaking. "Why don't we leave it here. May I check your kitchen before I sign the final approval."

His request pulls me out of my head. My kitchen is always clean and ready for inspection of any kind.

"Go right ahead." Ian heads to the back. "Ian." He turns. "Thank you." The tip of his head is the only indication he gives me.

Whew, glad to end that conversion I turn back to my bag. All I want is a bath and a glass of wine.

"So the bartender dumped you already?" A venomous voice rings out stopping me in my tracks. Ice gathers in my veins and a chill runs over the hairs on my arm.

Noah. Jeez, not now. I'm having a business meeting. "What are you doing here?" My voice is shaking but calm.

His earlier attempts at confronting me were annoying, this time something in his voice makes the hair on my neck stand on end.

Standing in front of me in a matching three-piece suit and loafers, the same cocky smirk on his face. Nothings changed but now I wonder what I found charming to begin with. He always dressed in his expensive suits. Now, I see what is really beneath.

"What? You text me to come. Said you wanted to talk. Why are you here with another guy?" He questions. Huh?

"No way I asked you to come here. I have nothing to say to you. Why would I send you a message?"

"Bullshit, the text is right fucking here." He pulls out his phone. I don't move closer. Something about this isn't sitting right with me. "Take the fucking phone, Katy." he snaps.

"No. You need to leave now." I squeak out.

Ian emerges at that moment from the kitchen. "Katy, you okay?" He levels his gaze on Noah the second he registers his presence. "Is there a problem here?"

"No problem. My girlfriend and I are having a miss understanding. You can mind your own business."

"Funny, you don't look like Connor McKinnon. Last time I checked, he was Katy's boyfriend. You should leave." Ian tells him.

"Do what he says Noah. I'm not your fucking girlfriend. We broke up weeks ago, just go." What a spineless needle dick, calling me that.

"Then why did you text me begging to start over? What game are you playing here Katy?" He snarls.

He's lost his damn mind. "You need to leave." Ian commands.

"Who do you think you are?" Noah's eyes blaze red and I swear I can picture steam blowing out his nose.

"Ian Dewitt. You must be Noah. The asshole who never learned how to speak to a lady." He peers over at me for confirmation and I nod. "Thought so. It appears the ban from my restaurants around town hasn't helped you with your manners."

"Excuse me!" Noah roars. Shit, this is going bad fast. He turns his anger on me. "Me getting banned from the prestigious places around here is your doing. You fucking bitch." He screams. "I don't know what kinda game you're playing. You pleaded with me last night to take you back. Now I find out you are spreading lies about me all over town."

It takes every bit of strength and force of will I possess to keep me from jumping back.

"No, that was all me. I don't take kindly to people coming in to my place of business and speaking to anyone, let alone a woman the way you did. Now leave or Katy will call the cops." Ian steps in front of me, blocking Noah's way to me with his body. "Katy, call Hadley PD. Now."

"This is bullshit. Katy, lose my number. Don't fucking message me ever again. Damn crazy bitch." Noah turns to go but stops with his hand on the door holding it half open. "You are nothing. You'll always be a stupid little bitch I used to get my dick wet. An inexperienced child who can't do anything for herself." The door slams shut with his exit.

Noah's words slice into my skin sinking deep. The rational part of me screams he's full of shit. But that other part whispers he may be right. The bank loan is like proof shouting at me.

Warm fingers wrap around my arm and I jump, every muscle ready for escape.

"Hey relax, it's only me. He's gone. You alright?" Ian asks in a soothing voice. I force the tears welling up behind my eyes to stop.

"Katy do I need to call someone?"

I shake my head, pulling my attention from the door to him. "No, I'm fine. I'm going to lock up and go home."

"Let me call Connor." He reaches in his pocket for his phone.

"No. Please don't. I need to process what happened, and he will want to fix it and go after Noah. He'll only end up in trouble."

Ian hesitates. Connor will be livid when he finds out but I'll handle it then. I'm too raw and extremely confused after Noah's words. They shouldn't bother me, but after that fiasco of a party, my ego is vulnerable.

"You need to tell him. I won't lie to him, Katy." His voice is stern.

"I'm not asking you too. He's my boyfriend, not my husband. We don't tell each other everything."

"You want to keep secrets, fine but I won't keep anything from him if he asks me. He's my closest friend."

"Thank you. I appreciate it." And I do. So much of me desperately wants to run to Connor and tell him everything that happened, but a small part of me is holding back. Afraid of what he'll think. If I'm being honest with myself, a dark piece of me wants to keep this from him. I'm still not completely ready to put all my faith in him with every aspect of my life after the whole Kelly thing. I need more time.

"Grab your bag, lock up and I'll walk you out." We tell the night baking crew goodnight and close up the store. On the way to my car, Ian stops me.

"Don't let pride and your past ruin your chance for a future." He isn't looking at me though and his words sound like they are coming from someone with experience.

"Care to share?" He shakes his head in reply.

"About as much as you want to share about your problems." I swallow, uncomfortable with my question.

"Goodnight, Ian. Thank you for everything."

"Goodnight, Katy. Remember what I said. Don't let your past crap ruin your future." With that he stalks off like a dark knight to his car but doesn't climb inside until I'm safely tucked in mine and pull out of my parking spot headed for home.

Damnit, what I am going to do. *Go tell Connor.* Can I trust him with my heart? *A little late for that.* Ugh, I need my girls. Tomorrow, I'll talk to my friends. They will tell me what to do.

Katy

Chapter Twenty-Three

Veronica and Elise are seated with drinks when I arrive to The Falls Cafe, one of our many go to spots for lunch. A small eatery on Main Street. They change their menu with each season and sometimes for no other reason than the chef's whim. Like this month they are featuring specialty pizzas which is of course my favorite food ever.

My lips watered the second I read the sign on my way in. The place is also next door to Veronica's shop, making it easy to grab a bite together.

"Hey, you're the late one for once." Veronica teases as I drop into the seat next to Elise. Her hair is tied up in a tight bun and I'm positive there are a few pins sticking out. Someone was sewing before lunch.

"Ha, ha very funny. Enjoy while you can because you work right here and are always late." I stick my tongue out at her.

"Real mature."

"You started it." I giggle back.

"Seriously?" Elise scolds us while brushing back a loose piece of hair on her head. Unlike Veronica Elise's hair is thrown up into a pomp on her head. It's almost sickening how good she can make a messy bun while V and I look like hobos anytime we try. "How old are you two?"

"Five!" We say back in unison.

"Hey, where's Lily?" I ask, realizing we are short one and her purse isn't in her seat.

"She hasn't gotten here yet. Elise, did you talk to her this weekend?" Ask Veronica.

"Not since she stormed out of Common Place. I'm worried about her. Katy call her, maybe she'll pick up for you."

The phone goes straight to voicemail. "She's not answering. Let's enjoy lunch and I'll try to reach out to her again later."

We order our food and continue like normal.

"How did Saturday finish? Did you and Connor make up?" Elise asks, concerned.

"Wait what happened? Why am I out of the loop?" Veronica pouts.

"Untwist your panties we didn't leave you out intentionally. Elise only knows because Jameson called her." She smiles. I fill them in about our everything including our make up sex, which was hot and heavenly. Then I arrive to yesterday with Noah and they cringe.

"What the freak. I'm so glad you dumped him. What is wrong with him?" Elise says.

"Katy, I don't understand. Why didn't you want Ian to call Connor? He'd come to your rescue." Veronica adds.

"I can handle my own messes. Plus with all the drama from the party. Connor doesn't need to be thrown into more of my bullshit." I whisper.

"You're afraid to lean on him. You don't want to ask for help because you love him." Elise's analysis on my hesitation isn't wrong but I'm not admitting to anything.

"Need help? With what, not Noah," I ask puzzled.

They both gape at me, smiling. Elise speaks first. "Honey, something is going on with you. You've been super stressed since your birthday. You don't even seem super excited about Ian's contract more like relieved. We aren't blind you're keeping a secret." She touches my arm. "You don't have to give us the details now but we're here when you're ready."

Of course, they knew something is wrong. I can never hide a single thing from either of these two. My heart fills with warmth knowing phenomenal people are in my corner.

"I second what Elise said. When you want to talk we're here but sweetie, you need to tell Connor. If we noticed, he noticed too. Take a chance, tell him everything going on. Then tell him you love him. Cause you do." Veronica swoons on her own words. The truth of her words statement hits me hard. Leave it to my two besties to see through my crap and unravel my tangled thoughts.

"You're right. I love him. Okay, fine. I'll talk to him today. What would I do without you guys. I love you."

"Love you too!"

"Now that we dealt with your issues. Veronica, what is going on with you and Parker? Did you talk to him?" Elise's voice raises with the question.

She blushes so hard I think her face is about to match the color of her hair. I can't help but chuckle.

"If you can't discuss sex with us, how the hell are you gonna talk to him?" I urge.

"Katy. Will you be quiet that isn't ladylike. But yes I talked to him. He got defensive, said the sex we are having is fine for him, and he doesn't understand what I want."

"Did you tell him more orgasms?" Oops, that came out a little loud. Elise and Veronica go red. They glance around the restaurant.

"Will you keep your voice down. I don't need gossip to spread about my lack of excitement."

"Honey, if you aren't orgasming and if you are faking it, he might be thinking that but doesn't want to say." I whisper.

"Lord, kill me now. I cannot believe you dragged me into this conversation." She takes another glance around the room. "Okay, tell me, how?" V whines, "He did seem a little miffed after our last time." She wiggles her eyebrows at me. A snort threatens to come through but I keep it down.

"Katy. Tell me," Veronica whines.

"Okay, okay. Sorry. Anyway, if you are faking when he's inside you — assuming he's made other woman come before — he'll suspect something if you don't squeeze him." I say as softly as possible. Veronica tilts her head in a mixture of confusion.

"What do you mean, squeeze him?" She asks her face scrunching up.

My face drops. Oh, crap. Damn her grandma for not telling her anything about sex.

"Say it. You can't sugar coat that." Elise says. Ugh, why me.

"Oh come on V. You read steamy romance books. They describe what happens."

"Wait that's true? All those descriptions are real." Veronica face flushes and she bows her head. Shit, me and my giant mouth.

"Ugh, I'm sorry. Forget I said anything. You know me and my dumb mouth."

"No, you aren't trying to be mean. It's just..." Veronica wrings her hands. "My grandma always said the M word is wrong and you are not allowed to touch yourself down there. Guess I always kept her judgements with me. I've never." Elise and I both reach out to her. Her lack of self pleasure is a talk for another day. Today her heart is all that mattes.

"V, I'm not saying Parker isn't the one. If he is you two will figure this out and if he isn't, you will find your forever with the right one. The One will give you mind-blowing orgasms."

"She's right." Elise whispers. "Only two men in my life have made my body come alive, and Ryan is one." We both know who the other guy is, but no one mentions her relationship with Jameson.

"I'm so happy you found Ryan. He is such an amazing guy." Veronica swoons at her own words. "I don't think

Parker is the one, but I'm lonely, and he helps me not be, I guess."

We finish up our meals in relative quiet, but I can't handle this heavy silence among us, so I decide to be crass.

"Babe, if you are ever lonely you call me and I'll give you an orgasm." Her eyes bug out, and she throws her napkin in my face.

"OH MY GOD. Really, Katy. I'm gonna pass, but thanks for the offer." I blow her a kiss, and we break into a fit of giggles.

Veronica's phone beeping brings us all back to reality.

"Shoot, I hope Beth is okay." She answers the call and after a quick conversation and a promise to be on her way, she hangs up.

"Something wrong?"

"Yes, a client wants to speak with the owner about special alterations she won't let Beth help her at all. Would you ladies mind grabbing our after lunch coffee and dessert to go and bringing it over?"

"Of course. Put your wallet away today is on me." I tell them.

Elise and I enter Veronica's store, self titled Veronica's with our coffees and desserts in hand. Her place is adorable. Couture wedding dresses line all the racks in the front of the store. V keeps a section of affordable gowns as well so brides of all budgets can look and try on items without worry. No matter your price range a fitting here is a memorable experience.

Fresh pasties and a chilled bottle of champagne are served free of charge at all fittings. Everyone in Hadley Falls shops here for wedding, party, and event dresses.

Veronica opened the business after her grandfather died and her grandmother gave her the down payment. She told her to do what she loved and start living. V could still live a little more. When it comes to her baby she is a bad ass boss babe though and takes no shit from anyone.

We make our way to the bridal seating knowing there won't be brides in today. The gold table and beige chairs make a relaxing space to enjoy our coffee and dessert. Her setup is perfect. Those seated can view the bride in the mirror on the mini stage but guests can't see themselves. Thank god. We lay out our food waiting for Veronica to finish up with her client.

"I cannot wait to try wedding dresses on one day. Katy, I think Ryan might be the one." Elise is glowing.

"I'm glad. About time one of us gets over their bullshit and you deserve the best. " Her smile falters.

"Shit, I'm sorry. I didn't mean to put my foot in my mouth."

"No, you're right. Thanks for never forcing me to talk about things I'd rather not." Elise whispers.

"I could say the same to you. I'm here if you ever want to. No pushing."

"Same girl, same."

"What on earth are you doing at a bridal boutique?" A woman screeches. All the warmth leaves my body. Oh, no.

Maggie McKinnon. Ugh.

"Maggie, how nice to see you again. Joy, Kelly." I say, plastering a fake smile on my face.

"Are you going to answer my question, what are you doing in a bridal shop? Connor didn't propose to you." Connor's mother snips.

Wow, crazy much. What on earth did I ever do to this woman? "My friend Veronica is the owner of this dress shop. What are you ladies doing here?" I ignore her Connor comment.

"Oh, we are picking up dresses for Casino night." What night?

"Casino night? Who is having throwing the event? Sounds like fun."

"Oh, Connor didn't tell you? No I guess he wouldn't since he is going as Kelly's date." Her words snatch my breath. What the hell? Connor is taking Kelly to an event. This is news to me. A cold chill goes through my body.

"Don't be so surprised Katy. Connor has always been mine. Did you think he liked you? Oh, how pathetic. Why are you shopping here anyway, do they even carry your size?" Kelly taunts and Joy and Maggie fall in with snickers. "Connor is taking me to the McKinnon Casino Night Fundraiser as his date. Don't you see you were only a bed warmer. A man like Connor doesn't want to take someone like you in public."

Images of our dates flash in my mind. *Don't turn everything.* Noah's words from yesterday scream in my head adding to her venom. My control snaps and my fist flies without thinking. The thud of flesh hitting as I connect with

Kelly's perfect face resounds through the room. She's lucky, I missed her nose by less than an inch.

A small scream rips through the store. "Agh! You punched me. I'm calling the cops. You're going to be arrested for assault." Kelly bellows.

"I'm sorry. I was in the back getting your dresses. What happened?" Says Veronica entering from the store room. She gives me a nod when their backs are turned.

Elise speaks up. "Kelly, is it? You should be more careful where you walk." She smiles at her in a I'm smiling but I hope you choke way. My hand is on fire, damn punching someone hurts. Fuck.

"You are finished. Do you hear me? The whole city will hear about what kind of crazy woman you are." Maggie spits in my face. Tiny droplets of her spit hit me with each word.

"I'm done, that's rich. Be my guest and tell Connor what I did because I don't give a flying fuck what you do. You made it clear I'll never be enough."

Maggie's jaw goes slack and I think for a second it might fall to the floor. "How dare you speak to me like that. Veronica, if you don't hand over the footage, right now I will never be in here again and I will ruin this little business. There are other dress stores. What are you going to do?"

Veronica doesn't miss a beat. "I'm so sorry Mrs. McKinnon my video camera isn't working. Jameson said someone is coming out tomorrow to fix it for me."

"Agh, I have never." Maggie turns to me. "You will be sorry when I'm through with you no one will shop at your little bakery." She throws her dress on the counter and all three of them storm out.

Their exit sounds with the door jingling shut.. My legs give out and I collapse in a giant mess of tears and chocking sobs on the couch. All the stress from the bank loan, Noah's weird visit yesterday, my worry over trusting Connor and now this. And my hand fucking hurts. One knuckle is turning a shade of blue. Oh fuck me. My mind is running the conversation on repeat.

"Shh. Everything will be okay. Come on, take a breath. Here drink water." Elise wraps her arms around shoving a water bottle in my hand. Veronica is on the phone with someone.

"Oh my god. Can you believe them? Maggie's a tough cookie but I can't believe they had the balls to say those things to you. Don't worry about your bakery honey. I dress most of the big money in this town, and they can't stand her lately." Veronica hand rubs smalls circles on back trying to help calm me down.

"Hey. Ryan hasn't said anything to me about Connor getting back with Kelly. They were lying, hoping to bait you."

"What about this fundraiser?" I ask. Veronica's face falls into a look of guilt.

"What is it?"

"That is real. They ordered those dresses at the end of April. A lot of their customers who attend their fundraisers every year did too for a casino event. I'm sorry."

My stomach drops out. "I'm going to be sick."

"Hey, breathe sweetie. Go home and talk to him, get to the bottom of this. If you give up, they win."

"You're right. Okay. Let me clean up." The sobs are under control until the bathroom door closes and a fresh set of tears pours out.

How did I let this happen again? I became the butt of a joke, again. *No, you don't have the whole story.* Don't I? Connor used me to get his ex back, there isn't much else to it.

When I leave the restroom Cam is here in his EMT uniform and a first aid bag at his side.

"Someone need assistance?" He says raising the bag with a soft smile on his face. The man is such a sweetheart, falling for him would have been so easy but there was no spark. He's a great guy, loves to travel and treats ladies with respect. He'll make someone happy one day.

"You called Cam? Ha. Alright, at least someone is smart." I hold up my hand, squinting. My fingers are already a darker shade of blue and swollen. Great, the exact thing I want, something to remind me of today.

"Sit and let me take a look. Please." He urges me to sit and examines my hand. All I think about is how perfect this is, a broken hand to go with my broken heart.

Connor

Chapter Twenty-Four

The pub is fairly empty when I arrive. Not surprising considering the time. Of course Ian is already here working on Nicole. He always tries to get her to go out with him, but she always refuses him. I don't even think the guy likes her, more like proving she has a crush on me. Today is no different. He may be right.

"Ian I can't. The boss would kill me." She says.

"You mean you still think you have a chance with him?" Ian replies to her. He saw me walk in so now he is baiting her.

"Who says I don't?" Nicole snaps her whole demeanor turning frigid.

"Don't play dumb. Connor is off the market. Wouldn't be surprised if he starts ring shopping soon." Asshole. Uttering those word to Nicole is going to put her in a foul mood. Joking or not.

Nicole scoffs at him. "So not funny. Connor is only getting his dick wet. She's fat. Who willing wants to go home to her?" Anger burns in my gut. What the hell is her problem? Screw her jealousy. I never gave her a reason to think we were anything more than employee and employer, but she won't get over her crush.

"Hate to break this to you but I willingly take Katy home every night. There isn't a single thing I would change about her."

Nicole whirls around to face me. "Oh boss, I didn't see you there. I'm sorry it's just she isn't very pretty."

"Are you fucking blind woman." Ian snaps at her and I take a step back in surprise. "Katy is one of the hottest pieces in this city. She may not be a cover model but who wants something airbrushed?"

"Did you insult me?"

"Don't think so." Ian takes a sip of his whiskey. Nicole shrieks.

"Nicole, why don't you head home for the day."

"What. I've only been on three hours, I still have four left on my shift."

"I'll work tonight. You need to go home and change your attitude. Bad mouthing customers is bad for business." Ian jumps in.

"Connor, he can't send me home. Those are my hours he doesn't even work here." Her voice is getting higher with every word. I'm waiting for dogs to start barking.

"Nicole. He can, Ian owns part of the place. Go home, cool off and I'll pay you for the rest of your shift. When I say cool off I mean go home and figure out a way to remove whatever fantasy where you and I end up together out of your head. We are never going to happen." Her eyes go wide, and her mouth opens in a slight oh.

"Connor please? She isn't enough woman for you. Katy doesn't know you, not like I do. How can you still want that chubby bitch over me?" My vision goes red. Who the fuck does this woman think she is?

"Get out." My deep growl rumbles through the bar. I'm surprised there isn't saliva hanging off my jaw like some rabid dog. "Turn in all your stuff with Jamie, right now and leave. You're fired."

"UGH. You can't fire me because I don't like your girlfriend! I'll sue you."

Ian cuts her off. "Go ahead and sue. I documented each time you threatened customers including Katy. You've been warned about your tone on multiple occasions. Did you really think all those times you were reprimanded they weren't documented somewhere?"

He holds up his hand at her.

"Before you say another word, I have all the videotapes from the security cameras. Every incident documented where you were rude and out of line with a customer. I have both incidents where you were extremely rude to Katy too. So go ahead, try to sue but we have cause. Now go turn in your stuff and get out." Ian says the last words with a menacing edge to his tone.

"You think this is over." She screams, her voice three octaves higher than normal. "I'll make you regret this Connor McKinnon." Thankfully Jamie enters from the back.

"Perfect timing. Jamie please have Nicole turn in all her things to you and escort her out of the pub. She no longer works here and is banned from the property. Please make the bouncers aware she isn't allowed on the premises even as a patron." I instruct.

"Make sure you cut her a check for final hours before she leaves. No reason to have her come back."

Jamie falters for a second then hops into gear at my nod. "Yes sirs. Nicole, let's go. I'll need you to sign some papers before you leave."

"Like hell you will! I'm not signing shit. Fuck this place and fuck all of you." She throws her key card down on the bar grabs her purse from under the cash register and storms out.

Thankfully, we aren't officially open for another two hours or this scene would have been very public.

"Um, boss. I'll be in the back doing paperwork." Jamie says, sensing the tension.

"Fine. Come out around five to help finish set up. Ian is going to help work Nicole's shift."

"Sure thing." The girl half salutes me then heads into the back office.

"Can't work it yourself, got a hot date?" Ian ribs.

"Yes. Why you'd you snap so fast at Nicole?" I ask him, picking up the discarded rag Nicole left on the counter to finish cleaning glasses and wiping down the bar top.

"I'm over people bagging on Katy. People need to let her be."

"What aren't you telling me?" All humor is gone from my voice. I want answers and I want them now.

"Dammit. This is why I didn't want to make that fucking promise."

"What promise? Come on, Ian stop acting like a girl and tell me what you are hiding."

"Noah stopped by Katy's shop yesterday. Awful would be putting it mildly." Noah stopped by her shop, and she didn't tell me, what the fuck?

"What happened? Tell me everything. Katy didn't say shit." My fist slams down on the bar.

"Chill, I wanted to call you. Katy asked me not to. She was shaken up pretty bad." Anger turns my stomach.

"Stop skirting and talk." I grit out, my jaw is clinching so tight it hurts. "Now."

"Relax, there isn't much to tell. Yesterday, I was in her kitchen looking over her set up when I heard shouting. Noah was screaming at her when I went to check. The fucker tried to tell me he was her boyfriend."

He takes a swig of his drink. Keeping me on the edge of my seat. "Before you go all cave man. She told him off, and I told him to leave. He got angry cursed her out. He left when I threatened to call the cops. End of story."

I pour myself a shot and swig it back. The alcohol burns on the way down. "Why wouldn't she let you call me? Fuck why didn't she just call me?"

"She said she didn't want anymore drama. But I think she was worried you'd go after Noah."

"Damn straight. His ass needs to be taught a lesson" My hands flex itching to hit something. "I don't understand her. Why won't she let me help her?"

"No clue, but I'm glad she didn't call you. You would have done something stupid. Look at you. You're ready to go after him right now." Ian's words pull me out of my rage.

"Shit, you're probably right. She still should have told me."

"Maybe but did you see her last night? I thought you had to work late."

"We haven't talked since Thursday morning."

"There you go. You're over thinking this. Go home, be with your woman and talk to her. Don't go at her demanding answers though. Keep your temper in check and be calm. She might have her own reasons for why she didn't want to tell you but you need to talk to her. Not fuck her either, talk to her."

"Watch it."

"Don't. I'm not being gross. Your problem with Kelly was too much sex not enough talking." He tilts his head to the door. " Go, I can handle the pub tonight. Grab a pizza or something and take care of your woman."

"Sweetness. You here? I'm home." Pizza, a six-pack of beer, and a six-pack of coke for Katy. She didn't answer the phone on the way home, so I guessed. I hope everything is okay, I'm a little on edge after talking with Ian. I'm more than a little but the drive for food helped mellow my mood.

"In the kitchen." Katy replies but something is off. Her cheeriness is missing. I head towards her and stop, almost dropping the pizza and drinks. Katy is sitting at her dinner table. A bottle of whiskey and a glass half full resting in front of her. Her left hand is in a soft cast.

"Sweetness, what happened?" I put everything down and rush to her.

"Nothing important. Did you bring pizza?" The smell of liquor rolls off her breath.

"Yeah and something to drink. You want a coke or beer?"

"Coke. I can mix it with my whiskey." She hiccups.

"What happened to your hand and why are you drinking alone?" My hold on my temper slips and the words come out harsh.

"Can we just eat, please? I'm not in the mood to talk." Something is definitely wrong. Katy is a chatter box no matter what. But I give her the space she wants and serve us dinner. "One piece or two."

"One." The word is clipped.

"You okay? You never want only one."

"Connor, I..." My phone rings, cutting her off. Her face falls slightly before she schools her expression into a cold, lifeless one. I look to see who's calling. Mom. Damn, what does she want. "Hold on. I'll only be a second." Katy nods, then take a swig of her drink.

"Mom can I call you back? I'm a little busy."

"Connor. Good I caught you. We need to talk it's an emergency. Can you come over?" She sounds frazzled. What is wrong with the women in my life today?

"I can't Mom. Katy and I are having dinner. If this is important, then tell me now or I'll call you later."

"Fine, you need to dump that girl she's violent." My mom's voice breaks. She must be joking, but her voice has me concerned.

"This is getting insane."

"No, listen to me. We ran into her today and she attacked us. She punched Kelly in the eye, for no reason! And she practically told me to eff off in a store full of people. Connor, she has issues you need to distance yourself from her." I pull the phone back from my ear like I've been bit. Katy hit Kelly. There has to be an explanation, she wouldn't. But she might after this weekend. *Possibly, but for no reason.* That doesn't sound like her at all.

My mom is still going on about all the things Katy said to her and how mean she was. I'm not hearing a single word. Anger is coursing through me. We promised no more secrets, and she is still keeping shit from me. First Noah and now this.

"I have to go Mom," I tell her before ending the call. Fuck Ian's way of doing things. Confrontation it is.

"Did you punch Kelly and call my mom a bitch?" I growl. Katy tenses, her face goes pale, like she's seen a ghost. "Is that how you hurt your hand?"

"Connor, it isn't what you think or what I can bet she said. Hitting Kelly was an accident. Kind of. Honest, and the words I said to your mom spilled out without me thinking. You weren't there, they said vile shit, and I lost my temper."

Her words rush out in a single breath. "Please, believe me," she pleads with me, tears spilling down her cheeks.

"How can I believe you." I roar at her. She freezes, her eyes are hollow and her lip quivers. "First, I find out from Ian that Noah not only stopped by your bakery and made a scene, but he threatened you. But you didn't call me or even tell me. And now this. Why do you keep shutting me out?"

Silence. Katy stares at the glass in front of her like I didn't even speak. This woman drives me mad. All I want is to help her and she won't let me.

"Katy." I urge.

"I'm trying to okay." She snaps turning to me, her voice is strained, and I think she's holding back a sob. "You don't understand. Opening up to people is hard. Elise, Lily, V they are the only people I've ever talked to, besides my grandma. No one else. The times I have, always end the same. Me getting burned and my heart can't more shit." She screeches, her voice cracking.

"Bullshit excuse and you know it. We said no more secrets, but you refuse to tell me what's going on with you. I've been through this shit before and it blew up in my face. Not this time Katy." Keys in hand I head for the door.

"Connor, please." She begs as tears pour down her face.

"Then tell me everything. That's all I'm asking. Just fucking talk to me. Be open and honest with me." I plead expecting my words to break through to her, but they seem to do the opposite. She shuts down completely. Her face goes slack and her eyes go cold and vacant, like she isn't really here anymore.

"I can't." She whispers, shaking her head.

"Then I can't do this." The door slams shut behind me. Katy's wail pierces the wood. Her sobs shred me, but I don't stop. If she won't open up there is nothing for me here.

Connor

Chapter Twenty-Five

I burst through my brother's front door. Thankful it's open, and he isn't in an intimate moment with his latest conquest. Nope, he's sitting on his couch, wearing sweatpants, with his laptop and a beer.

"The hell. Connor, what the hell are you doing here?" He barks at me. I ignore him and head straight for the wet bar. I need a fucking drink. I grab the Powers whiskey off the wall and I take a large gulp.

"Slow down. You're chugging brand-new bottle dick. You finish it, you owe me a new one. The fuck is wrong with you?"

"Consider us, even." The edge of my mouth lifts in a smirk.

"Fine. Still doesn't answer why you're here ruining my night. Use a fucking glass will you." He gets up off the couch and heads toward me, dropping his rocks glass on the counter next to mine. "Might as well fill me up. Shit must be bad if you're here chugging from the bottle. Spit it out. What did you do?"

"Nothing." I snap at my brother. "Why me? Is Katy a saint or something?"

"Didn't say that, but you have a tendency to growl at people. So who did what?"

I pour another drink and give Jameson the rundown.

"Damn. She hit punched Kelly. For real?" All he took away from this is Kelly got hit.

"Jameson, what the hell?"

"Okay. Why are you mad at Katy for hitting her? I'm not following."

"Dammit Jameson. I'm not mad at her for that." My brother gives me a look. "Not really. I'm angry she's keeping secrets. Noah stopped by her shop, and she didn't tell me. She runs into mom and my ex, but she keeps silent."

"Did you ask her why she didn't tell you?"

I stare at Jameson. "She gave me some excuse about how opening up is new to her."

"Okay, so give her time. She has reason to be the way she is." Jameson's knowledge of Katy's past is pissing me off. It's like he owns a piece of her I can't touch because she won't let me. I'm aware I'm acting like a jealous ass, but I want to understand her.

"No. I went through the not opening up shit with Kelly look where it got me. Now mom is claiming all this shit. What am I supposed to do?"

"You are getting the two confused. Kelly didn't keep shit and her feelings from you to protect herself, she lied and manipulated you to further her own wants. Huge fucking difference."

I open my mouth to disagree but all my conversations with Kelly and Katy run through my head. He's right.

"Damn."

"Yup, little brother. I wondered how long it would take you to remove the blinders. She played you for a long time but you said you were happy. Graham and I didn't want to push."

"Thanks for that. As much as it blows to say, you're right. Kelly and Katy are different. Doesn't help me figure out what to do about everything." Now I sound like the one with excuses.

"Stop caring about what mom thinks. She will never like anyone other than Kelly. Especially not someone that stands up to her. We are her babies and you are her golden child. Her way of showing love is to criticize but lean on you. She will never change and this year it seems to be getting worse." I'm speechless.

"Got any beer and food? I'm starving." I ask, trying to switch the subject, but I'm also hungry. Didn't eat a single slice at Katy's house. Jameson hands me a beer and places an order of Chinese from our favorite local spot.

"Delivery should be here soon. Now sit your ass down, I have a story to tell you. I was hoping she'd tell you because Katy will kill me for spilling this but she's being stubborn so I'll risk it." My brother sits back on his sofa, closing out his computer before as he starts.

"Something bad?"

"No, but it might help you understand why she's so closed off. You know Katy is younger than her friends and two years under her graduating high school class."

"Yea, that's about all Katy told me about high school. Big deal, she's smart and graduated early. Her friends don't seem to mind."

"The girls don't, they love her. Elise more so. She's like Katy's big sister. Look, in high school, Jackson let Katy hang with us no matter what. It kept her close but that didn't go over well with the girls in any grade. The entire jr. varsity and varsity football team treated Katy like one of the guys."

"How did I never meet her?"

"You would have if you hadn't been helping at Uncle Casey's house so much my junior and senior year." Understanding clicks. I missed a lot of my brother's lives those two years. It was a rough time for my Uncle but I wouldn't trade the time we spent together for anything.

"That makes a lot of sense." I smirk.

Jameson chuckles. "Even back in the day she could hold her own like one of the guys. She fit in well and don't tell Jackson, but most of the team wanted a shot at her by the time she hit her junior year. No one dared try though because of Jackson."

"Did any get a chance?"

"No interrupting."

"Fine. Continue." I wave my hand.

"One girl in particular hated Katy with a passion. She constantly pulled pranks on her. One prank she set Katy up to get stood up. Jackson went bat shit when he found out and told everyone she was off limits."

"She's mentioned Jackson is over protective, but he's that over barring?"

"Oh, it gets much worse. The next summer when we went into our Senior year and Katy became a freshman, she started to come out of her shell. Guys were starting to notice. Jackson put out the word. If you wanted to date Katy you had to go through him first. You've seen him he's a giant motherfucker, even in high school you didn't want to mess with him."

"Wait, I thought Jackson is shorter than you?"

"He is. The asshole is five ten and can still take me down. Not the point. Katy's entire four years at high school consisted of her doing nothing other than hanging with the girls or studying. All the guys she thought were her friends stopped talking to her. She'd like a guy, and they would never ask her out. Every boy friend zoned her, it was killing her on the inside. So I made a point to hang with her."

Jameson stops and pours himself a drink before continuing. "Jackson treated her like she couldn't make a right decision and I said as much. Once I started hanging with her at her house, I figured out why pretty quick. Her mom questions her every move."

"I've witnessed her in action. She's tougher than mom."

"You have no idea. Back then the kitchen was her escape. Her grandma taught her everything and praised Katy for her skills. Once she learned a recipe, her gran never questioned her if she did something different. She let her experiment, which is why Katy is so comfortable in a kitchen."

"Damn." I shake my head absorbing everything he just told me. Jameson just nods his head in response.

"She isn't used to someone asking her to say what she wants. She's always been told to go with the flow and not make waves. Trust me I understand you needing her to confide in you, but come on Connor."

"Come on Connor, what? I'm not demanding the world. I only want her to open up." This conversation is making me hungrier, I pull open the fridge. The damn think is empty. The door bell rings. "Hell yes, I'm starving."

Jameson grabs the food and we serve each ourselves and head to the table.

"Tell me why my request is so over the top?"

"Bro, you messed with her trust what ten days ago. Today she finds out from Mom you're taking Kelly to a fancy event. Not any simple event either. Only a giant fundraiser your family's business puts on and you are going with your ex. Did you even tell her about it? How fucking hurt do you think she feels? No wonder she didn't tell you anything. You're lucky I haven't kicked your ass."

My head snaps up from my plate. "What the fuck are you talking about?"

"You promised mom you would go with Kelly to Casino night. They threw that in her face today." My heart beats faster, steam is gushing out of my ears. "Gotta love when mom leaves out the important details to suit her needs. Tell me she told you all this."

"She didn't." My mind goes back to the kitchen when Katy went to speak but shut down right when my phone rang. "Son of a bitch. Katy didn't say anything either but explains why she was getting hammered alone when I got there."

Jameson lets out a whistle. "What time did mom call, afraid of Katy?" Jameson asks placing air quotes around afraid.

"I'm not sure what time she called. I just got to Katy's so maybe six ish. How in the hell do you know so much when I'm in the dark?" Jameson walks over to his computer and pulls up a file.

"What are you looking at?"

"Security footage for Veronica's shop. After Mom left, V called me and told me what happened. She asked me to delete the entire day. I guess Mom demanded the video to call the cops for assault. So, Veronica said the camera is being replaced tomorrow. I did her a favor on our end. Now, I'm the only one who can access the footage"

"Wait a second. They want Katy arrested for assault. Show me the clip Jameson. Now. I need to see what went down." I command.

"There you go." He turns the laptop toward me and the scene plays out. The time stamp says 12:45pm. Each word out of my mom and Kelly's mouth makes me more pissed off than the last. What the fuck. A thought occurs to me as the screen turns black.

"Jameson, the app we use for tracking hours. Does it track your location all the time?" A light goes off in Jameson's eyes.

"Ah shit. Hold on." Jameson turns the computer back around and starts clicking away. "Damn, she's ruthless."

"What?" I grit out knowing what he's about to tell me.

"Someone in IT is doing favors for Mom. Your account has an alert set to go to Mom's phone when you arrive at Katy's house or her bakery. She waited for you to arrive at Katy's house. You saw the video Mom was mean, not scared. She needs to stop meddling."

I finish my half full glass in one gulp. I'm an idiot. I asked Katy to trust me, and she finds all this out. No wonder she clamped shut.

"Jameson, I fucked up. Again. I walked out on her. I'm so stupid. What the hell am I going to do?" I rub my hands over my face. A headache coming on. My shoulders are tight and aching.

"You need to decide what you want. Kelly or Katy? McKinnon Security or the pub? You need to figure this shit out before you talk to her."

Jameson's advice is sound, but I want Katy. Tonight, I was a complete idiot for trusting my mom. Forget Kelly, after hearing the words she spit at Katy I don't want to deal with her ever again. "I don't need time. I want Katy. How the hell do I gain her trust back?"

"Give her a day or two to relax before you call. I'm sure you've figured out by now she's a thinker. She'll want to process everything, her way. Let her but don't leave her alone. Text her, tell her you're sorry and you miss her. Words won't work, but actions will. She's fairly forgiving when she loves someone."

My ears perk at that. "Katy never said she loves me." Jameson hurls a cushion at me from the sofa.

"You brother, are an idiot if you don't realize that girl loves you. She probably didn't want to tell you about today because she's hurt. And I can guess why she didn't tell you about Noah."

"Why?" I growl out.

"Because you would have done something stupid like go attack him and end up in handcuffs."

I scoff. Jameson throws up his hands in challenge. "Am I wrong?"

"No, I would have hunted him down and beat his ass. I still want to." He raises his fork like see before shoveling a giant bite of food.

"You're proving my point. Give her a day or two. She'll come to you when she's ready. But like I said, don't ghost her either. She may not answer, but it will help."

"How the fuck do you know so much about her? Sometimes you talk about her like you and her had something." My jealousy over my brother's past with Katy peeks its ugly head.

"Not with her. You missed some shit when you were helping Uncle Casey. A lot happens in two years."

"Elise?" My brother's eyes go wide and his jaw ticks. Yep. Elise. Wonder what the story is there.

"Not gonna talk about her. Besides, she's happy with Ryan."

"Okay, I'll let it go, but one day I will make you tell me."

"Fine, but not today. I'm going to bed. Take the guest room." Jameson heads off to his room leaving me with my thoughts.

Shit, I can't believe I screwed this up again. I'm not the only one at fault but Jameson's right why should she trust me after everything. I've only given her pieces after the fact not beforehand. She keeps getting blindsided and that is my fault.

A pit forms in my stomach. Forgetting about the stupid fundraiser could cost me Katy. My mind goes back to the day my mother asked. Did I say yes? The memory clicks. No, I told her I was dating someone. Not possible to misunderstand my answer. What the hell. Jameson is right mom will always manipulate us into doing what she wants every time. I need to talk to Katy, make this right.

Jameson's words stop me. So I listen to my brother's advice and send a text instead.

> **CONNOR: Sweetness, I'm sorry. When you want to talk, I'm here.**

...

For a second I think a response in coming but the dots go away, leaving me to feel like the asshole I am.

Katy

Chapter Twenty-Six

This is the worst week ever. A piece of my heart broke off when Connor walked out my door. One click of a door and I felt the walls slam into place. Honestly, I felt them erecting while Cam checked out my hand. The conversation with Maggie and Kelly played out on repeat. My shield is why I didn't fight for Connor when he confronted me. All my fire was dried up. My phone beeps pulling me from my thoughts.

CONNOR: I miss you. Can we talk?

Another text from Connor. The fifth message in as many days and I want to answer, but I can't. My heart and if I'm being honest with myself, pride is stopping me.

Indecisiveness is clouding my brain, I miss him, but he lied. According to his mom he planned to take his ex on a date while we were together. A sigh escapes, thinking about them is giving me a headache.

Why didn't I open my mouth, demand answers about the things Kelly said? Regret washes through me, that's the worst part of it all. The chance to ask him why was right there and I missed it. Instead, I did what I always do. Locked myself up tight and refused to budge. For my friends I'll go toe to toe against anyone, but for me, I clam up and stay silent.

Shit balls. Why do I do this? I never use my mouth when something is important, and I'm always left feeling like utter crap. Growing up constantly being told "you're overly emotional and don't understand" because I'm so "young but advanced". The best oxymoron ever, I'm smart but too young to comprehend. Yea right. My parents didn't get me and instead of saying so my mom made me fit in the box she needed me to.

My grandma always blamed herself that she treated my mother to harsh when she was little. Now she does the same to me. A tear slides down my cheek, thinking of my Gram makes my heart hurt.

Looking at the mess surrounding me isn't helping. Surrounded by pots, pans and metal trays, cleaning and reorganizing my kitchen at its finest. Although, I think I'm making things worse. The pantry is empty, the contents are scattered on my kitchen table. A bunch of canned food I won't eat is set aside to donate to the local food bank. There is a pile of old cook ware I am donating to the local high school to use in home economics class and bake clubs.

After the fight with Connor I took a day off, cried all the tears I could shed. When the tears dried up I drowned myself in pizza and ice cream. After I recovered, I picked myself up and busted ass getting everything ready for delivery of Ian's order.

Last night Ian's order was under control. So, I told Meghan she is in charge and I'm taking the day but I will stop in later this afternoon to double check everything. We're closed today to make sure everything is ready for delivery. Ian's order is massive with tons of variables, I want everything triple checked.

Thankfully, Ian employs pastry cooks who know how to handle a dessert. After delivery tomorrow I'll do a mini demo for his staff, to show them how to plate for service. This opportunity is the one thing keeping me going. Ian has the ability to help this idea take off. My cheeks pull up at the realization that after tomorrow's delivery I can pay off the loan with the bank. A happy sigh escapes me. All will be okay, my baby will weather this storm and I can dive into a new plan.

Numbers don't lie. After a few months of consistent orders with Ian I should be able to secure a loan from the bank and space to create Platted by Katy. This is my secret project and I can't wait to unveil my ideas to everyone. Is this what Connor meant? Not opening up about things like this? Looking back, I screwed up not telling him about Noah but I worried he'd go after him and be in bigger trouble. Noah is a slick bastard who would use his connections to get Connor in trouble.

Focusing on Connor pulls at my heart. Stupid heart. What I am supposed to say? Oh, hey, you wanna take the gorgeous blonde to a public event over me, okay sure. What did he want from me, to open up after he hid things, huge things?

KNOCK KNOCK!

What the? I make my way to the door and a man I don't recognize is standing on my porch. He's an older man, maybe early fifties, he's dressed in a three-piece suit and carrying a briefcase.

"Can I help you?"

"Ms. Heart? Gerald Breza, I'm your grandmother's attorney." The memory clicks, yes I met him once at the reading of her trust.

"Yes, hello, Mr. Breza please come in," I say, waving him inside. "What can I do for you?"

"Can we sit? There are a few things we need to discuss."

"Sure, let's use the living room. My kitchen is overrun at the moment."

"Moving?"

"Oh no, cleaning and organizing. Would you like a cup of coffee, water?"

"Nothing for me, thanks." All business he opens his briefcase and pulls out a giant envelope. Sorry I didn't give this to you when we first met. Your grandmother left very specific instructions for this had to be delivered today and not a moment sooner." He places the envelope in front of me.

Taking my time I slowly dig through the contents. Inside is an acceptance letter to Hadley Falls College for their night school culinary program. Huh, the paperwork is thick, so I skim for details. From what I gather, my grandmother submitted my desserts and a video she had made of my accomplishments.

There is a note from the program director lining out my start date, and when I need to contact her. She's a customer of BreadLove and loves my food. A warmth slides into me, only my grandmother could pull this off.

"How did she?"

He hands me a small envelope with my name scrolled across the front in my grandmother's handwriting. "This should tell you everything." My hand shakes as I take the cream paper from him. Emotions are swirling inside me.

"I'll leave you alone, but if you have any questions, call my office Monday." I move the papers to stand, but he stops me. "Please don't, I can see myself out. Enjoy your day Ms. Heart."

The front lock clicks into place as he closes the door. Inside the envelope is a hand-written letter in my grandma's beautiful cursive.

My Dearest Katy

If you are reading this, it is as I feared and this cold is something I don't recover from. Know my heart is breaking not being by your side. I love you so much my sweet granddaughter.

You are a shining light that always brightens the day of those around you.

Although, I hope you got rid of the wretched boy you were dating and finally found your true love when you read this. Yes, your grouchy grandmother is also a secret romantic.

Don't you dare tell your mother!

Close your mouth which I'm sure is wide open in shock after you looked through the contents of the package Mr. Breza left you.

I apologize again for not being here. If you knew about all this ahead of time your mother would have found a way to talk you out of it. Or talk you into giving her the bakery while you went to school. Don't be annoyed I shared the videos the girls made of you baking with Susan at Hadley Falls College. She is a great customer and helped me get all the paperwork started on your admittance. You only need to go in and sign the student forms and you are ready to go. She is as excited as I am for you to start.

About the loan, I am sorry. I thought I had more time, and I did save a small portion to help you in case I died before you started school. Assuming you needed help. Mr. Breza left a check in the packet for five thousand dollars. This will mean you still owe twenty but I have faith in you.

The loan covers the tuition for your school. I meant it to be a huge surprise but God had other plans and I think your grandfather missed me. Silly old man, bet he begged the Holy Father to call me home, so he could spoil me in kisses.

A small piece of advice I feel I must tell you is this, trust those around you my sweet girl. I know you don't trust well, nor do you open up but you can't hold on to love if you aren't willing to trust the fall. The right man will make a lot of mistakes, but we all do, your grandfather did, me too. No one is perfect.

Don't be like me and think you must do it all yourself. Be like you, the strong willed, beautiful woman you are but ask for help when you need to. It isn't weak to lean on the ones you love.

I must be going now. Remember, I will always love you and I'm always with you.

Love,

Grammie

P.s. Give your mom grace I wasn't always the kindest or warmest with her, and she doesn't always know how to show her love. I tried to do better with you. I love you my sweet girl.

For a second I feel as though my grandma's arms wrap around me. Tears roll down my face but so much is beginning to make sense about the loan.

My grand mother's message hit home. She never liked Noah, not a surprise but I wish she mentioned her dislike for him before she passed. There is so much I wish she told me. I feel so silly. For so long I refused to let anyone in all the way. Even my friends I keep at a distance never letting them see in all the way.

None of it was intentional but I see now how many times I waited to let them in until I didn't feel vulnerable anymore. The letter opened my eyes in more ways than one. Without realizing I created my own isolation bubble. Well that ends now. Connor first, the girls next.

Not wanting to waste another second, I gather up the documents, put them back and place them on my bed before I rush out the door. There is only one person I want to tell this amazing news to, Connor.

If my grandma were here, she might have saved me a few days of misery. Keeping so much to myself is a mistake. Yes he messed up but so did I. Connor deserves to be heard same as me. His earlier message gives me hope and I send up a prayer to my Gran.

My palms are sweaty and there are a million butterflies flapping about my stomach. I love him and attempting to deny the fact is foolish. Not anymore. Time to tell him everything and apologize for being so stubborn.

I park in the rear and head in through the back door, thankful Connor keeps it unlocked. In my rush, I burst through the door without knocking.

Instantly I'm frozen to the spot. The scene in front of me can't be happening. Kelly's hands are on Connor's belt buckle, undoing the leather. Her lips firmly planted on his.

Bile threatens to rise into throat, my stomach heaves like someone punched me. A gasp escapes my lips. The sound restarts time and Connor pulls away from Kelly. His head whips toward me.

"Katy." He pushes Kelly away. "This isn't what you think. Let me explain." Connor takes a step back from Kelly. She smirks at me, fucking smirks like silently saying I win. Screw this, I'm done being the doormat for every guy I meet. All the rational thoughts I had about hearing him out are gone. They went out the window the second I walked through the door.

"Are you fucking kidding me? So you can feed me more bull. You text me an hour ago that you miss me, yet here you are with her."

"Excuse me." Kelly scoffs. My head snaps to her, jaw tight, and I release every bit of venom building up in my body.

"Yes, excuse you. What kinda woman goes after another woman's man? And don't give me the "he was mine first" bullshit. You left town two years ago. We were dating when you came back and you made it your mission to steal him. Well, you can have him I don't date cheaters."

"This is not that Katy, let me..." Connor tries again to clarify, but I can't. My heart is shattering into a million pieces and every ounce of sweetness and love is bleeding from my body into the carpet. All my anger and venom is transforming into a ball of pure hate.

"Screw your explanations. Blow smoke up someone else's ass," I say swiping away his hand reaching for me. "You are such an asshole." I'm screeching and my voice aches from my words. "The night of the party told me everything and I ignored my instincts." My voice cracks and a sob vibrates through my entire body. My teeth dig into my bottom lip, trying to hold my pain in check. "I'm so stupid. I thought..." It comes out as a whisper. My lungs are too tight to form deeper sound.

"Katy, please." Connor begs.

A deep breath helps me regain my courage to look Connor in the eye. "Her hands were on your belt. Her lips were on yours. Nothing left to explain."

Feeling completely humiliated I rush out the door. All I want is a pizza and a pint. Scratch that a gallon of cookie dough ice cream with caramel drizzle. I'm so lost in my head I smack into a wall of a hard-muscled body. Damnit, of course. "Jameson. Move." He grips my arms, I push against him.

"Katy, what's wrong?" Concern and worry lace his tone but I keep pushing back.

"Leave me alone, Jameson. Some things never change." He releases me at my words.

"The fuck?" is all I hear as I race out of the pub for the last time.

The drive to the bakery is too short. If I could leave town and go for miles I would. Or cuddle up to gorge on my favorite foods. But I'm a business owner, so I can't always do what I want. That fact is truer today when a giant order is waiting to be approved by me. A delivery that will save my business once the check clears. Assuming everything is perfect and can leave tomorrow morning for Ian's.

Most of the items are refrigerated and since he only wants one to two nights' worth delivered at a time, we made certain things ahead of time. The rest like bread and pastries will be baked tomorrow morning and dropped off first thing.

Weird. Meghan's car is in the parking lot, but they should be done until the overnight shift starts at nine. What is she doing here now?

Panic grips me. Thoughts of all that could go wrong today flash in my mind. Oh, crap, I can't loose this order. Leaving the car without bothering with my phone or purse, I only grab my keys and take off inside. The staff entrance is open but it's quiet.

"Meghan." I call out but receive no response. She could be in the walk-in fridge or by the ovens. Near the end of the corridor by the office I spot a baking tray full of desserts on the floor. Oh, no, no, no.

Three tall racks are scatted on their sides, the contents splayed across the concrete floor. Shit. *The fridge.* I run to the refrigerator section and the orders for Ian and Connor are smashed into crumbs. Someone dumped everything. My heart is pounding in my chest. Where is Meghan and what the hell happened? Heads will roll for this.

Something crunches under my feet as I head to toward the ovens, glass. This isn't happening. The front of my bread oven is smashed, shards of glass lie everywhere. The gauges are demolished too. Who the fuck would do this? At the end of the row, Meghan laying unconscious. Oh, god, I'm on my knees next to her prone body in a heartbeat.

"Meghan sweetie, wake up. Shit, shit." I reach into my back pocket for my phone, I come up empty. Fuck, my car. "I'll be right back, Meg. Hang in there." Please, let her be okay. I make it two steps, before something smashes into my back and my entire body feels like a live wire then everything goes black.

Connor

Chapter Twenty-Seven

Thirty Minutes Before...

Ten days since our fight. My mind won't stop replaying our last conversation. Fuck, I'm an asshole. Our blow up playing on repeat in my head showed me one thing. My anger clouded my judgement. Instead of being there for Katy I turned on her.

I gaze down at the papers in front of me. My attempt at work is failing miserably. My eyes keep darting to my phone willing the thing to ring or ping with a response from Katy.

Ten days of silence, since I spoke with her at all. Listening to my brother blows and I think he made an error. My home is so damn empty and silent without her laugh filling the place. I messed up. If I had been open with her from the start about my personal stuff we might not be here. The only one to blame for Katy not trusting me is me. A small knock on my door tears my attention away from the books.

"Come in."

Kelly struts in. "Hey Connor, can we talk?" Damn, Katy got her good. Her eye is a mix of yellow and purple bruises spreading down to the tip of her nose and across her bridge. Wow. *Don't wince. Don't make a face.*

"We don't have much to say." I close my laptop and come from behind my desk to lean on the front.

"I want to talk about us." She fidgets in place and points to her face. "Can you believe what Katy did to me? She's crazy."

All I want to do is tell her off. Any leftover feelings I thought I had are dead. I didn't handle things right with Katy, but Kelly actively tried to ruin my relationship. And for what? Because she thinks we belong together after all this time.

"So I heard. You can't tell with your makeup on."

"Yes, you can," she says through sniffles. "Thanks for trying to be nice."

"So what's up?"

"Umm, your mom said you broke up with Katy after she told you what happened. That true?" She asks, her voice adding an edge of breathy lust.

"Not exactly."

"What's that mean? Never mind. Things are weird between us but I love you, Connor." She blurts. "The day you dumped me was the worst day of my life. Pushing you so hard was a mistake but you need to understand..."

"Stop." I hold up my hand, "I don't need to understand anything. We were in a relationship. Forget that, you were one of my best friends. Opening McKinnon Pub shocked a lot of people I understand that but instead of supporting me you tore my dream down. All because you didn't listen to all the times I said how much I needed, wanted to have something of my own."

Kelly moves closer, putting herself in my space. "Connor, please. One last chance. We were always supposed to end up together." I take a second to consider my response. She uses my pause as an invitation to pounce, smashing her lips to mine. Her fingers go straight for my belt buckle. I attempt to buck her off but she's persistent and her fake perfume is choking my senses.

A loud gasp fills the room. My heart drops out of my chest. *Katy*. Kelly's grip loosens and I push her off me. Tears are streaming down Katy's eyes and Kelly is smirking, almost gleeful to cause so much pain.

"This isn't what you think. Let me explain."

"Her hands on your belt. Her lips on yours. Nothing left to say." She turns to rush out the door and smacks into my brother. "Jameson. Move." He ignores her, grabs her arms trying to steady, but she struggles.

"Katy, what's wrong? What happened?" He asks her concerned. The vicious glare he shoots me makes my balls pull up.

"Leave me alone, Jameson. Some things never change." He releases her likes she's hot to the touch, and she bolts out the door. Dammit.

"The fuck?" he demands turning to Kelly. His gaze goes to my half undone belt. "Give me one reason not to beat the shit out of you, little brother." Jameson's eyes go dark.

"You can't speak to him like that. This is his business," Kelly stutters, dumb mistake. Jameson levels one look at her, and she stops in her tracks.

"Leave. My brother will deal with you later." He points to the door.

"I'm not going anywhere. Connor and I are discussing unfinished business." It comes out bratty as fuck and the urge to scream at her to leave pulls at me.

"Out now. If Connor wants to talk to you later, he will." Kelly's head goes from me to Jameson. "Move your ass before I throw you out." Jameson grinds through clinched teeth. Kelly's mouth gapes open. Shit, Jameson yelled at her. He never yells at woman.

"Connor." She pleads.

"Just fucking go, Kelly. There is nothing left to say." A sigh escapes me.

"Fine." Kelly whines while storming out of my office.

"You got one shot little brother, one. Start talking before I beat your ass." Jameson roars.

"Kelly came to declare her love. I took two seconds to choose my words. Two seconds, and she pounced. Her hands went right for my belt buckle. As soon as my brain started working again I pushed her off, right as Katy walked in. Go ahead and hit me. At this point I fucking deserve it and so much more."

"I'm not gonna hit you, yet."

"Hit me. You didn't see her. A piece of me shattered on the fucking floor right along with her." I stare at Jameson expecting his fist to come flying at my face.

"Then what the fuck are you standing here for? Go after her."

"She isn't going to listen. If she didn't trust me before, now she thinks I betrayed her. Worse cheated on her."

"So, we are McKinnon's we don't take shit laying down. Make her listen. Don't give her time like last time. Go after her right now, but only if you want her."

"She's the only damn thing in my life I want more than my pub." I say pushing against Jameson's shoulders.

"Then why are you still here."

Fuck it, I grab my keys and bolt for the door. There is only one place she'd go today. Her bakery with Ian's order is due tomorrow, no way she went home. We exit the pub to the parking lot and my tires are slashed. Fuck me.

"Damn she's evil. This was all Kelly." The woman is crazier than I thought if she thinks this childish shit is gonna win me back.

"Fuck her plans, I'll drive." We head to Jameson's Audi, slip in and speed to Katy's bakery.

"So you trust me."

"Of course, you're my brother. Plus, no way you pick Kelly after the things she said."

Something is wrong. The back door to Bread Love is swinging open. Katy's car in the lot but her phone and purse are inside. Leaving her phone to avoid calls I can see, but her purse no way.

"The lock seem messed with to you?" Jameson takes two seconds to inspect the door.

"There are scratch marks on the keyhole. Does she normally leave the back door open?"

"No, they always keep the back shut and locked. They had high school kids trying to run in to steal cooling pastries last year." Jameson shakes his head. Dumb kids. The door creeks slightly. Jameson throws his hand out stopping me.

"Wait, we need to be smart about this. Put your phone on vibrate and go-slow. You don't want to spook a burglar or something. I'll call 9-1-1 if we need to." We head inside, moving at a snail's pace and staying extremely quiet. A muffled voice is coming from the open area towards the middle of the shop. Jameson signals me to keep quiet and low. Voices are coming from the middle of the bakery.

"You're a whore, aren't you? You'll spread those legs for anyone. So tell me how long do you have to sleep with a guy before they pay your bills?" The woman mocks. "Admit the truth. The only reason you went after Connor is because you needed someone to pay your stupid bank loan. All so you can keep your precious bakery. You don't deserve him."

The voice sounds familiar, but I can't place where.

"Are you insane? I'm making the payments because I work my ass off." Katy yells. A loud smack sounds, Katy whimpers. My blood boils. I'm gonna kill whoever is hurting my woman. *Hold on Sweetness*, I say a silent prayer, I can't lose her.

"Don't you fucking lie to me." The voice screeches.

"Fuck you. How the hell do you know about that? No one knows. Not even Connor." Katy hurls back. Hatred dripping from every word.

We make our way following the raising voices. Katy is there. Feet tied to a chair, tapping away. They are bouncing hard enough to cause her legs to shake. A patch of matted hair stuck is to her face. From this far away I can't tell for sure, but I'm positive it's blood. Fear hits my gut.

"You expect me to believe your bullshit?!" All I can make out is the silver revolver pointed right at Katy's chest. My anger turns cold at the sight. Just hold on baby, we'll get you out of this.

"Not bullshit." Katy says, breathless. "Why are you doing this?" The strain in her voice is scaring me.

My phone vibrates in my pocket.

Jameson: HFPD is 5 out. Move slow.

"Because you fucking stole my life. That little stunt you pulled acting innocent, so Connor would like you. No worries though, I'm gonna take care of you right now. Connor is mine." A phone rings out.

We gasp turning to the noise. "Oh goody, more fun is coming. Excuse me." The footsteps back away. Every thing inside me wants to run for Katy but my gut and training kick in, shouting at me to wait. My phone vibrates with another text.

JAMESON: *don't fucking move.*

No shit. The bells from the front door jingle.

"Hello, Katy?" a man's voice calls, "This better not be a joke." Footsteps grow louder. Please be the cops.

Not the cops, Noah walks into the back of the bakery in his normal three-piece suit and loafers. One look at Katy and his entire mood changes.

"Katy. What happened?"

"Like what I did, baby? Now we can make her pay." Nicole says stepping out of the shadows. Noah jumps back. My brain short circuits. This can't be happening.

Noah turns to Nicole. "Babe, what are you doing?" Babe? Rage boils in my blood. He called her babe. They're a couple.

"I'm making life better." Nicole lifts a can of gasoline. "Remove her and all our problems go away." She giggles. The sound is eerie and so unlike her.

"Nicole, you can't be serious." Noah urges. "There has to be another way."

"But you said you hate her. You said everything would be better if she disappeared." Noah face contorts into a snarl.

"No one said anything about murder. This is insane." Noah shouts, taking a step towards Katy. "I'm not going..."

BAM BAM.

Noah sucks in a breath and falls to the floor. Holy shit, Nicole fucking shot him.

"Fine. Not like I need you," she says to Noah's prone body. "The plan works better with you dead. Now you can take the fall." Nicole lands a kick to his abdomen. He lets out a huff.

"Noah?" Katy croaks out.

"Oh shut up, you bitch." Nicole screeches, turning on Katy. "Is your pussy magical or something? Making these men fall all over you. Now Ian too." Nicole smacks Katy with the gun. A whimper leaves her lips as her head flies back, blood flies on landing on the floor.

Spit flies from Nicole's mouth. "You had to be miss perfect and take what's mine. So tell me when did you start fucking Ian?" She smacks Katy again. A whimper escapes from her.

Fuck this, I go to move. In an instant Jameson is there, grabbing my arm. I whip my head back to look at him with fire in my eyes, his expression stops me, its grave. He points to the ovens. Shit, Meghan is laying on the floor not moving, a pool of blood around her head.

"We gotta be smart. Chris and Ryder are going to wait for my signal and roll up without noise." Jameson whispers. I give him a nod, I trust my brother. Sweat breaks out on my neck, my skin feels too tight over my muscles as my body anticipates what's coming.

"None of it matters anymore." Nicole's voice is cold and unfeeling. No trace of the sweet waitress I hired three years ago. An amused laugh comes out of Katy. "Is something funny, bitch?" Nicole demands.

Katy is still laughing, harder now than before, her chest and shoulders are moving up and down in time with her laughter. "Very, you're so twisted your absolutely fucked." Nicole's face flushes a deep red.

"You're tied to a chair about to go up in smoke with your bakery and you're calling me fucked. Honey, did I hit you harder than I meant to?"

My girl doesn't even still at her words, the laughter is rolling off her. Nicole smacks her across the face again, causing Katy's head to whip to the side. When she rights herself, there is a new trail of blood coming from her lip. I fist my hands at my sides. *Just wait.* Jameson signals to me his plan and I watch him slink away for a better angle. My eyes are glued to Nicole and Katy.

"Connor had what two years to make a move or take you up on one of your advances? But he didn't, ever. Didn't you wonder why?" That's right, baby, keep her off her game. Don't give in.

Jameson moves around the other side of the bakery for a clearer shot at Nicole.

"Why don't you tell me?"

Katy shrugs.

"No, I wanna know why." She stomps her foot. "Tell me." Nicole raises the gun at Katy. "I'm not kidding, quit fucking laughing and spit it out."

This your chance. "I'll tell you why, Nicole." I say stepping out of the shadows.

"Connor. What are you doing here?" Nicole turns her head towards me but keeps the gun pointed at Katy.

Katy's lip quivers slightly.

"Could ask you the same thing. Why are you doing this, Nicole?"

"For us, baby. You couldn't date me like you wanted while I worked for you. For months I was trying to land somewhere better so we could be together." Nicole pauses and wipes the tears from her face.

"But then she came along and ruined our chance. She tricked you into feeling sorry for her. How sick to use some giant loan being held over her bakery to make a move on you and your family's money. Noah told me the whole thing, she trapped you."

Nicole takes a breath and turns back to Katy. "Why did you take what was mine? I told you from the very beginning, you're nothing"

"Looks like you're a shit shot." Noah groans startling Nicole. He's on his feet, shit I didn't even see the man move. Nicole jumps pointing the gun upward. Everything slows. Noah dives at Nicole. She brings the gun down towards my chest, pulling the trigger.

A loud bang fills the kitchen. Fuck. Something barrels past me, knocking me into the floor. I anticipate the pain from the bullet. Red blood is coating my skin but nothing hurts.

Noah groans. "Katy." He's on top of Nicole, pinning her to the floor. Jameson comes up from behind and rips the gun from Nicole's grip. Noah rolls off Nicole. Fuck he's bleeding. Blood rushes from his abdomen.

"Connor, the towels." Katy urges, swinging her head towards the stack. I grab a handful and rush to put pressure on Noah's wound. Fucking hell.

He coughs and blood covers his lips. "I'm so sorry," he murmurs.

"Don't talk, you're making it worse." I put pressure on his wound, he coughs more blood. Shit. "J we need an ambulance. He's gonna bleed out."

"Noah, don't die." The pain in Katy's voice cuts me like a knife.

Nicole screams drawing all eyes on her. "You piece of shit, you'll pay for this. I thought you were man enough. You're pathetic."

I ignore her vile words and turn to Katy while holding the towels to Noah's wound.

"She's annoying, babe." Katy says as her head sways and her eyes roll back into her head.

"Sweetness!" The scream leaves my throat raw. "Jameson, call 9-1-1 we need another ambulance."

As if I conjured them, the police bust in the front door. Four police offices file in, guns drawn aimed at Jameson and me. It's utter chaos for a split-second as Hadley Falls PD shouts for everyone to follow orders and get on the ground.

My brother ignores their demands. "Riker, will you quit pointing your gun at me and detain this one? We need three medics Meghan is down by the ovens with a gash on her head, Noah has a gun shot wound and Katy is unconscious."

"Please help her." I shout. My palms are sweating, the fear of loosing her is twisting in my gut. Riker takes one look around and changes everything. I've never been so happy to lay eyes on that jock in my lifetime. He yells something to the officers and everyone lowers their weapons.

Two paramedics rush in, one goes to Meghan and one rushes to Noah. A second set of EMTs enter and rush towards Katy. They remove her from the chair and set her down atop a stretcher. Her chest rises and falls, my only clue she's still alive. Thank god.

Katy

Chapter Twenty-Eight

"Damn woman, only you would add a sprained wrist to your broken knuckle. You know you almost broke the bone again, right?" Cam says to me from the back of his rig.

"Yep, I missed you so much I hurt myself to see you again. Lost your number, so figured this would be the easiest way." I snark back and down the bottle of water he handed me when I woke up in the ambulance. "Fuck, remind me never to take hit on the head again," I say tucking the water between my legs and rub the back of my neck.

"Sure thing. Can we be serious, head injuries are no joke. The hospital needs to check you out." Cam urges.

"No. Wrap my wrist and give me an ice pack. Give me whatever I need to sign but I'm not going to the hospital."

"Listen to your paramedic, Katy." Jameson says, coming around the open door of the ambulance.

"How's Meghan? Is she okay?" the question burst out, my heart is racing as thoughts of her laying on the floor not moving go through my head.

"She's on the way to the hospital. They need to run tests, she's still unconscious."

"And Noah?" Dear god, let him be alive.

"On his way to surgery. It doesn't look good. Now, you ready?"

"I'm not going to the hospital, I don't have a concussion. Please, J, I want to go home. Call Elise to check on me or something."

"Katy! Where is she?" My entire body stills at the sound of Connor's gravelly voice. Flashes of Kelly kissing him, her hand on his belt jump into my head. Too many emotions are swirling in my head to processes everything, I need time.

I shake my head at Cam and Jameson. "Please, Jameson, I can't." A sob sticks in my throat. Cam moves closer rubbing circles on my back giving Jameson a hard glare.

"Shh, breathe Katy. Jameson will keep him away. Here." An oxygen mask over goes over my face. The extra air helps clear the fog. The tightness is easing. Jameson doesn't make it very far, their voices carry through the ambulance wall. "Everything will work out, Katy." Cam is talking but I'm not listening. My brain is too focused on the conversation happening outside.

"What do you mean she doesn't want to see me?" Connor demands. "Katy!" The shout wraps itself around my heart.

"She's not ready, Connor." Jameson's gruff voice cuts in. "The girl is recovering from an attack. Give her a second to breathe. Do that and I'll explain everything to her. Trust me."

"Don't let her out of your sight, Jameson. Keep the paramedic away from her too. She's still mine." The force of his words pierce my anger, a little.

Jameson chuckles, "Who do you think is with her in the ambulance? Relax, I'm taking her home after she signs a form refusing to go to the hospital." A loud thump rings out like someone hit the side of the van.

"You better call me Jameson. I'm fucking serious."

"I'll take care of everything. I always do."

Jameson's head appears from around the corner. "Well, he's pissed, but he went home. We need to talk." His hand flies up in protest. Dark ink peeks out past his rolled up sleeves. When did he get more ink?

"Before you yell. No, I'm not going to defend my brother." Oh crap. I shake my head pulling myself back focus on Jameson's words. *Maybe you should go to the hospital.* No.

"However, unlike you, I stayed for an explanation and you need to listen." His eyes dart to Cam's arm. "Take your hand off her back and grab those papers. She's coming home with me. Katy, sign that crap and lets go."

Cam grumbles something about bossy McKinnons, I can't help the tug pulling on my lips, Jameson always has my back.

My liquor cabinet is like a beacon honing me in. Jameson is right behind me as we enter my home. Who cares, all I want is to wipe the stench and bullshit of today out of my mind. Nothing relaxes me more than some liquid gold. My fingers wrap around a bottle of whiskey, not bothering to check the label. Anything will do, as long as it numbs the pain.

"What do you think you're doing?" Jameson says from behind me and for a split-second his voice sounds identical to Connor. *You're the one who refused to speak to him.* Ugh, shut up.

"What's it look like? Pouring a drink." I pull two glasses down and pour two fingers in each. The bottle isn't even capped when Jameson wraps his arms around me, reaching for both drinks, draining them.

"Hey what the fuck," I growl.

"Katy, you have a head injury. You should be at the hospital. I'm willing to let that go, but you can't drink, at least not tonight." He leans into me and places the glasses on the bar behind me. My body sinks into him. Strong arms wrap around me, and we both stay locked in place for what feels like forever. The hug is soothing and reminds me of Jackson. Tears prick my eyes. Awesome, now I miss my brother too.

"Let me call Elise and you can go home." I only said it to change the course of my thoughts, but Jameson tenses. "Hey, you alright?"

"Always Little Heart."

"What ever happened between you two?"

Jameson pulls away with a squint. "She never told you?" His eyebrow scrunches. "Huh, she sure is one hell of a woman."

"What's that supposed to mean? What did you do?" The tip of my nail digs into his chest.

"I'm ordering some pizza. Don't call Elise, I'll crash here tonight."

"Oh pizza. Nice dodge. One day I will find out. But, you can keep your secrets, for now. Add dessert when you order the food. Then you can tell me whatever it is you need to explain for your brother?"

"Deal. Now go rest." He waves me off and I make my way to the couch. Plopping down, I let my oversized pillows swallow me up and I drift off to sleep before he finishes ordering.

"Katy, wake up. Pizza's here." Jameson says, slowly shaking me out of my slumber.

"Ugh, how long did I nap for?" My mouth tastes like cotton. Yuck.

"About an hour or so. Pizza place was busy." I sit up and shake myself awake. Jameson hands me my phone.

"I'm not calling him Jameson."

"How hard did you hit your head? Ian called you half a dozen times, and he text me right now. You might want to call him back."

"Oh shit. His delivery, his first order is tomorrow and the whole thing is ruined. What am I going to do? Crap, if he cancels, I'll have to refund him and I'll..." My lips clamp shut. No one is aware of the bank loan. Ian is the only exception, but only because the man knows everything.

"You'll what? What will happen if you refund him?" He crosses his arms shooting me a glare that pins me in place. Fuck.

"Nothing. I'm gonna call him from my room."

"Not happening. Normally I don't put my nose in someone's business. In this case, if something is wrong and I don't help, your brother and mine will kill me. Now spill."

"Alright, fine." I cross my arms over my chest and sit back down. "The Monday after my birthday, I got a call from the bank saying my grandmother took out a loan on the bakery. Only, they said it hasn't been paid since her passing, so they demanded the balance due in full."

"Huh, something sounds off there."

"You're telling me, but no one will budge. They gave me until July first to pay off twenty-five thousand dollars, or I'll lose the bakery. I didn't tell anyone because BreadLove is my baby. My problem to handle. Can you imagine the fuss my mother will put up if she finds out."

"Yes, but you could have come to me."

"Maybe." More like never. "The same day the bank called I ran into Ian. We set a meeting to collaborate. My wheels started turning and I thought I could save the bakery and keep my secret." The more of my secret I share the lighter I begin to feel. I didn't realize how uncomfortable and heavy this whole mess was.

"You suck at keeping secrets. Connor knew something was up with you. That's why he's so upset about you not opening up. He's known something is eating at you, but it frustrated him you wouldn't let him in or help."

"He doesn't need to help. The bakery is mine. I'm not some damsel in distress." The words sound childish the second I say them aloud.

Jameson gives me a knowing smirk, "Katy."

Damn it, he's right. If I hadn't been so stubborn, Connor is the perfect person to turn to. He owns a business too, and he understands not wanting outside help. "Ugh, why do I do this?"

"Don't be so hard on yourself, I get the need to show your family how capable you are, but Connor doesn't care. No owner in this town would think less of you. Fuck, I run a million dollar company and I don't think any less of you. I never could. Katy you are so strong, you didn't wallow. You used an idea you've been talking about since high school to pay the loan off. The whole thing is brilliant. All I'm saying is you need to learn to lean on your friends more. Bet you didn't tell the girls about any of this." He tips his head to me. I purse my lips and bite the inside of my mouth. My cell phone rings in my hand. Crap.

"Answer it." Jameson orders.

"Hey Ian," I say pacing my living room.

"Katy, how are you? Chris told me what happened. I'm sorry you're going through this. I knew Nicole was crazy, but I didn't think she was insane." His words fly out in one quick breath and I'm not sure I caught his entire sentence.

"You talked with Chris. Any news on Meghan?"

"Riker said she's awake and recovering. Prognosis is positive. How are you?" A sigh of relief rushes out of me. She's gonna be okay.

"I'll be fine. Hoping I can get back to work soon." *Please don't cancel, please don't cancel.*

"At least everyone is okay, the outcome could have been worse."

"So true. Ian, I'm so sorry about your delivery. She destroyed every bit. I'll do whatever I can to make this right." The line quiets.

"Katy, don't worry. This is what owners pay insurance for, to claim the damage. I'm not pulling my order because of this mess. Let's postpone the first delivery until you reopen, sound good?" No way, postponed. Keep the order. My feet refuse to move.

"Katy, you still there?"

"Crap, sorry. I'm still here. Sounds great thank you so much Ian."

"You don't deserve to suffer because of what Nicole's actions. I'll be in touch with you next week."

"Wow, thank you."

"Don't worry about it. Goodnight Katy, please rest up." He says kindly.

"Will do. Thanks again." The call ends and I slip my phone in my pocket.

"Did the prick cancel his order? Do I need to raise hell?" Jameson pounds his fist into the counter. I can't help the laugh I bark out watching him go all over protective. "Uhh, did I miss read your face? So, not a bad talk since you're laughing."

My mouth forms an "O" shape as I attempt to control my laughter. "Yes, all good. Ian isn't pulling his order. We are moving the delivery date to when I reopen. Even better news Meghan is going to be okay. Ian spoke with Riker."

"Amazing." He holds his hand up for a high five. I take it and he grips my hand. "Now, what are we going to do about you and Connor?" My joy falters. Boo.

"You had to go there?"

"I'll let you do the same if we are ever in a reverse position, deal?"

"Oh fine. I love him Jameson, like over the moon, walk through fire, love him. The reason I went to see him was to tell him. Plus, I got news and wanted him to be the first person to know. My Grandma's attorney stopped by with a packet she had made up for me. It explained the money but not why the payment needed to be due so soon and not made in monthly payments. I'm still confused about all of that. But inside was also a check for ten thousand dollars and a letter from her explaining everything."

"And?" I purse my lips into a thin line. I'm unsure of where Connor and I stand. Something in my bones is screaming at me not to tell Jameson. Not before Connor or it will put the final nail in the coffin of our relationship and hurt him. I'm mad, but I won't be spiteful.

"I can't tell you. Not because I'm holding back, but because Connor needs to be the first to hear the news. I'm pissed beyond all hell at your brother, but a small piece of me is hoping we can fix us. Before you say anything I realize I said I don't want to see him, and I don't. Today showed me he needs to figure out what he wants before we talk. Right now, I need to figure out where to find this last ten thousand dollars, so I don't lose the bakery."

Jameson folds his arms across his chest. "Funny, I told him the same shit earlier. He said he only wants you."

Connor

Chapter Twenty-Nine

Thump, Tump. The constant pounding of my brother's heavy mental workout mix fills the air, pushing me harder. My fists beat the bag over and over until my knuckles are raw. Two hours and still going strong.

The treadmill, weights, battle rope. I've hit every part of this gym. Hopefully exhaustion can force my mind to stop turning. All I can think about is the hurt on Katy's face when she walked in my office. Now I'm taking my frustration out on heavy bag.

"You gonna beat the bag until you drop?" Jameson yells over the music coming up behind the bag leaning into it the rubber.

"Need something?" I ground out. It's been a week since Nicole attacked Katy and the bastard still won't tell me what they talked about that night.

Fuck that night. She should have been on my shoulder. Instead, Katy shut me out and refused to speak to me. From what she walked in on in my office I can only imagine the ideas she ran through in her head. But she didn't let me explain, she still won't.

Jameson keeps telling me she needs space to sort some legal stuff after Nicole or something. Legal crap I should be by her side for. My punches land harder. I'm pissed off at the world. My hand connects with flesh. Oops.

"Fuck, I know you're pissed but I'm not the bag fucker." He pushes the black leather, hitting me in the shoulder. "You done killing yourself? We need to talk."

"About?" Jameson shoots me a glare, dipping his head close to mine.

"Not here. Go shower and meet me in my office in twenty." The fuck is he being so secretive about?

Twenty minutes later, I'm sitting in the black chair in Jameson's office stationed in front of his massive wooden desk. He sits behind the dark wood in a high-back chair which resembles more of a throne. The metal accents make him appear like a modern day Hades in his black suit with emerald green pocket square. He pushes a button under his desk and his glass doors frost over. My brother dresses way too fancy for this job.

"Whoa, when did you put frosting glass in?"

"Last month after I caught my receptionist feeding mom information."

"Fuck. Well, good for you." Several moments of silence pass, I gape at him. He wanted this meeting, so he can tell me why I'm here.

"I didn't want to talk out in the gym because the walls listen. You aren't happy here anymore." I go to speak, but he stops me. "No, hear me out." He hands me two thick manila envelopes. "Open them."

The first one is a bank loan paperwork. The name on the documents sticks out, Lilith Bowen, Katy's grandmother. "What is this?"

"Remember when Nicole mentioned something about a loan?"

"You're joking, I thought she was being crazy."

"Same here, but I pushed Katy on the subject after her anxiety spiked over the possibility of Ian canceling his order. She caved."

I'm on my feet pounding my fists on Jameson's desk in an instant. "What do you mean, she told you? She won't tell me anything, but she'll talk to you?"

"Calm down. The only reason she told me is because I demanded answers. Stubborn woman still refused to tell everything, said you had to be first, so I didn't push. Can I finish without you losing your shit?"

"Yes."

"Good. Right after you two started dating she got a call about a loan being past due. She never received a bill, nothing. The bank didn't care and demanded the balance in full." Jameson holds up his hand. "Let me finish before you spout off," My teeth bite into my lip. "She explained all this and it still didn't matter. The branch manager gave her sixty days to pay twenty-five thousand in full."

"Oh man, she doesn't keep that much on hand."

"She told them and they wouldn't budge. From what I can gather, right after the bank called she got the meeting with Ian about the dessert gig. After you expressed interest in ordering too. With your contract added in she was on her way to making it all work. Katy's doing a fantastic job too. Ian is keeping his order and paying in advance giving her almost the entire amount."

"Wait, Ian didn't cancel his order?"

"No, ask her about it," He waves me off, refusing to say more.

"Okay. Why didn't she tell me and how did you get a copy of this?" Damn her stubbornness.

"I bought the note from the bank. Turns out Noah is close friends with manager and loan officers at the local branch. They fudged something to mess up the bills. I don't know all the particulars only that it all amounts to fraud. Noah planned to rush in and save the day. Make Katy indebted to him. Fucking prick."

"Wow and her parents liked that guy. The man is lucky he's recovering in the hospital after what he did."

"He was a pro at hiding himself. Give her mom a break. To her Noah appeared to be a well-educated man with a good job wanting to take care of her daughter."

"You talk like a parent. Maybe you're spending too much time around mom and dad. You need your own place, bro." Jameson's eyes darken, I cough, and he glares at me. Jameson has his own place. My parents happen to live on the same land, and my mom loves to fret over her boys as she calls us.

"Funny, asshole. Katy doesn't know what I did. I want you to tell her."

"She won't accept, she'll be angrier than shit for you coming in to save the day and mad at me too." Jameson cocks an eyebrow. The realization of my words hits me, she didn't want to be saved. *She isn't some princess waiting for prince charming.* No she's a queen needing her king.

"Glad something is sinking in. But I'm not forgiving anything. Katy will still pay me back but I'm not demanding she pay in full by the end of the month. When you speak with her, tell her to call me to set up a time to discuss repayment. She won't refuse a payment plan." My brother's a genius. He found a way to help Katy without her feeling bad at all.

"Fuck, I'm an idiot. This entire time I thought she didn't tell me what was bothering her because she didn't trust me. But, she didn't tell me because she didn't want me saving the day." Jameson tips his imaginary hat in my direction.

"More or less. She's always felt like she's had to prove herself, so I think she wanted this handled under wraps."

"Give you two guess why." I rub my hand over my jaw, thinking of her mother's comments at dinner.

"The other stuff she won't tell me, including what the loan funded. Open the second envelope." Jameson orders, closing the door on the Katy conversation. I pull the papers out. A business sales contract, for McKinnon Inc.

"I'm lost?"

"This is between us, but I'm taking over McKinnon Security as of July first the start of our fiscal year. Dad is retiring and handing the business over to me. His only demand is I buy you out. The paperwork inside is a contract to buy your third."

Damn. Jameson is taking over the company, and he wants to buy me out of my share.

"You want to buy me out? Why?"

"For one, you don't want the job. You can still use the facilities I don't give a shit. But be honest brother, you always felt like you had to do this. Running this place is my dream. Your passion is your pub and you belong where you're happy. Time to focus on your business without the guilt."

My eyes lock on the sale amount line. "Holy shit. This can't be right, Jameson."

"It is. McKinnon Security is only part of the McKinnon Inc banner."

"Right but how can you afford this?"

"I have my ways which don't concern you. Take the check."

"Alright but why is the first I'm hearing about a McKinnon Inc banner. Did I miss something?"

"Kind of but its mostly the corporation name, nothing to worry about. Everything is correct, technically the papers say you are selling half of your portion to me. You keep the other half which will earn you a monthly draw as an owner. You would receive fifteen percent of all profits issued to you every month. I'll keep you in the loop of what's going on but you aren't required to report to the office daily. What do you think?"

"You run it and I give minimal input?"

"More or less." Jameson confirms nodding his head.

"I'm in. If you need me for anything here you call me."

"Deal. If you want to have a lawyer look over the contract."

"Fuck lawyers, I trust you." I let out a huff, shaking my head.

"What?"

"I've been trying to figure out a way to tell dad I'm done. The pub needs to be my first priority." The confession slips free. Jameson chuckles.

"Dad puts Ian to shame on the knowledge department. You can't keep secrets from him, I learned that a long time ago. He's been waiting for the right time to talk with you. Your phone call with him a while back helped him decide now is time. The lawyers have been working on this for weeks."

"What about Graham? Dad is giving him the same offer?"

"Not exactly. This situation with Graham is tough." Jameson shakes his head.

"How bad?"

"Bad. He's fucking up constantly. Showing up late and being an overall pain in my ass, but I can't figure out what's going on with him. He's so close to losing his job and his home. I'm too close to the whole thing and Graham's worked here his whole life he capable of hiding things."

"Damn, what are we going to do?"

"As far as the business goes, Dad and I worked something out. Graham's portion of the sale in a trust for when he turns his life around. The money is growing interest until he's ready. He got the same deal you did, his fifty percent will deposit into the same account every month. Once he is clean for a year I'll transfer the money over to him."

"Sounds pretty fair. He's gonna hate you."

"He needs help Connor and if he has to hate me to get it then I'm okay being hated. Won't be the first time." Jameson says. The tone is odd and almost sad, not like my brother's normal attitude.

"I know." We fall silent. I wish a magic formula existed to help Graham. Everyday feels like the brother I grew up with is drifting further off into the distance.

"Do me a favor, don't breathe a word of this to anyone. I don't want him knowing he could receive a windfall if he gets clean. Mom too, she'll scheme to help him. He needs to get clean and sober for him, not money." Jameson says.

"Sounds fine but I have one question."

"Shoot."

"You just bought thirty percent of a multi million dollar company." His eyes darken.

"Your question?"

"Where the fuck did you get that kind of money?" Jameson smirks. He looks more devilish than I ever thought possible.

"None of your business, little brother. Now, you gonna keep this to yourself?"

"One condition." My brother's lip twitches. I swear he loves to negotiate.

"Name it."

"I want to tell mom." Jameson lets out a low whistle.

"Alright saves me from having to deal with her. Deal." He holds out his hand, and we shake, agreeing to all the terms.

"One last thing before you go. About Katy. She told me why she went to your office that day." He stays quiet. Fuck, does he need to make this so dramatic?

"Spit it out." I growl leaning over his desk.

"She went to tell you everything. About Noah, the bakery troubles, the whole story with mom." My mouth hangs open, and I stare at Jameson. For the last week I wondered why she stopped by my office.

"She came to fix things?" And she walked in on Kelly's hands on me.

"Katy said she found something out. I don't know anymore, you are the only person she wants to tell. From what I know, she still hasn't told anyone. So pull your head out of your ass and go after your woman."

"Mom we need to talk." I announce walking into my mother's kitchen from the side entrance. My eyes bug out at the sight of Kelly sitting at my mom's dinette in a blue sundress, makeup and hair hanging loosely around her face.

Mom is wearing a dressy blue tunic and black slacks with those strappy shoes she likes. It's like I entered the twilight zone. Seriously, when did they start coffee dates? Did they have them when we were dating? I shake the thought, refusing to go back to the past. My mom's face brightens when she sees me. "What a pleasant surprise."

"What are you two doing?"

"Having coffee, like old times. We used to do this once a week before Kelly left for Italy." That sure answers a lot.

"It isn't a big deal, coffee with another fun lady. Now can I help you with something?" My mom's voice is sweet, but the slightest hint of annoyance is hiding below the surface.

"I came by to talk to you about the family business and the Pub. Is Pops around?" Leaving it there. Not having this conversation in front of Kelly.

"Jameson, Connor needs to speak with us." Mom calls.

"Hold on, I'm coming." My father's baritone rings from the hallway.

"He'll be a second, but go ahead. Kelly is family too. Especially now since you're done with the baker. So glad you came to your senses. Now if you can just find someone to run your silly little bar we can go back to normal." There it is, the venom I knew was hiding. Sweat coats my palms and my eyebrow twitches. Don't blow up at her. Talk calmly.

"Maggie will you stop." My pops chides her as he enters from the hallway. She gives a sheepish grin in return. My father smiles at her knowingly. I so don't want to know what unspoken words are going on between them. That's always been my parents, in love like teenagers.

"Go ahead son, what did you want to talk to us about?"

"I'm leaving McKinnon Security to focus on McKinnon Pub full time and I'm going to work things out with Katy." I finish with my chest puffed out. The shackles of family duty fall away and for the first time I feel free.

My mom's squawk cuts the quiet in the room. "You can't. Jameson, tell him that's not possible. You own the company, we are not letting the boys take over yet. He can't leave." My mom shoots me a glare, and my father runs his fingers through his hair. Oops, guess he didn't tell her the news. More likely he had, and she chose not to listen.

"I'm proud of you, son. Finally, going after what you want." He slaps me on the back, and my chest gets fuller. Pops is proud of me. I turn to my mom and Kelly and both of them need a shovel to pick up their mouths off the floor.

"Jameson." My mom screeches.

"Maggie, I told you in January I wanted to retire this year. We can talk about this later. For now, Jameson Jr. is in charge starting now."

"What about Graham. Did you forget about him?" My mom's voice is going shrill.

"Enough." My father commands. "Later Maggie. I'm not discussing this in front of company." His gaze falls to Kelly, and she shrinks into herself.

"That's all I needed to say, so 'm heading out. Bye."

"Connor, wait," Kelly shouts to me.

"Yes." I grit out, turning to face her.

"Can we talk? Clear the air." She bats her eyes at me, pushing her hip out. Is she serious?

"No, we don't have anything to say. We aren't the same people anymore and I won't hurt Katy by staying friends with you."

"Oh..okay. I understand." Tears well behind her eyes and her voice catches. She puts her head down as she walks out of the house, calling bye to my mom.

I follow her out but before I can close the door all the way I catch the beginning of my parents' argument.

"Jameson, you better fix this. He belongs with Kelly and working with you, not at some greasy pub and not with some baker." Her screeching carries through two rooms. Damn.

"Maggie." Pops roars. "Listen to yourself. Truly listen. You are so caught up in the fantasy you've created, you haven't stopped to ask what Connor wants. He wants his pub, and Katy. If you don't get on board, don't think for a second he won't cut you out. Our boys love you, but you are pushing them to do what you want too hard. Leave them alone to grow up and live their lives. Please, woman, I beg of you, don't push our boys away." He pleas.

I shut the door without making little noise as possible not needing to hear more. There is only one thing left on my to do list. Pulling my phone from my back pocket I ring my best friend. This last task is going to require help.

"Hello."

"Ryan, I got plan."

Katy

Chapter Thirty

Today is the day. My bestie is about to get the surprise of her life. I couldn't be happier for her, even if I'm a giant mess inside who would rather curl up and cry. My life is a wreck. The police are still investigating Nicole. Noah is in the hospital recovering but under arrest. Jameson offered to be my go between with the officials, so I jumped at his offer.

Why did I agree to hold my stalemate with Connor? It took me days to get over myself, then Jameson asks if I can wait. Ugh! I'm going insane. I didn't push him away to be hurtful. My brain needed time to sort everything out. Mostly I wanted to focus on how to get this last five thousand dollars to save the bakery. Hopefully Connor won't pull his order. Five thousand is enough to gather up by the end of the month. *Stop worrying. Today is about Elise.*

RING!RING!

"Crap." Pain shoots up my arm. And now I burned myself. Note to self, no curling irons when your mind is going insane. Ugh. My phone rings again. The read out says Ryan.

"Hey Ryan. You ready?"

"Hey gorgeous, I was about to ask you the same thing." Ryan is cheerful as always, not a hint of nerves. The man is smooth.

"Not fair, why do I sound more nervous than you?" I let out with an awkward laugh. "And shouldn't I be asking you if you're ready? This is your day and all." His warm chuckle through the phone makes me smile. They are perfect for each other. He's so sweet and kind exactly like Elise.

"I guess you're right, but I feel great. Cool as a cucumber as always. Seriously though, how you holding up? Heard from Connor?" His tone goes from fun-loving to a concerned brother in the matter of seconds. The thought pulls on my heart, making me miss Jackson.

Oh, crap. Jackson. He is gonna be such a dick after my mom fills him in. I will not survive his I told you so. At least she's only called once, somewhat frantic after the incident at the bakery, she hasn't pushed for many details.

Tears are building behind my eyes but I refuse to let them fall. *Don't ruin your makeup.*

"Um Katy, you still there?" Oops.

"Yep, still here sorry got lost in my head. And no, I haven't talk to Connor but I miss him so much Ry. I was going to call him, but Jameson told me to give him a few days because of something going on with the family business. Is it something serious? I'm kinda driving myself crazy here. Is he coming today?" I ask twirling the curling iron cord around my finger.

"I'm not aware of any family stuff. Will you be alright if he shows?" My heart instantly starts racing at the thought of seeing him.

Two weeks since the whole mess with Noah and Nicole has giving me lots of time to think. Pushing Connor away was a mistake. All I could picture was Kelly all over him and I froze. I put this cavern between us and I can't figure out how to close the gap.

"I'll be fine. We need to talk, I need to apologize for being so stubborn." A soft chuckle rings through the phone, and my face scrunches up. "You are not laughing at me Ryan."

"I swear I'm not, but you said you need to apologize and you're stubborn. I'm pretty sure hell is freezing over because girls never admit that. Ever." His boom of laughter pulls me right out of my melancholy mood and giggling right along with him.

"And here Elise tells us you're so sweet. You're like all the other guys."

"Hey now, here I'm trying to be a gentlemen and you go and say something so cruel." He mocks offense. I snatch my lip gloss off the counter and add the last touch of makeup. Perfect. "Everything will work out Katy. Have faith." His reassurance helps a little.

"Thanks, Ryan. Enough about my crummy love life. Today is about you and Elise. We should be to the tasting room by twelve thirty."

"Okay, sounds good. Thanks again for helping with this Katy."

"No need to thank me, Elise would do the same for me if the situation was reverse."

"I'm sure she would." Ryan chuckles. "You two are more like sisters than friends."

"Oh I know. She's the best."

"She sure is. I'll see soon."

We hang up. *He's right, you know, everything will all work.* Hell yes it will, because I'm not quitting. After lunch, I will find Connor and tell him everything.

"I'm so glad we are doing this. It has been too long since we had lunch, only us." Elise beams as we head down the small private road that leads to Hidden Hills Vineyard & Winery. She is beautiful with her hair styled in beach waves hugging her cheeks.

The woman is finally going to let her hair grow out, for now. Elise loves and hates her hair length. She always cuts it short hates it, declares no more cutting grows out her length and the cycle starts all over. Her makeup is flawless as usual in neutral tones with a hint of a smokey eye. I don't look half bad myself in a yellow and green floral sundress dress that hugs my curves, flaring out at my hips. My hair flows down my back in long curls and I added a touch of makeup. I might have dressed up, hoping to see Connor. No biggie.

"You're right, I can't remember the last time we hung out. I'm so glad you could take off work today. And this weather, is perfect." Elise works at one of the best lingerie stores around. She's the head designer, so she never gets time off.

"I'm lucky Brandi was in a semi-decent mood when I requested the day off. That woman is nuts. Sometimes I wonder why I work there. Then I remember they are the closest shop. Driving into Los Angeles every day would be horrid."

"Did you say horrid?" I raise my eyebrows at her. "No more British TV for you." We giggle. The smile on my face is real for the first time in a long time.

Hanging with Elise reminds me of old times. I'm beyond grateful for her. She has this ability to always lighten my mood talking about nothing and everything. Jameson was right, I needed to lean on them sooner.

We pull into the Winery restaurant parking lot. Thankfully, Ryan remembered instruct everyone to park elsewhere. Hidden Hills is a popular winery and lots of locals and tourist visit, however an entire parking lot full at noon on a Saturday would be a super suspicious.

"Is Faye joining us?"

"Maybe, she said she was going to try, you know how busy she gets." Elise nods in agreement. I'm trying so hard to be cool on the outside. This is it, Elise is about to get the surprise of a lifetime.

The front of the winery is beautiful. Faye styled the entire building to resemble a California Mission. The front is red brick with a bell tower the color of sand. The combination is gorgeous. Large wine barrels line the front door, giving the entrance a rustic appeal. Looking into the distance on my left, I expansive greenery of the vineyard spans rows after row of beautiful foliage through the hillside.

"After you, sweetie." She smiles at me and thanks me while I hold the door for her.

The inside is stunning, filled with racks of wine bottles and a fresh cheese case for charcuterie platters. Small tables for parties of two and four line the small wall on the right. They are set up to enjoy tastings and food.

Faye's been holding out on us. The whole inside has been updated since last time we were here. The bar used to be a light oak. Now in its place is a dark cherry wood that wraps from the right wall all the way across the room. *Connor would be in love with the place.* Thinking of Connor sends a shooting pang to my heart. I will not cry, this is not my day. I take a deep breath to clear my head.

"Let's skip the tasting room and head around to the restaurant first. I'm starved." Elise chimes in. Damn it. I was hoping to taste with her first before getting the thumbs up from Ryan. I hope they are ready for us.

"Sure. Lead the way."

Ryan, please be ready, I send out a silent prayer. The plan is for him to be in the dining hall on one knee waiting for her. I sent a quick text when we pulled up, but he hasn't replied yet. We step inside the restaurant section.

My eyes go wide. Standing in front of everyone with a shit-eating grin is my big brother Jackson Heart.

Jackson stands there looking like a real action hero with his sharp jaw, dimples and short but long on top black as night hair. A complete contrast to his light grey eyes. He's wearing an olive green Henley t-shirt, dark blue jeans and shit kickers. Wow, I think he's almost doubled in size since he was home last. His chest is puffed up from muscle and those back muscles are peeking up above his shoulder.

"Holy shit!" I squeal.

"Language Katy." My mom shouts but I ignore her and run into my brother's arms. I can't remember the last time I saw him in the flesh.

Umph.

"Damn girl, you are solid. How many bags a flour do you lift a day now?" Jackson gives me a squeeze, taking all my air with his tight hold. "Oops, sorry." He releases me and pulls me away from him. "You look good, Little Heart. You didn't think I'd miss this, right?" Elise's engagement proposal, huh?

Ryan comes around with a typical bright smile plastered on his face, but this time he is wearing a mischievous grin. What the hell?

He wraps me in a hug. "What's going on?"

"Please don't hate me, he begged me." Ryan whispers back.

"What?" Am I on a funky game show or something? What the hell is going on?

Jackson steps away, reveling Connor in his place.

I gasp, grabbing at my heart.

"Katy, I've been such an idiot." His rich voice soothes the butterflies trying to escape my stomach. "I used to think all I wanted in life was my pub. Until you. The night you walked into my pub and asked for two fingers of whiskey was the day I started falling. Your heart is bigger than anyone I've ever met. You're always willing to walk through fire for those you care about. I messed up more than once and I'm a stubborn ass. But I hope you can forgive me. I love you, Katy Heart."

"Connor." His name comes out breathless, closer to a whisper. He loves me. He said he loves me. My heart is jumping inside my chest. This man I pushed away and made so many mistakes with said he loves me. Tears are rolling down my cheeks.

"Wait, please. We've had a rocky two weeks, but you are it for me. The only woman I ever want to call mine." He drops to one knee. "Katy, I'm being open and honest with you right here in front of everyone. I love you more than anyone on this planet. Will you marry me?"

My entire body is stuck gaping at Connor as he opens a box with the most beautiful ring I ever saw. A square-cut diamond, surround by two Irish knots with a band of small diamonds. It's elegant and beautiful, perfect.

"Yes. Of course, I'll marry you. I love you." Connor stands, sliding the ring on my shaking finger. He gathers me up in his muscular arms and kisses me deeply.

The entire restaurant erupts in cheers and laughter, followed by congratulations from all our friends and family.

"Don't cry, Sweetness." He tells me wiping away my tears.

"They're happy tears. I can't believe you did this." His gaze goes over my shoulder to Ryan and Elise standing behind me. I release myself from Connor to give my best friend a ginormous hug.

"How did you do it? This was your proposal?"

Elise is smiling from ear to ear. "Ryan proposed to me last night at this most romantic private dinner imaginable." I steal a glance back at Connor over my shoulder, remembering our own private dinner. "The whole night was amazing. After I said yes." She holds up her ring finger showing me her ring. A Princess-cut diamond the size of her finger. Damn, Ryan knows how to buy a diamond. "He explained everything to me, including Connor's idea for today. So we made it happen."

"Thank you so much for everything. There are no words, you totally got me." I give her another hug.

"Enough explaining." Connor growls, wrapping his arms around me, dipping one hand to pull me close and cup my ass. Warm heat floods my center, making my nipples pebble against his chest. Connor leans down and whispers in my ear. "This dress is fucking sexy as hell on you."

"Thank you. You should see what I have under." I tease.

"Later, we have guests." He whispers, his breath tickles my skin. Throwing him a puppy pout I reach up and kiss him on the cheek.

The room is full of chatter. All our family and friends including all of Connor's cousins are mingling. Warmth fills me and I send up a thank you to the heavens. Funny how so much can change in a few hours. Jackson makes eye contact with me, smirks and heads our way. Crap, the inquisition.

"See a ghost Little Heart? You're pale." Jackson asks as he approaches.

"Umm nope, I know you. Play nice." I order glaring at him. He barks out a laugh.

"Funny, I always play nice. So, this is the man who thinks he can handle you for life. You better not be breaking her heart." Jackson as protective as always. "What was all that talk of being stupid? Did you hurt my little sister?" I open my mouth to snap at him, but Connor squeezes my side.

"Babe, he's looking out for you. If I had a sister I would probably act the same way." I force my drink to stay down. "I won't lie to you. Katy and I have had a rocky month."

"The rocky stuff isn't your concern, Jackson. I'm okay. Can you please be happy for me?" Using my eyes to silently plead with my brother.

"Fine." He kisses me on the forehead. "I don't care if you are Jameson's little brother, you hurt her I'll kill you." I glare at my brother, but Connor holds out his hand to him.

"Fine by me. Jameson will willingly help you too. He always has her back."

"Where is the asshole? I wanted to catch him before I head out."

"Head out? You've been her like an hour." He did not come home for a damn day after being away for years.

"Sorry. The boss called with job assignment this morning but don't sweat. I'll be back in October, I think. It isn't like you're getting married this year." He taunts.

"I don't want to wait. You better not miss it. I won't forgive you." My eyes narrow at Jackson. I love the oaf, but I'm sick of his running. He needs to stay for longer than a freaking weekend.

"Katy, we'll talk about this later." His voice is harsh and leaves no room for argument. Not that I could say anything because my best friend Lily runs up and hugs me ending our disagreement.

"Oh, my gosh. You're engaged." She wraps me in a hug and starts bouncing up and down. "I can't believe it. Connor, you are one lucky man." Lily beams at him. She stiffens slightly like her body only now realized my brother -- her forever crush -- is standing right next to me.

"Jackson, hi. Been a long time. Back for now or forever?" She rambles, her cheeks go flush, and she tucks her hair behind her ear. I'm not the only one who notices though because one glance at Isaac says it all. His jaw ticks, his fists are balling at his side. Great. I sigh. He better behave, I will not let him ruin my day. Once again I'm left wondering what the hell Lily sees in this guy.

"Jackson, you remember Lily Grey, one of my best friends."

"Hey, wow. You grew up. Last time I saw you weren't you in like ninth grade?" Jackson says in a flirty tone. Oh, no. He is not hitting on her in front of her jealous fiance.

I cough. "Jacks, this is Isaac, Lily's fiance. He works at the same firm as my ex Noah." I let slip intentionally, knowing my brother will pick up on the hint I'm dropping.

"Not anymore, the firm let him go after the crap with you." He sneers. Hold up, is he upset with me over being attacked? Connor and Jackson stiffen at his words too, oh shit.

"By crap you mean your crazy co-worker's girlfriend trying to kill her or him attempting to destroy her bakery and reputation. You can't possibly be angry at my sister." Jackson stands up straighter, filling out his almost six-foot frame. Isaac sinks back barely and throws up his hands in defense.

"Hey man, I didn't mean it like that. I'm only saying he doesn't work with me anymore."

"Since he's about to be on trial for fraud it doesn't matter now does it?" Connor throws in.

"Can we stop talking about him. He will not ruin Katy's day. Hey babe, there's Dean and my mom. Let's go say hi." Lily pulls Isaac away.

"Good seeing you again." Jackson calls to her.

"You too." Lily says over her shoulder as she drags Isaac over to her mom and stepfather. Isaac throws a sneer back at Jackson. Fuck, I hope he doesn't take his anger out on her. We made up but she still won't admit anything to me. He must be hurting her or at the very least grabbed her arm.

"Let her make her own decisions, Sweetness. Lily can handle herself." Connor whispers in my ear, pulling me from my thoughts.

"I hope you're right." The twist in my gut says he's wrong.

Connor

Chapter Thirty-One

Our friends and family are chatting away. Music is playing in the background and everyone seems happy. Except the rather tense moment with Isaac and Jackson. I hope Katy's wrong about the abuse. No one deserve

We make our way around the room, thanking everyone for coming.

"Katy." Calls a deep female voice. We both turn and Veronica comes rushing up, her boyfriend Parker, I think, following in her wake. "Congratulations! I am so happy for you. When Elise called me and said plans had changed for today, I didn't know what to think and now three of my best friends are getting married." She says in a single breath. Wow, I thought Katy talked fast. "So Connor, do you and Ryan do everything together, or alike I should ask?" Veronica wiggles her eyebrows, referring to a naughtier topics I think.

"Honey, that's a little inappropriate." Parker snips. Damn, what is with these dudes. Lily's boyfriend is a total ass and Parker has a stuck up attitude.

"Wouldn't you like to know." Katy arches an eyebrow, and making them both squeal. My dick twitches knowing exactly where her thoughts are going. Parker appears uncomfortable with the turn in conversation. "Oh Parker, relax, what do you think we talk about at our weekly coffee date?" The man turns white as a sheet at her statement. Holding in my laughter is getting hard. What is with this dude?

"In my family what happens in the bedroom is a private thing not to be shared with others." Oh shit, he said the worst thing he could say to Katy. Veronica knows it. Her eyes go wide and she shoots me a pleading look. Too late, Katy is already wearing a sexy fucking smirk.

"Whoever taught you that wasn't getting it good." Parker coughs on his own spit. I bite my cheek to keep control. "Oh relax, Parker. We never repeat what we talk about. Veronica doesn't talk about your sex life anyway because you're a private person." She shrugs. "Connor, there's Pops we should say hello."

"We'll talk Tuesday at lunch, honey. Congratulations again." Veronica says, leaning in to give Katy a hug. She discreetly whispers something to her. I bite back a chuckle.

"Congratulations to you both." Parker says nodding. His skin is more normal than before, but he's still annoyed.

I pull Katy close to me, and lean down whispering in her ear. "Sweetness, I think you almost gave him a heart attack. Great lie, by the way." The side of her lip goes up in a grin.

"No clue what you're talking about." She replies throwing me a wink.

We make our way over to my Pops who is juggling two plates and a glass of wine.

"Enjoying the food dad?" He smiles at his food.

"Your mother told me to hold these." My pops sets the plates down on the nearest table and holds his hand out to me. "Kid, I'm proud of you. You got yourself one hell of a woman here. I'm glad you didn't ruin it." He nods at Katy. They're both wearing giant smiles.

"Your son is pretty amazing. I think I lucked out too." She burrows into me as the scent of fresh-baked bread fills my nostrils and I lean down and kiss the top of her head.

"Congratulations to you both." My father says a look of pride on his face.

"Yes, congratulations to both of you," says a warm voice. "Katy, can I speak with you?" We both turn and yep, my mother is standing behind us. Katy squeezes my hand.

"Sure." I tilt my head to Katy. Her last encounter with my mother was awful and cruel. A part of me assumed she wouldn't want to talk to her for awhile.

"I'm sorry about before. The way I spoke to you the last time we ran into each other was out of line. There is no excuse." My mom bows her head to Katy. I glance around the room looking for Jameson, he needs to witness this shit. My mom never apologizes like this to anyone, not even Pops.

"You were looking out for your son. I said things I'm not proud of too. Let's agree to never speak of it again, okay?" Katy replies, sweet and genuine. She is mending fences with my mom. Once again this woman captivates me with her kindness.

"You'll forget so quick?" My mom asks. Katy nods then turns to smile at me. "Well, clearly she has a good heart Connor. Fierce for those she loves too. I like her. You got yourself a keeper. I am sorry about all the Kelly business, I overstepped." Tears rim my mother's eyes. "Forgive me," she asks Katy.

"Speak of it no more. In fact. Why don't we start from scratch. Hi, I'm Katy." My mother's face brightens filling with joy.

"Maggie. Welcome to the family sweetheart." They embrace. Katy steps back and my mother throws her arms around me in a bear hug.

"I'm sorry son. I love you."

"I love you too ma."

Graham approaches from behind my pops with two beers in his hands. "Did the biiitchhh finally apologize?" My younger brother Graham slurs, swaying slightly.

"Graham." My mom gasps. Her bottom lip is shaking and her cheeks are bright red. I can't believe Graham humiliated her. My head swivels, searching the room again. This time my gaze locks with Jameson. A quick nod and a head tilt is all he needs to be line for us.

"Graham. Don't be so silly." Katy says in a high-pitched voice. "Your mother is a sweet lady who loves her babies like a mama bear. No need for name calling."

Jameson walks up behind Graham and wraps his arm around Graham's shoulders. "Come on bro, time for bed. No more drinking for you. Sorry ma." He adds before walking away.

My pops heads our way and kisses her on her temple. "It'll be okay, love. He's struggling at the moment. The boy will find his way. Why don't we head home, or better yet let's head out to the cooking store you love so much over in Bailey Township? We can grab a quiet dinner after."

"You spoil me, Jameson McKinnon."

"Always will love." My parents stare at each other like they're the only ones in the room. Looking down at Katy I realize we have a love like them. She's the piece that was missing from my life all this time.

Katy

Chapter Thirty-Two

The party last two hours. Half way through my parents had to leave. I felt a slight pang they missed the rest of the fun. But I didn't let it ruin my night. They explained about some large party checking in a day early, sending the B&B in to complete chaos and them needing to help.

What kind of daughter and business owner would I be if I didn't understand wanting to take care of clients. My mom acting like a whole different person with Connor today helped kill any anger I felt. She was sweet and kind. *Maybe when a man saves your baby girl, you change your opinion about him.* Hope so.

Connor is driving back to his place. Or I thought he was. We turn right, going into Hadley Hills instead of turning left back into town. "Umm, where are we going?"

"For a drive." His hand reaches across the console sliding into mine and interlocking with my fingers.

"I'm not having sex with you up here." I'm only half serious. At this moment, I'm pretty sure Connor could get me to do anything. My body is missing his touch. The corner of his mouth turns up in amusement.

"You sure? Don't worry babe, call it a surprise." Another one? For a man who hates surprises, he loves to give them.

"What kind of surprise?" I press, tapping my finger to my chin. He lets out a chuckle.

"Now how can I surprise you if I tell you?" My lip pulls in a snarl and I stick my tongue out at him. We pull off the main road into the hills down a quiet street lined with giant, old Victorian and cottage style homes.

The block reminds me of a fairy village, plucked right from a story book. The older houses up here are beautiful. I always dreamed of raising my family in this neighborhood.

We pull into a driveway of a beautiful home. It has white with navy roofing and shutters in gray trim. The long drive away leads to a guest house and pool. Wow.

"What are you doing?"

"Go with it, babe. Come on." Connor slides out of the truck and comes around to help me down. Thankfully, because his new truck doesn't have a runner installed, and the drop is kinda far, especially in my heeled boots.

"Nice truck, by the way. The color is gorgeous." A prideful smile lights his face.

"Glad you like her." My body drops into his hold. Connor wraps his arm around my lower back guiding my feet to the ground. One hand dips below my waist giving my ass a squeeze. A moan release from behind my closed lips. We're so close, his breath is warming my cheek. "Fuck, I missed you, Sweetness."

The use of my nickname has me jumping for joy on the inside. Connor leans down and captures my lips in his. All the need and pain between us is explodes at this moment.

Warm fingers slide into my hair. His grip is so possessive and firm. Heat blossoms between my legs. Our tongues thrust together, sending goosebumps raising over my flesh.

Connor releases a growl as he sinks his fingers into my ass. My back bows, I pull away breathless. "I love you. Now tell me, what are we doing here?"

He drops his head down for a quick peck to my lips, smiling the whole time and leads me up to the front door. The handle jiggles in his hand before popping open. Connor walks inside without a care that he is trespassing.

"Babe! What are you?" My question dies on my lips. The inside is gorgeous. Talk about a complete contrast. Completely modernized, with vaulted ceilings in the living room and an open-plan concept. There is a loft jutting out overlooking the common space. I follow him deeper into the house.

The place is empty. We round the corner and a blow up mattress covered with a blanket is laying in the middle of a day room. A bottle of champagne is chilling in a bucket on the floor.

"Well, what do you think?" He asks, holding his arms open wide.

"What do I think of what?"

"Our new home. If you want the place."

"Seriously? Oh, my god, yes!" The scream echos through the empty house, bouncing off the walls. I throw myself into his arms laughing. Connor twirls me around twice before setting me down.

His body stiffens, and he swallows handing me a thick packet.

"Let me explain while you read. Please try not to be angry. It will all make sense when I finish." He says firmly. Now I'm nervous and kind of scared.

"Okay." I set the papers on the nearest counter top and wait for him to continue.

"Jameson went digging into the things Nicole said to you. He found tons of interesting things out. This is the new paperwork for the loan your grandma took out against the bakery. Jameson bought the note from the bank after he found out about the whole story. Before you get mad he did it to help you. Noah and your loan officer purposely kept notices and letters from going out. The asshole wanted to swoop in and save the day for you."

"What a fucking jerk. Ugh." Connor reaches for me. I let him wrap me in his embrace. "Baby, this was the news I was going to tell you."

"Wait? You knew Noah was doing all this?" His brow scrunches in confusion and its so cute.

"Not exactly. My grandmother's attorney came by with an acceptance packet to the culinary program at the college. Inside my grandmother left a letter explaining everything and leaving me with much-needed advice. As soon as I read her letter, you were the only person I wanted to tell. I realized how stupid I had been about everything. Thinking I needed to do it all myself. I thought leaning on you made me weak.

That you'd walk away if I did." Connor is silent for a moment.

"That's why you were at the pub to tell me first?"

"Yes. But when I saw Kelly kissing you all my old fears came back. Instead of letting you explain, I ran. I'm so sorry, Connor."

His arms squeeze tight locking me in place. He traces kisses from the top of my head before leading down to my lips. The kiss is slow and sweet. A fire stirs in my belly.

My entire being wants this man. I deepen the kiss, slipping my tongue inside his mouth. Forget all the other details I need him, now. "Make love to me, please."

Connor wastes no time. Without taking his lips off mine he pulls at my dress until he finds the hem. In one movement he pulls it over my head. Leaving me standing in front of him in a black lace bra, matching panties and my boots.

"Fuck me, you're beautiful." Connor growls. "Turn around, so I can see your sweet ass." I turn for him, bending slightly at my knees to make it pop out more. "I fucking love you, Katy."

When I turn back around Connor's shirt is lying at his feet, and he's standing before me shirtless in slacks and dress shoes. My gaze go straight to his glorious V shape leading to the thick bulge hiding behind his zipper.

Dropping to my knees I reach for his belt. Connor grabs my wrist, stopping me. "You don't need to, you don't owe me anything."

"Duh. Let me love on you. After, you can love on me. I want to suck your cock." Connor lets out a groan.

"Fuck, I missed your dirty mouth." He releases my wrist. "Do whatever you want, Sweetness." My fingers go to work removing his belt and pulling his pants down his legs. His dick springs free, already rock hard. A small drop of fluid is gathered at the tip. My tongue darts out, lapping up the drop.

A moan purrs out of Connor. "Fuck Katy." My lips wrap around his length and I slowly take him as deep as I can. I'm torturing him but I missed this. Ruling this giant of a man with my mouth and pussy gives me a sense of power I can't explain. No one has ever looked at me the way Connor stares at me.

"Sweetness, I'm gonna come." He growls grasping my neck, guiding me to take his length down the back of my throat. He fucks my mouth deliberately while I savor every minute of it. My tongue swirls over his member in a punishing pace.

"I'm coming." He slams his cock deeper. His release squirts down my throat, and I swallow every last drop, licking over the opening in his tip. The move makes him shiver. "Shit woman, you know what that does to me." I bite my lip and smile up at him while wiping at the corners of my mouth. He pushes me backward on the blow up mattress. "My turn." There is a pinch at my hip, the only hint I get before the sound of fabric ripping reverberates through the room.

"Hey! Those are my favorite pair."

"We've gone over this, just send me the bill. Now open for me and show me what's mine." He demands. My legs fall open at his command before my brain even registers.

Connor's eyes bore into my dripping pussy like a man dying of starvation.

"You're so fucking beautiful spread open for me." He descends on my pussy, lavishing me in long strokes with his tongue. His one hand spreads me open to give him better access to my clit, and the other reaches up to flick and pinch my nipple between his fingers. I scream out, not able to contain the pleasure coursing through from this mans touch and arch my back.

His hands glide down my back, gripping my cheeks in each hand. Cool air hits my tight hole. Connor spreads me apart, baring me to him then descends on my pussy. His beard scrapes my skin while he growls into me, pushing himself into my wet heat.

"Oh my god, Connor. I'm coming." My orgasm rips through me, making my body vibrate so forcefully my breath stops. My lungs burn screaming at me to take a breath. Holy hell, this man. "Connor, I need you in me now." I gasp. My fingers scrape has arms and back.

"Fuck babe, say it again." He commands with a smirk moving up my body. I'm about to smack the smirk off his face if he doesn't do what I say.

"*Connor.*" I plead, pulling him closer to me. The head of his cock brushes my opening. My body shivers in response. "Yes." Dark brown pools stare down at me, hooking my chin with his finger, making us lock eyes. His heat bores into me.

In his arms time slows. All sound beyond us fades away. This moment is all my body can focus on. Our bodies joined together and the waves of pleasure gliding over me.

"I love you Katy." Connor declares. His length slides inside me to the hilt as my pussy clamps down around his cock. "Damn baby, you're so tight." He gives me a second to adjust to his size before torturing me with slow, loving strokes.

Connor picks up his pace to punishing thrusts. He's pounding into my pussy like a wild man and I raise my hips to meet every thrust. My walls grip him like a vice setting off new pleasure throughout my body. Goosebumps cover my flesh, another orgasm already building.

Connor keeps up his pace for what feels like hours, sucking my breasts into his mouth, and biting on my nipples. He is gripping me so tight I'm sure I'll have bruises in the morning. Every cell in my body tingles, like a super charge is running through my veins.

"Yes baby, squirt all over my cock."

"Yes. Yes." He slams deep once more. My nerves erupt in sweet agony. I ride the high feeling my juices coat him while spilling down my ass cheeks onto the bed.

"I love when you drench me, Sweetness. Turn over." Connor pulls out flipping me to my knees and elbows. Without hesitation he thrusts inside me. His cock stretches my walls, filling me completely. My pussy clenches around him attempting to pull him in deeper. His length hits my cervix and I cry out.

"Right there. Don't stop Connor, don't stop." Hard muscles slam into me, each thrust more forceful than the last. The fever over taking my body is out of my control. I can't help the gibberish flying past my lips. All words have lost meaning, I'm riding the waves of every orgasm and spark the rushes through me.

"Yes. Come in me, Connor. I want you!" A loud roar erupts from him and his release coats my walls.

"Fucking amazing." Connor trails kisses up my back with his now softening cock still buried in me. "I love you, Katy." He purrs into my ear while he cleans up.

"I love you too, Connor."

I'm not sure how long we lay there in each other arms basking in our post sex haze. The sound of my cell phone going off brings us back to reality. Every part of me wants to ignore the call, but somthing nags at me to answer.

"Phone please." Connor passes me my phone. Lily's name is flashing on the screen.

"Hey sweetie, what's up?"

"Katy, I'm so sorry," Her voice is so low I can barely hear her. "I need your help, please. Isaac hit me. Katy, he coked me."

Lily

Chapter Thirty-Three

How did I let my life lead to this point, where the man I love turned into this monster? What did I do to make him hate me?

My eyes are burning so much blinking hurts. Tears run freely down my face. I'm such an idiot. Why did I open my mouth?

Attempting to stand the blood rushes to my head. My feet wobble from side to side, almost slipping out from under me. Ugh, my stomach hurts. Nausea rolls through me in waves like I'm on a ship. I limp to the mirror and stare at the face I haven't been able to look at in so long, my own.

What is staring back at me sets a fresh round of tears and sobs to come pouring out. My once golden blonde hair is dull and faded. Deep red patches of matted blood dot the left side of my face. My left cheek is throbbing, a large gash splits my face across the center of my cheek. My neck is a mix of purple and red bruises; he choked me.

More tears flow. How can Isaac be so cruel? Pieces of earlier are missing. The last thing I remember is him calling me a liar and punching me in the face. How long was I passed out for?

My fingertips brush at the bruises, my heart is breaking into a million pieces. The last few years play on a reel, raking my brain with how we got here. Two years ago we were happy, getting engaged. Life wasn't perfect, but things were nice. I thought I found my one, my happy ending.

Never in a million years did I think I could end up locked in my bathroom. Scared out of my mind, wondering how the man I love could ever do this to me. Something creeks somewhere in the house. All the blood rushes out of my face, a wave a nausea hits me so hard, I force the bile back down.

A quick glance under my shirt and I cringe at what I find. Purple and yellow bruises cover my stomach. Some are old but most new. Tears well up inside me again. "No." Now is not the time to be weak, I need to get out. My hands run over my pockets checking for my phone. Thank god. I speed dial the first person I think of.

"Hey sweetie, what's up?" My best friend sounds so happy. Maybe I should hang up, I can't ruin her happiness with my problems. She got engaged this afternoon. How can I ruin today? I'm about to hang up when the creaking sounds again from the hall, like hardwood giving under the weight of someone's steps.

What if Isaac is still here? The thought snaps me out of my pity party and I answer her, "Katy, I need your help, please.

Isaac hit me, he choked me." The last sentence is barley above a whisper.

Every part of me is ringing in pain. My fiance hurt me, he hit me. Put his hands around my neck. Was he trying to kill me?

"Where are you?" All business, nothing hysterical.

"I'm at home, locked in the first floor bathroom. Please hurry, I think he's still here. I'm so scared." My teeth are chattering, I can't stop them.

"I'm with Connor. We're on the way. Hold tight and don't move." Everything aches, my entire life is crumbling around me. Today all the hiding ends, everyone will find out. "Katy will be here in time. I will make it out of this."

What seems like hours later. The cold tile is seeping into my bones. I have to rub my arms to keep from shivering. Footsteps shuffle outside the bathroom door. My hand clamps over my mouth swallowing a gasp. Please let be Katy, please be Katy.

"Lily, its Connor. You need to open the door, honey." His calm voice unlocks tension I was holding inside. A mix between a sob and a cry slips free. My feet stick to the floor, but I force myself to move and undo the lock. Relief rushes over me as the door swings open and the big hunk is staring back at me.

"Someone call for a superhero." Connor's face splits into a giant grin, and he winks. I smile and wince back. Ouch. His smile falters. "Sorry. Can you walk?"

Screw his question I have my own I throw at him. "Thank you, where's Katy? Is Isaac still here?" The words come out in a rush. His lighthearted comments make me less nervous, but not much.

"Take a deep breath. Katy, is fine. She is keeping the car running." Before I can speak he holds up his hand, "The doors are locked, she is armed and knows how to use it. I got my ass covered. We need to leave now, before Isaac comes back."

Connor's body is strung tight, he looks ready for a fight. His hand is on the butt of the gun holstered at his hip. Whoa, I missed that before.

"Please get me out of here, forget about my stuff." Connor takes my hand and leads me to my car. He drives while Katy follows behind.

Realization of where we are headed hits me. "No. Not the hospital. No way my family can see me like this."

"Lily, you're hurt pretty bad. You might have a broken bone in your face and your wrist is broken. You can barely stand, there could be internal bleeding. You need to be checked out."

"Fine, but somewhere else. They'll call the police." I beg. "You don't understand. Please, anywhere else." Connor pulls the car over and turns to me. Concern is written in the thinning of his lips and the lines pulling at the edges of his eyes.

I sound crazy, but Connor won't understand. My family loves Isaac, and they will never believe me when I say he did this. Worse, two of his brothers work on Hadley Police Department and his dad is Chief. No one will help me through this, Isaac will do what he always does and walk away clean.

"Please." My voice is hoarse. Pain shoots through my skull, I wince because everything aches. This is my fault, I stayed. I deserve this.

"Lily, you need to be one hundred percent honest with me right now. Why don't you want a hospital? Don't lie to me." My first instinct is to make up some bullshit lie, but I think better of it. I take a deep breath, wincing only slightly at the pain in my head and stomach.

"My half brother is friends with Isaac. He is on shift until ten. Isaac's two brothers work on the Hadley Falls Police force. His dad is Chief Sanchez. This can't go anywhere, they'll protect him." I say in one breath. Connor draws back in a fury.

"Chris won't. He hates crimes against woman. Let me call him."

I shake my head. "Isaac told me they don't care. Please."

Connor lets out a huff. "What about Riker? He won't let anything happen to you."

"No cops."

"Fuck." Connor punches my steering wheel. "Issac told you a bullshit lie, I've worked with Chris. He would kill him for this. No way he stands for this shit. But, for now this stays between us. Let me make a call."

The McKinnon Security's Clinic felt like an eternity. Five hours of x-rays, stitches, and photos. I protested when Connor said they were going to Riker for documentation only. But he promised no one will lay eyes on them. They better not.

Connor and Katy want me to press charges, but they don't understand, I can't. I'm so grateful for them though. Recovering at Connor's house this week is helping me finally feel normal again.

The bruise around my eye and cheek are turning a morbid shade of yellow, but my throat is feeling better, and it's much easier to swallow.

My phone buzzes, the screen lighting to show another message from Isaac. He still thinks I'm coming back. He keeps messaging me things like; he misses me, and I'm upsetting my family.

What a mess I made of my life, almost thirty, no job, no place to stay. All my clothes are at the house I shared with Isaac, I have no clue when I'll be able to retrieve my things. Part of me doesn't care, letting go of all those things might be what I need.

A knock sounds at the door, Katy peeks her head in. "Hey, can I come in?" Concern is written across her face. A lump forms in my gut. Shame washes over me, I'm a horrible person for lying to everyone for so long.

"Come in. Thank you so much for all your help. I'm so sorry I ruined your engagement day."

"Don't you dare." Her tone is harsh, I swallow. This is what Isaac says I do all the time. I anger those who are helping me.

"Lily I'm sorry, I didn't mean to sound upset. You are like a sister to me, you can call me whenever you're in trouble. No matter what I'm doing."

Her voice is full of love and understanding. I don't know what I did to deserve her, but I'm so glad she's my one of my best friends. Katy hugs me close before taking a few steps back.

"Okay, I talked to Connor. Before you say no. You'll be helping me out huge. We leave for Connor's cousin's wedding tomorrow. We would love for you to stay until you get everything figured out." I stare blankly at her. They are offering me their guest house to recover.

Katy is such an amazing woman. Even after lying to her she is kind to me. "Are you sure? You guys just got engaged you need alone time. I can't intrude."

"And you won't. If I need or want alone time with my man, I'll make it happen." She quips back with a naughty smirk, pulling at the corner of her mouth. "Here's the deal. We leave for a week tomorrow. We need someone to come check the plants and our mail. This way you are helping me out while I help you out. Plus the guest house is far enough away once we are home, unless you come to the main house we'll hardly see each other. What do you say? Please say yes."

I hold back my tears. "Okay, yes. Thank you so much."

"Perfect, let me show you the guest house, and where everything is."

Katy takes over an hour to show me everything. Connor's house is enormous, and there are several buttons I had to learn. I might need to label them after they leave tomorrow. The peace of this house is helping me reconnect with myself again, and maybe I can revive the old me back. Or a newer better version.

Katy

Chapter Thirty-Four

3 Months Later

Someone pinch me. How is this my life? I woke up in Paris, France. The view from my hotel room balcony. Yes I said balcony is the freaking, Eiffel Tower. Like so close I could reach out and touch the thing. Absolutely breathtaking.

The air is crisp but comfortable. A soft breeze blows the leaves around the square below. The scent of fresh baked bread floats up from the bakery down the street.

The last six months have been like a fairy tale. No way would I have thought life could change so much if I hadn't lived through it myself. Noah spent three months in the hospital before taking a plea deal on the fraud and embezzlement. He and his banker friend were running tons of scams on people to get rich.

Nicole took a plea deal too. She is spending her time in a mental health facility. I hope she can receive the help and care she needs. I'm still angry she tried to kill me. But, after I heard about the evidence removed from her apartment, it was clear she isn't cruel. Nicole is sick, professional help is the only way for her to have a chance at healing.

I haven't forgiven her but the bakery opened its doors back up two weeks after the incident, thanks to Ian. He had people working round the clock to kick us back in business. The the lord for Jameson buying out my loan. I saved the bakery without having to ask my parents for the money.

Things have been busy since the reopening of BreadLove. Several restaurants and local eateries in Hadley Falls and the surrounding towns want us to provide them with treats and desserts. At BreadLove I don't have the capabilities to take on those orders, so I pitched my idea to Connor about Platted and he is all in . He offered to fund my project and become a full partner. I love our new path we each own our own business and now we own Platted, together.

We both decided BreadLove needed a full-time manager, I wanted Meghan, but she asked to stay assistant manager. I think she's still shaky from the whole Nicole thing. Thankfully Connor's older cousin Cormac was available and I hired him on as my general manager for BreadLove. His resume is perfect, full of managing experience. No clue how I got so lucky. Having him at BreadLove allowed me to take time to start Platted and go back to school to learn new techniques, after all, that is what my grandma always wanted for me. To be honest, I've always wanted to learn more too.

GAH! I still can't believe I'm on my honeymoon with the most perfect man for me. Yesterday was the most amazing day of my life. And somehow we pulled everything off in three months. Correction, Lilly pulled the whole thing off.

Don't get me started on Lily. Her strength amazes me. She threw herself completely into coordinating my wedding when I came home from Connor's cousin's wedding with my ginormous idea. I wanted to have mine in the fall this year, less than three months away. She might have a future career in event planning. Lily made the day perfect. Wine colored roses mixed with white and cream ones were placed everywhere. The arch was decorated in dark red roses and sunflowers, adding to the fall theme.

Veronica created the most magnificent gown I've laid eyes on. Rose petals were hand sewn on the bodice with a cluster of Roses in blush and cream a fixed on my left hip. Random petals and rose buds lay scattered over the skirt and blend beautifully into the bodice. Of course my dress wouldn't have been complete without the brand new cream and blue lingerie set Elise had made for my special day.

My favorite part of the day, no drama. Not a single critical word or fight. My mom spoke with Connor and I the night before to apologize for being so unpleasant since meeting him. I thought I caught a glimpse of a tear in her eyes when she said she was trying to do what's best for me.

Forgiving her wasn't easy but I remember what my grandma said, so I forgave her. Life is too short to hold a grudge.

RING!RING!

The screech of my phone dissolves the memory revealing the Parisian skyline. Jackson's name flashing across the screen and I try to remember what I told myself a second ago about holding grudges. Nope, I can't help the annoyance burning towards my big brother.

He missed my wedding, all because he refused to ask for the weekend off. *There was always a chance he'd have work.* Ugh, yes there was a chance he wouldn't be granted the time off, but the ass didn't even check. I'm not crazy either, Jameson knows his boss. Jackson never put in the paperwork.

The ass chose to miss my wedding. My phone rings again this time I decide to answer.

"Hello." My voice is clipped.

"Hey Little Heart. Congratulations, I know you're a McKinnon now but you'll always be Little Heart to me."

"Thanks Jackson, what's up?"

"Hey, come on, don't be mad at me. I tried to make it, I couldn't." Why does he have to lie? Tears sting the back of my eyes, I won't cry. Him not showing up is his problem, not mine. "Good news though, my job assignment is ending this week, so I'm coming home for an entire month."

My anger vanishes at the promise of a month to torture him. "No joke. A month?"

"Yep, only problem I have now is no place to stay. I don't want to stay with mom and dad. Last time wasn't pretty."

"Ha! You're telling me. Mom still mentions it." I snicker. My brother getting caught having sex at twenty-something years old because the girl couldn't keep her volume under control is teasing gold for a baby sister. "My condo has a tenant otherwise I'd offer the place to you."

"Damn. Dad mentioned you have a guest house? Got room for me there?" He asks. I catch the hopefulness in his voice. "Come on sis. We can catch up so much easier if I'm close by."

I almost mention Lily staying there, but decide against full disclosure. If he wants to play the lie game with me, I'm about to do the same. Oh, I'll tell her he's coming to stay in the other room. I would never do that to one of my besties.

"What a great idea. I'll have it prepared for you, when are you arriving?"

"Seriously? Thanks, sis. I should land October fourth."

"Oh, perfect. We arrive back on the fifth. I'll have everything ready for you, and I'll make sure there's a lockbox with a key."

"Thanks, Katy. I'm sorry I missed your wedding." Guilt and regret are thick in his tone. He is sorry and I almost feel bad for what I'm about to do. Almost. The sound of rustling sheets inside my room is my signal to end the call. Time to go.

I end the call telling Jackson I'll see him soon and shoot him a quick text with the information he needs. A cat ate the canary smile crosses my face and I can't help the naughty joy coursing through me, Jackson has no idea what he's in for.

Connor

Chapter Thirty-Five

"Why are you smiling like that?" I ask Katy, walking up behind her, naked and a little chilled. I should probably put clothes on, but the balcony's edge is covered in shrubbery. No way anyone can see my junk.

My wife. Fuck, that is good to say, sits at a little table and chairs with the city of Paris behind her, she's the most gorgeous thing in the world. Turns out even on honeymoon Katy starts her morning the same every day, with a cup of coffee and a pastry. This morning is no different, she's enjoying an almond croissant. Her long curly locks are blowing loose in the breeze and a mischievous smile is on her face.

"Like what?" Her mouth forms into a smirk.

"That. It's sexy as fuck, but what put it there?" She looks up at me, finally notices that I'm naked and her smiles turns sultry.

"Nothing worth telling right now. Come here, you." Katy crooks a finger at me. I'm in awe by how much this woman is made for me.

She has this naughty little side she only shows to me. Getting her riled up is fun as fuck too. I follow her command and bend down to claim her lips. My tongue slips into her mouth and I show her exactly what I'm thinking.

Small fingers pull at my bare chest, trying to mold me to her. Katy stands as I lean further down, so I use her momentum to pull her up into my arms. She wastes no time and wraps her legs around my waist. We don't stop kissing even as I walk us into the bedroom and place Katy on the bed. She lets out a satisfied sigh. "Mm, you taste yummy."

I smirk at her. "You taste like coffee and sugar, Sweetness. Now that you had your breakfast I'm about enjoy you for mine. You look fucking hot in this lingerie." I growl at her.

"Elise is talented, isn't she?"

"You need to order more when we get home. From now on I only want you to wear her stuff. Nothing but finest lingerie until the end of time for you." I wink, didn't think her smile could any bigger but there it is.

Anytime I compliment this woman she blushes from head to toe. I'll never tire of watching her skin change color under my touch and words, more so when I have her naked and open for me. "You ready wife?"

"I'm at your mercy, husband."

Fuck, my dick goes hard as granite at her words. The word husband on her lips sets something primal off in me and I fucking love the rush. Her lace bodysuit has a button at her pussy, giving me easy access and allowing her to keep this sexy scrap of material on while I devour her.

Her nipples pebble at my touch, pink little points straining against the white fabric. I lean over her, pulling her breast into my mouth, licking and sucking on her through the fabric. Katy whimpers. I trail kisses down her abdomen and through her small patch of brown curls until I arrive at her bared opening. Laying a long breath over her slit I love watching her twitch as her ass cheeks clinch from my teasing.

"Connor, please." She moans. I descend on her wet pussy, laving it in kisses and sucking her sensitive bud into my mouth. She bucks her hips, moaning into the hotel suite. My arm wraps around across her waist to hold her in place.

"Like that, baby. Damn, your tongue feels so good." She whines. I apply more pressure to her clit, and slip two fingers inside her hot sheath, her walls squeeze me, and she moans in satisfaction. Her juices coat my fingers in her wetness with each pump into her channel.

Her pussy is heaven, her musky scent fills my senses, driving me wild knowing she is all mine. I trail my soaked fingers down to her ass, slowly probing her puckered hole.

After a few pumps, my finger slides through her tight ring of muscle and slide my tongue into her soaking channel at the same time. She screams my name and a flood of wetness squirting into my mouth. I fucking love when she does that.

Katy's entire body is covered in a light sheen of sweat, her breasts are heaving. Rosy pink buds stick up trying to poke through her bodysuit. Katy looks down at me, a hint of a smile at the corners of her lips. Aw, my woman is still embarrassed about the squirting.

"That was fucking hot, Sweetness." Her smile goes. I will always make sure she is never embarrassed over sex especially when I think she's hot as hell.

"On your knees." I demand. She complies, putting her ass in the air and shaking her hips to tease me. Using my fingers I spread her cheeks, getting a look at her dripping pussy and little hole. Claiming her ass one day is going to be fun. Not today. My palm comes down firmly against her flesh and the responding squeal makes a drop of a liquid leak from my tip.

My hand grips my aching cock and I place the head at her entrance. Teasing her slit. She tries to push back against me but I hold her at bay for a second before pushing myself inside until my pelvis is seated against her ass. Her pussy pulses and tightens around me adjusting to the intrusion.

"I fucking love this pussy." The growl echoes through the room. Each thrust pushing my need higher than before. Last night was the night for love making, now I'm claiming her and leaving my mark. I stare down at my dick moving in and out of her pussy. My thumb slides around to her clit. The slightest bit of pressure is all I need to send her over the edge.

"Yes, Connor. Oh, my god. I'm coming." She moans and her pussy grips me like a vice. Oh yea, the pressure sends me into overdrive. My pace quickens until I'm plowing into her as she orgasms around my length.

After her second orgasm, I take my soaked finger and explore her tight little asshole. Making sure she's coated in wetness, I slide one finger in, stretching her and pressing against her ring of muscle. Once her body relaxes I add a second finger.

"Fuck baby. I'm so full." There's my dirty girl. I love hearing her naughty little mouth say the dirtiest shit when I'm inside her.

"That's it baby, take my dick while I stretch your ass. I'm gonna claim that hole one day soon too."

"Yes, baby. I want you. I'm yours."

"Damn straight babe and I'm yours." Those words send her into oblivion, my orgasm is right behind pulling my balls up and surging through my cock. Hot jets of come fill her as she screams my name.

Hours later, after several rounds of mind-blowing morning sex, Katy is laying in bed passed out. Room service is set to be delivered in an hour. Should be plenty of time to let her sleep. I should crawl into bed with her but I'm wired.

Too many things are running in my mind. I'm pacing the carpet. More like creating a personal runway with how many times I've walked this damn spot. There are a million moving pieces going on at home. We are in the middle of launching our joint business. Platted is currently under construction and the only reason we are honeymooning right now. Who knows when we'll have a chance for a break next.

Hell, BreadLove and McKinnon Pub are busier than ever. Tall tales of our story are running like wild fire through the town. The rumors are making both our establishments a sort of romantic date spot. Katy tells me hush and enjoy the business, which I do. But I still find it weird.

I turn around making another pass and my gaze lands on Katy's form sleeping peacefully. Rays of light shine in from outside highlighting each curve of her body tucked under the sheet. Damn, I'll always be in awe that she is mine. Katy owns every inch of my heart. From the first night she walked into my pub, she shook up my life and all for the better. I would do anything for this woman and I will spend the rest of my days showing her how much she means to me. Katy Heart is mine and I am hers, forever.

The End

Epilogue

5 years later...

"Babe. We need to go. My contractions are five minutes apart. I am not having this baby in our car." I holler for Connor. That man, you'd think he'd know to move his ass since the last child came in a flash.

The day little Kade Jameson McKinnon came into our lives was a crazy one. We barely made the trip to the hospital in time. And I ended up being in labor for all of twenty minutes before I had the most precious, adorable bundle of joy wrapped in blue placed in my arms.

A wet tear slides down my cheek. Damn these hormones. I've been an emotional mess from the day I peed on the stick and found out our little family of three was becoming a family of four.

"We won't be late. I was letting your mom know where everything is. I'm ready." Connor says, coming from the kitchen, still holding a sleeping Kade in his arms.

"Um babe, I think you are carrying a little extra cargo." I nod my head at our son as I put my hands on my hips

"Huh?" He looks down. "Shit."

"Everything is okay, here give him to me. I want to cuddle my grandson as much as I can before my little granddaughter arrives." Says my mom in the sweetest voice to ever leave her lips.

What they say is true, babies change people. My mom sure changed a bunch since Kade's birth. One look at him and all her walls came crashing down. I smile watching my mom with my one-year-old son passed out in her arms.

My father comes out from the hallway. "Hey kid, I think you need to get this lovely lady to the hospital before she does give birth in her car." My dad claps a hand onto Connor's back, laughing. He leans in to whisper to Connor but speaks loud enough to hear. "If she gives birth in her car, she will make you buy her that new SUV she's had her eye on."

"On second thought, let's wait," I tease. Connor's eyes bug out.

"No new cars here, little lady at least not until Christmas." He winks at my father. What was that about? I don't get to think because another contraction sends a sharp pain up my back and tightens around my belly.

"Connor, let's move."

"I got you Sweetness. Everything is in the car."

We better make it. Giving birth in a car ruins the seats. Plus, I don't want to end up as a crazy news story in the Hadley Falls Gazette. I can see it now, 'Local business owner gives birth on the short drive to hospital', ugh, the thought makes me grimace.

Thankfully, we arrive at the hospital with plenty of time to spare. Three hours later, a lot of pushing and little miss Arya Margret McKinnon is born. She's a tough one and completely different from my experience with Kade, which probably means she will be my handful. I honestly can't wait.

Being a mother to a little boy was an experience I'd never want to change, and now I start a different journey with this new bundle of joy.

I'm watching Connor sit with her in the giant chair they keep in the rooms for dads. He wouldn't notice if the world ended right now. He is so mesmerized by her. They are gonna be trouble. She already has her daddy wrapped around her tiny little finger. Connor glances up at me. "You did good babe. She's precious. How you feeling?"

"Okay. Happy she's here because, that one, was hard. Did you talk to your dad?"

"Yep, he's on his way."

A knock sounds at the door. Speak of the devil, standing in the doorway at his six-three height and graying head of hair is my father-in-law wearing a huge smile. "Is that my granddaughter?" He asks, grinning. Connor scrambles from the chair.

"Pops, come here I want you to meet Arya Margret McKinnon." Pop's mouth hangs open in confusion. I nod my head, smiling at him.

"You heard right, Pops."

"Beautiful name, son." He takes Arya from Connor and coos to her. I think I'm melting in place watching these two men fawn all over her. "Hi Ari, I'm your Papa. We are going to have so much fun together." Pops takes a seat in the chair. Connor comes over to me and wraps me in a hug.

"He is so happy baby, thank you." Connor whispers in my ear. Happy tears flow down my cheeks.

"I didn't do it, she did." I gesture to Arya. "She is gonna be one spoiled little girl."

"That she is. I love you, Sweetness."

"I love you too, Connor." He hugs me tighter and kisses the top of my forehead. I have never been more content and happier in my life. All because I finally opened up, and learned to lean on someone. Putting my trust in this man to protect and cherish me for the rest of my days is the best decision I ever made. Whatever life throws at us we can handle because we have each other. Forever.

Coming Soon...

Trusting Me

Lily & Jackson's Story

Lily Grey is hiding from her abusive boyfriend and the pressure her parents are exerting for her to marry him. Approaching thirty, she finds herself lost, desperate for her parents approval, but not at the cost of her own safety. Isaac was always a mistake, a poor second choice for the man she really loved—her best friend's brother. Sadly, he never gave her a chance. Isaac is cold and manipulative, and he has Lily in his sights. He wants her back. Where better for Lily to hide than her best friend's guest house?

Jackson Heart needs a break from his demanding career, and too much travel. His cheating ex-girlfriend wants him back, for all the wrong reasons, and he's had enough. His sister's away, and if he can avoid her bestie, Lily, he'll be fine. He's longed to start something with the petite blonde but not at the expense of her friendship with his sister. If he slinks into town quietly, where better to lay low than his sisters guest house?

Talk about being in the wrong place at the wrong time! What could be worse than finding a naked Lily in the bed Jackson expects to find empty. How can they resist each other after all these years? When they let down their guard at last, the attraction is undeniable, and they don't fight it.

Can the lovers turn one night of passion into a lifetime together? Complications arise as Jackson and Lily work to avoid their pasts and build a future together. Will the pain of the past get in their way?

Continue the steamy saga as four friends work through their pains and pasts to find their happy endings In book two of this sexy series.

TRIGGER WARNING: This book contains references to past domestic violence.

About Author

Hey, I'm Ashley – Contemporary Romance Author and lover of all things sweet, steamy and yummy. I'm a sucker for a growly alpha male – probably why I married one. I'm just a girl who loves creating her own world and crazy characters.

I currently live in Nevada with my little girl and growly husband. I've got a thing for wine labels, desserts, and all things sparkly. Can't forget the pens though, office supplies make me giddy. When I'm not chasing my little around you can usually find me sipping coffee with headphones writing or with my nose buried in a book.

We are very family oriented. You can most likely catch me at a hockey game or chilling with family around the grill with a cold beer. Don't get me wrong I love a good girls weekend or better yet a weekend alone with my hunky husband.

Fantastic hubby aside at my core I'm a dreamer and a creator. My favorite part of the day beside my family is sitting down to dive into the world I've created. I can't wait to share it with you!

<3 Ashley!

Let's Get Intimate!

Want to stay in the know?

Click Here to Join my Newsletter to stay up to date on new releases, exclusives, giveaways, and more!

Want to to get to know me and the Hadley Falls World even more?

Click Here to Join Welcome to the Falls - Ashley Kay's Readers

Made in United States
North Haven, CT
17 February 2022

16203906R00219